volumes & villainesses

A Cozy Fantasy

Tales from the Broken Claw
Book Three

don jones

praise for volumes & villainesses

"Volumes & Villainesses" is a true delight, a perfectly brewed cup of tea on a rainy afternoon. Jones has crafted a world that feels lived-in and loved, where the magic is not a grand spectacle but a gentle, humming part of everyday life. The characters are so endearing and their quiet moments so genuine that you'll find yourself completely swept away by the charm of the Broken Claw. This is a story that comforts and captivates in equal measure, leaving you with a warm feeling long after you've closed the book.

— TheList

What a triumph of subtle world-building! Don Jones weaves a rich tapestry of fantasy that is both unique and deeply believable. The magic system feels organic and grounded, tied directly to the rhythms of the town and its people. This is not a book about saving the world, but about understanding it—the quiet power of a magical library, the history in the stones of an old building, and the wisdom found in forgotten tales. It's a testament to the fact that great fantasy doesn't need to be epic to be powerful.

— Fantasy Reader Magazine

With "Volumes & Villainesses," Don Jones has proven once again that he writes from the heart. The characters feel like old friends, their struggles and victories resonating deeply. The story is driven not by dramatic conflicts but by the quiet, heartfelt moments that reveal who these people truly are. It's a book that finds the extraordinary in the ordinary, exploring themes of belonging, friendship, and finding your place in the world with a gentle, yet powerful, hand.

— Longtime Reader

also by don jones

stories of witchkind®

<u>Age of the Adherents</u>:
Daniel Scratch • Master of the Tower • The Fifth Axis

<u>The Order</u>:
The Order of Some • The Conspiracy of One • The Truth of All

———

Clara Thorn
Clara Thorn, the witch that was found
Clara Thorn, the witch that fought
Clara Thorn, the witch that won

———

Endless Sky®
Truthsayer • New Worlds • Old Bones

———

Tales from the Broken Claw
Pubs & Pegasi • Anvils & Avatars
Volumes & Villainesses • Teas & Tribulations
Watchers & Windstorms • Stitches & Snake Oil
Peacekeepers & Púca • Cuts & Catastrophes
Gears & Gateways • Bandages & Banshees

———

The Never: A Tale of Peter and the Fae

Bob Constantine (no relation)

A House of Forgotten Quests and the Dragons That Lie Within

————

Find more at DonJones.com, including a free fantasy trilogy, a free superhero duology, two collections of short stories, and even more short stories and flash fiction.

Sign up for the author's newsletter at DonJones.com (click the "Freebies" link) for notifications of new novels, and ample opportunities to get free ebooks by becoming a beta reader!

contents

Urwald

Darkehame
Darkestore
Forrest
North
Pointe
Common
Towne
Gray Foal Pass
The Mistral Mountains
Elgindam
Strongfast
Lake
Evendiam
Celestrum
Smallhaven
Scintas
Demonbane
Range
Westhold
Lake
Midton
Holderdown
Magefell
Stormport
Skyreach Range
Salten Sea
Kithwellen
Lake
Trenton
Flameheight Range
Trenton
The Mountedives
Dunereach
Highseat
Shorehaven
Farreach
Bright Islands
The Forbidden
Continent
Amber Sea
N

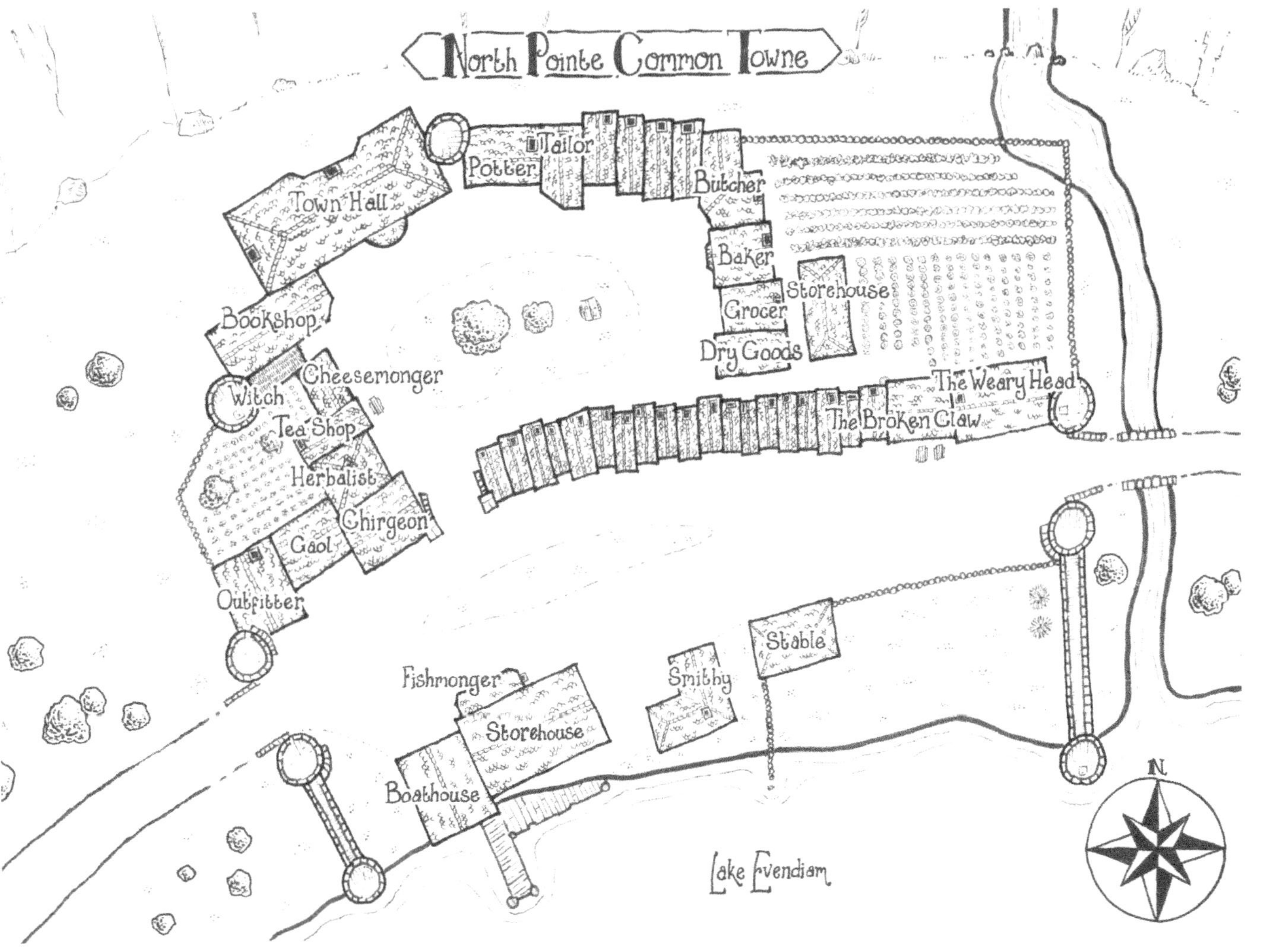

North Pointe Common Towne
Town Hall
Tailor
Potter
Butcher
Baker
Grocer
Dry Goods
Storehouse
Bookshop
Witch
Cheesemonger
Tea Shop
Herbalist
Chirgeon
Gaol
Outfitter
The Weary Head
The Broken Claw
Fishmonger
Storehouse
Boathouse
Smithy
Stable
Lake Evendiam
N

foreword

My initial release of this book coincided with a difficult time for my then-editor. I wound up "going it alone" for much of the manuscript, only bringing in a new editor after I was done. That wasn't the best decision, but I was going through some "stuff" of my own at the time. In any event, the result was a number of inconsistencies in the narrative, a great deal more repetition than my original editor would have let me get away with, and a not-entirely-satisfactory reading experience.

With this edition of the novel, I've engaged the same original editor to help me re-structure and clean things up. I think it's a better novel for that effort, and I hope you agree. If you'd previously found *Volumes & Villainesses* unsatisfactory, and you've given it a second chance, *thank you*. I've always tried to deliver a great read, but I've definitely learned the lesson that good editors make better writers—and to avoid writing when I'm not in the right head space.

I hope you enjoy the story.

Don Jones
May 2026

one

. . .

MORNING in the bookshop was always a kind of ritual for Vamir. He liked the quiet before the real business of the day began, when he and Polyocular—Poly, for short—had the run of the stacks. The shop's only window faced due east and was composed of a hundred uneven panes, each stained a slightly different hue. The sunlight arrived in waves and patches, and by eight bells the whole shop was checkered in delicate pools of blues, reds, and golds. The place was never truly bright, but always alive with color and the scent of old paper and leather, with a trailing topnote of herbal tea and dust.

Poly was already at work. The puffball creature perched atop the endcap of a shelf labeled "Forgotten Epics," eyes shut, chest gently rising and falling. Its blue feathers seemed to glow in the slanting sunlight. One stubby wing-arm hung over the shelf's edge, brushing the spine of a particularly battered epic as if it needed comfort in its old age.

"Dreaming of breakfast?" Vamir murmured, as he set a copper kettle atop the stove behind the sales counter.

Poly opened its largest eye, blinked twice, and chirped. The kettle gave a perfect whistle on cue, and Vamir poured the hot water over a mesh pouch of dried linden and apple blossom, breathing in the gentle fragrance. The routine was always this: open the shop, check the returns bin, tidy the shelves as much as possible, make tea, and then— if Poly so desired—share a bit of honey on seedcake for first meal.

The shop was rarely busy in the mornings. Travelers who had stayed overnight in the inn tended to head out straightaway, often at first light; those arriving from the closest towns to the east or west would rarely appear before noon. And so the bell above the shop's door was silent, except for when a breeze rattled it. Vamir took his tea and a heel of seedcake to the back table, where sunlight fell in a golden ellipse across the ledger and a stack of new arrivals. Poly hopped off its shelf and waddled after, landing with a gentle fwomp beside him.

He paged through the ledger, tallying which of the townsfolk had neglected to return the latest pulp serials. The names were familiar, their excuses already forming in his mind: Barnaba the mapmaker would blame a rainstorm, or a sudden surge in cartographical commissions; Makota at the bakery would swear the book vanished clean off her nightstand, likely filched by her kits; the constable, when she bothered with fiction at all, kept a rotating stack of political thrillers from ancient kingdoms under a loose floorboard in her gaol and never remembered to bring them back. Vamir smiled, imagining their sheepish faces.

Poly emitted a soft whirr, its third eye fluttering open for a heartbeat. Vamir obliged, breaking the seedcake in half and offering the slightly larger piece to his companion. Poly accepted with a gentle nip of the beak, crumbs scattering across the tabletop.

Outside, the world was quietly industrious. Through the colored glass, Vamir watched the slow procession of townspeople: little Galhani from the tea shop, a tray balanced on one small hand; the two kits from the bakery, racing circles round the biggest tree; the blacksmith's son, Darby, clutching a package wrapped in brown oilcloth, eyes wide and eager. Their movements made strange, kaleidoscopic patterns on the shop's walls.

He spent the rest of the morning cataloging. The new arrivals— four modest crates, delivered at dawn by the town's blacksmith—were a mixed lot: two volumes of travelogues, a somewhat saucy memoir by a retired forest knave, and a thick compendium of local insects.

Vamir ran his hand over the embossed spine of the memoir, then flipped to the title page, where the author had inscribed, in a shaky hand, "To the endless curiosity of strangers." He chuckled, and placed it on the display table, just in case anyone in town was feeling adventurous.

While shelving the travelogues he paused at the "Histories — Local & Regional" section, where a slim blue volume occupied the end of the bottom row—his grandfather's, one of the few things that had come with him from the forest. He'd shelved it there years ago, in the way you shelve something you're not sure what to do with: present, findable, neither displayed nor hidden. He touched the spine briefly, the way you touch a familiar thing without meaning to, and moved on.

Lunch was a ritual, too: bread and cheese from the morning's market, a handful of dried berries, a bowl of savory broth prepared the night before. He set Poly's portion on a window ledge, where the creature could preen in the warmth and look out at the world. The air carried the scent of roasting vegetables, and somewhere in the square, someone was playing a tune on a battered flute, the notes rising and falling like a lazy summer wind.

Contentment was a subtle thing, Vamir thought, and easily overlooked. It lived in the pauses between tasks, in the unremarkable sound of a kettle heating on a stove, in the way sunlight illuminated motes of dust like gold.

He had just settled into his first bite when the shop's door rattled, the handle jiggling as if caught in a conundrum. Vamir gently pressed his teacup down, licked honey from his thumb, and called, "Give it a firm twist and a gentle shove! The latch is slightly—"

There was a decisive click, and the door swung inward, jangling its array of chimes. The day's first customer stood blinking on the threshold, as if uncertain whether to step inside or treat the shop like a warren and wait for an invitation.

Vamir recognized the type. The young man wore the green-brown traveling coat of someone newly arrived, unaccustomed to both the chill and the local etiquette. He was tall, thin, and not quite comfortable in his own limbs; he looked around with an expectant anxiety. A satchel bulged at his hip, crowded with the uneven shapes of hard-bound notebooks. His hair was blond, tousled from sleep or wind, and he wore a faint bruise at the base of his jaw—evidence, perhaps, of a minor scuffle with a doorframe or an overeager handshake.

"Good morning!" Vamir greeted, rising from behind the counter. "Come in, please. The light's a bit sharper than it looks, but your eyes will adjust."

The young man stepped over the lintel and the chimes sang again. "Sorry—I always underestimate these old locks. Is this the bookseller's shop?"

"The only one along the trade road, unless you count the moldering scrolls Tyran sometimes digs up. I'm Vamir. Proprietor, collector, cataloguer, and—when it suits—confidant." He made a little bow, then indicated the still-steaming kettle. "Tea?"

The customer's relief was palpable. "Yes. Thank you, yes. I'm supposed to be—well, I suppose I am—here for a book. But I didn't expect to find the shop so open."

"Always open at dawn." Vamir poured a second cup and gestured for his guest to approach. Poly watched the exchange with all three eyes, blinking each in sequence.

"My name's Rev," the visitor offered, as he accepted the cup and sniffed its contents with evident suspicion. "Short for Reverence. My parents are—"

"Religious?" Vamir guessed.

"Optimistic, I think," said Rev, and sipped. The tea was still too hot, but he braved it. "I'm from the magistracy. Northern branch."

Vamir was not surprised. In his experience, the only people who arrived at this time with empty notebooks and a sense of purpose were magistrates, scholars, or those tasked with errands that could be accomplished before anyone else was awake to witness them. "And what book does the magistracy require of me this morning?"

Rev set his cup on the counter and produced a crumpled parchment from his satchel. He flattened it with both palms, smoothing the edges with nervous care. "I need a copy of 'Customs and Kinship of the Ogre Clans.' The most current edition—preferably annotated."

Vamir pursed his lips. "That's not a common request. Most

scholars prefer to avoid the topic unless it's strictly necessary." He shot Rev a sidelong glance. "May I ask: is this about the boundary dispute, or are you planning to negotiate with the ogres themselves?"

Rev's cheeks colored. "The latter. I'm to serve as intermediary. Warren—your blacksmith—said I should come here first. He said you'd know exactly what I needed."

Vamir smiled, pleased at Warren's confidence and his own reputation. "Warren is seldom wrong. And you're lucky—the annotated edition is newly arrived. Let me fetch it. Poly?"

Polyocular shook itself, all three eyes wide now, and launched from its perch in a flurry of down. It glided silently down the row, then hooked left toward the "Clans & Kin" shelves, landing amid the dense stacks like a dart hitting its mark. Poly's head disappeared between two thick folios.

"It always knows?" Rev asked, watching with undisguised fascination.

"It always finds what the customer needs," Vamir said. "Whether that's precisely what they asked for is occasionally a separate matter."

They rounded the end of the aisle, where Poly's feathered tail stuck out from the narrow gap between "Beastfolk: Myths and Realities" and "The Collected Correspondences of Trog Marrowbinder."

"Let me," Vamir said, and reached delicately into the shelf, withdrawing Poly and the book at once. The creature gave a pleased warble, then spiraled up to Vamir's shoulder. The book, bound in thick, navy-blue leather and edged with heavy parchment, was precisely as Vamir remembered—its pages bristling with little cloth tabs, each marked with a different color of ink.

"Here we are." Vamir passed the volume to Rev, who cradled it in both hands with a reverence worthy of his name.

"It's heavier than I expected," Rev said, flipping the cover. "And annotated, you said?"

Vamir pointed to the tabs. "Marginalia by three of the leading experts. Pay special attention to the passages about hospitality and gift-giving."

Rev nodded, already turning pages. Poly perched atop Vamir's head, its feathers quivering as it watched the newcomer scan the volume.

"Thank you," Rev said at last. "This is—well, it will guide me greatly. May I—?"

"It's a full silver, I'm afraid."

Rev laughed—a bright, clear sound—and tucked the book under his arm. "Done." He fished a coin out of a pocket and laid it gently in Vamir's outstretched palm. Then he hesitated, looking over the spines of the other books, as if there might be some other treasure he was missing.

Vamir noticed. "If there's anything else—?"

"Actually," Rev said, "Barnaba the mapmaker. I'm supposed to see her next. Is her shop open?"

"It is, unless she's lost track of time. Happens often when she's drafting a new map. But you can't miss it—three doors down, on the left, right beside the weaver's place." Vamir leaned in, lowering his voice just slightly. "If you see her looking distracted, offer her a fresh apple. She can never refuse one."

Rev grinned. "Thank you. I'll do that."

He started for the door, then paused. "And, um—does the ogre actually eat people?"

Vamir laughed, the sound a low and musical thrum. "Warren? Only if they're particularly rude. You should be safe."

Rev smiled, nodded his thanks, and stepped out into the morning, the book clutched to his chest. The door swung shut behind him, clinking the chimes once more.

Vamir remained in the aisle for a moment, breathing in the complex perfume of paper and dust and the memory of a good conversation. He reached up to scratch Poly under the chin, earning a satisfied trill.

"He's a good one, that Rev," Vamir mused. "He'll make a difference, I think."

Poly made a small, affirmative sound, and then darted off to resume its watch atop the next shelf, already searching for the next mystery to solve.

"Hmm," Vamir said, responding to a gentle, mental nudge from his shop. "Maybe I should help a bit more."

Rev did not get far down the lane before Vamir, having quickly secured Polyocular with a crust of seedcake, caught up and called his name. The wind had shifted and now funneled up the trade road from the west, carrying with it the competing aromas of bread, earth, and the faint but inescapable whiff of horse from the stables opposite the pub. Rev turned at the sound, a book still wedged under one arm and an air of mild surprise lighting his features.

"Thought I'd introduce you myself," Vamir offered, catching up with a pace that was unhurried but somehow efficient. "Barnaba is a dear, but as I said, easily immersed in her work."

The rest of the morning passed in the easy way of good introductions well made—Rev meeting Barnaba, the map acquired, practical advice exchanged about ogre etiquette and mountain passes. Vamir guided, connected, smoothed the way between people who needed to find each other, and stepped back once the work was done.

That, he had long since decided, was what he was for.

two

. . .

BY THE TIME Vamir reached the bakery, the square was already blushing with color and sound. The overnight fog had retreated to its usual perch along the ridge, leaving the air bright and brisk, just sharp enough to remind him that spring was only pretending to have won out over the tail end of winter. Above the doorway, the new hand-painted sign ("Makota's Hearth: Breads & Sweetling Things") bobbed gently in the breeze, its gold-leaf letters shimmering with promise.

Inside, the bakery pulsed with warmth, and with the complicated scent that lived at the intersection of yeast, honey, and butter. Baskets lined every inch of counter space: tall loaves mottled with seeds, sugar-dusted brioches, half-moons glazed to a high sheen. Someone had set out trays of tiny round pastries in alternating rings of orange and blue, each no larger than a coin, their centers piped with pastel creams. Several townsfolk stood in the narrow aisle, hands around mugs or shuffling coins from pocket to pocket, all absorbed in the serious business of breakfast.

Makota herself stood behind the counter, wrist-deep in dough. Her fur was a pale tan, the color of raw wheat, and her ears flicked with pleasure at each new customer's arrival. She wore a blue linen dress today, with a broad white apron tied around her middle. If she noticed the streak of flour running up one cheekbone, she gave no indication. Her tail curled around the chair at her station, rhythmically flexing with the tempo of her kneading.

"Good morning, Vamir!" she called, eyes crinkling above her upturned whiskers. "You're late. We sold out of the brownseed rolls a candlemark ago."

Vamir placed a hand to his heart in mock distress. "The only reason to leave one's bed, and I've missed it. Tragic."

Makota made a tsk noise, but her eyes twinkled. "I saved one. For you." She nodded to her right, where a smaller Felis, likely no more than twelve or thirteen, crouched behind the counter, watching Vamir with an expression that was equal parts suspicion and delight. The kit's ears were jet black, contrasting with the rest of her cream-colored fur, and she had a smudge of jam on her nose.

"Sora, will you fetch Mr. Vamir's roll from the warming drawer?" Makota said, glancing sidelong at the kit.

The girl straightened and disappeared into the back, returning with a small parcel on a wooden paddle. She deposited it in front of Vamir with ceremonial solemnity, her tail flicking in a way that made it clear she was both shy and proud of her role.

"Thank you, Sora," Vamir said, bowing slightly. "You have a true baker's touch."

Sora grinned, exposing a row of needle-sharp teeth. "Mama says I'll run the bakery myself one day. If I don't eat all the profits first."

"Both are honorable ambitions," Vamir replied, and unwrapped the roll. It was still warm. He bit into it, savoring the honeyed, earthy taste, and allowed himself a low, contented sigh.

Makota resumed kneading, but kept one eye on the queue. "Busy already. The trade road's in a mood today. I can smell it."

Vamir nodded, mouth full. "I saw more carts than usual near the stable. A couple of travelers camped under the cider apple last night. Something's coming." His tone was calm and even—the townsfolk had seen enough strange arrivals over the past two years that he didn't think much could faze him anymore.

Behind the counter, Sora's brother Kene darted in and out with baskets of fresh rolls, making sure the display remained as full as possible. He was older, more cautious, but no less energetic. His fur was a deep orange with white striping along his arms and tail, and he wore a bandana in lieu of a proper hat.

"Did you hear the rumor?" Kene asked, arranging a tray of pastries with delicate precision. "Someone said the old mill sent three wagons of flour down the road at once. All the way from the north end."

"Never happened in my memory," Makota said, nose wrinkling. "Not unless the granaries are expecting trouble, or a very good harvest. And it's too early for harvest. But it's true. Warren's going to help unload them for me."

Vamir accepted a mug of tea from Makota, enjoying the bite of ginger in its steam. "Maybe the magistracy is planning another census. Or the ogres are coming to barter, and they're worried about running out."

Makota shrugged, then shaped a coil of dough into a perfect spiral. "Nothing good ever comes from the north, except flour and a few of your favorite books."

"And the occasional traveler who needs directions," Vamir added.

As if on cue, the bakery's bell gave a jingle that cut clean through the air, startling even the most entrenched of the morning regulars. In the doorway stood Samantha Godsdotter, her white hair loose around her shoulders, her face half-shadowed by the morning light. She wore a thick, dark traveling cloak that covered her entire frame, and the set of her mouth implied she'd had little patience for interruptions today.

Sam stepped into the bakery, nodded to Makota, then locked eyes with Vamir. "Didn't expect you to be here," she said, but there was humor in her voice.

"Where else would I be?" Vamir said, standing up and brushing crumbs from his lap. "Your tavern isn't open until midday, unless you've changed the rules."

Sam grinned. "You'd know if I did. May I join you?"

"Of course." He slid the second chair out from his table, offering it with a flourish.

Sam sat, draped her cloak over the back, and eyed the remaining half of Vamir's roll. "Did you save that for me, or are you going to finish it before I can?"

Vamir broke the roll in half and passed it to her. She ate it in two neat bites and licked her fingers clean, which gave him a rare moment to observe her up close. The scar on her face, which ran from brow to jaw and intersected her left eye, seemed more pronounced in the early light. Vamir had read somewhere that such scars could be mended with magic, but suspected she wore it as both history and warning.

Makota approached, wiping flour off her hands. "Coffee?" she asked Sam, who nodded. In the time it took for Makota to pour a mug, Kene had run another basket out to the front display, and Sora had darted up to the high shelf to retrieve a jar of honey.

"You heard about the traveler?" Sam said quietly, not quite a question.

Vamir raised an eyebrow. "Only what Warren said, yesterday. That someone new had arrived, very late."

"Showed up at my place late last night indeed," Sam continued. "Didn't even wait for the sun. Asked for water, then started in on the details. Says he's looking for something in the Mistrals. Something that can only be found there, and he's already lost two in his party trying to get here."

"That sounds—" Vamir began, but Sam cut him off.

"—unusual, yes. He's not a typical quester. Didn't want to share the details, but he's desperate. I think he's scared of something. Or someone." Sam sipped her coffee, which brought a momentary pause to her words.

Makota, who had been eavesdropping without apology, chimed in. "Did he have an accent?"

"West. Couldn't place it exactly." Sam thought for a moment. "Maybe the lowlands. Or across the valley."

"He's in the bookshop now?" Vamir asked.

"Waiting outside. I told him you might not be open for a few candlemarks, but he said he'd wait."

Vamir stood, folded his napkin, and set his teacup back on the table. "Then I shouldn't keep him."

Sora appeared beside him, eyes wide. "Are you going to help him?"

"I'll do my best," Vamir said, and ruffled the kit's fur between the ears. "But first, I'll need another roll to keep up my strength." He winked.

Kene wrapped one in a napkin and handed it over, solemn as a priest.

Sam finished her coffee and rose to leave as well. "I'll check in at midday, see if you need anything."

"You can always bring more coffee," Makota said, grinning.

Sam shook her head, but the smile lingered as she made her way out the door.

Vamir thanked Makota and her children, tucked the spare roll into his pocket, and stepped out into the square, already running through the catalog of what books he might need for a traveler with a quest to the Mistrals.

———

The bookshop's facade caught the first light in a way that made the window glass look smoky and uncertain. Vamir could see the shape waiting outside long before he got close enough to recognize him as the traveler Sam had described. Even from a distance, the man's presence was an interruption—where everyone else on the square gave way to the meandering patterns of morning, this man simply stood still, boots planted on the stone like he'd grown up from the very foundation.

Vamir offered a polite wave as he drew closer. "You must be my early riser."

The traveler's gaze flicked from the sign to Vamir's face, assessing him with the slow caution of someone who'd spent too many nights waiting for trouble. His coat was a nondescript grey, patched at the elbows and cinched too tight at the belt. His hands were big, with old scars puckering the knuckles and one index finger curving at a strange angle. He looked like a man who'd been on the road for sennights and hadn't yet found anything worth smiling about.

"My apologies," Vamir said, fumbling with the shop key. "Bakery was generous this morning. I can have you in and out in half the time, if you're in a hurry."

"Take your time," the man said, voice rough as gravel but polite. "It's quieter when no one else is around."

"Quiet is our specialty," Vamir replied, pushing the door open with a practiced shove. The bell above the lintel gave its customary three-note greeting, and the traveler ducked inside with a nod of thanks.

The bookshop was dark, save for a few scattered pools of golden light thrown from the stained glass windows. The shelves pressed close, towering over the aisle in a way that made even Vamir feel small on certain mornings. Every available surface had been claimed by a book, a box, or an impromptu stack of notes. The air was thick with paper and old glue, and the morning's chill faded to a comfortable, library-cool temperature almost immediately.

"Coffee or tea?" Vamir asked, setting the key behind the counter.

"Nothing," the traveler replied. He hovered in the entryway, as if waiting for an invitation to proceed. His eyes darted up and down the stacks, searching for something. Or someone.

Vamir took pity. "This way, please."

They made their way to the back table, where Polyocular was still dozing among a pile of catalog cards and a battered volume of natural history. The creature's feathers fluffed and fell with each tiny breath. Its beak nestled under one stubby wing, the third eye hidden beneath a halo of down.

The traveler sat without waiting to be asked, back straight, hands folded in his lap. "My name's Yoren," he said, the words dropping like pebbles into a well.

"Vamir," Vamir said, settling across from him. "How can I help?"

Yoren looked around again, dropped his voice a notch. "I need to know about the Mistrals. The real Mistrals—the ones that built the towers in the mountains above your town. I was told you'd have the records."

Vamir paused, then nodded slowly. "It's not a common request. Most folks are content with the legends."

"I don't have that luxury." Yoren's mouth twitched, almost into a smile. "I need to know what's true. I need to know how to get in, and I need to know what happens when you do."

Vamir leaned back, drumming his fingers on the table's edge. "I've read most of what's written, but the records are inconsistent. The Mistrals kept to themselves, even when they traded. Most of their history is oral, or lost. Long-lost, in fact. Even the most recent legends are hundreds of years old. What is it you're hoping to find up there?"

Yoren hesitated. "I'm supposed to retrieve an object for someone. But no one will tell me what it is, or why it's important. All I know is that it's old, and it's dangerous, and if I don't get it, someone worse will."

"Classic quest," Vamir said, not unkindly. "I'll get the books."

Polyocular lifted its head as Vamir stood, one eye opening and blinking blearily. The other two joined, forming a slow, synchronized stare that followed Vamir as he wove between the aisles. Vamir reached up, gently stroked Poly's head, and coaxed it onto his shoulder. The creature gave a reluctant chirp, then yawned, showing a surprisingly pink tongue.

"Help me out?" Vamir whispered, and Poly gave a barely perceptible nod.

The shelf of Mistral legends was buried at the far end of the room, nearly touching the ceiling and almost impossible to access without risking an avalanche of unrelated material. Vamir's ladder creaked as he ascended. Poly balanced expertly on his shoulder, using its stubby wings to keep steady.

"Let's see... 'Voices of the North Wind,' 'The Seven Towers,' 'Rites and Riddles of the Ancients'..." Vamir read each title aloud, Poly shaking its head at the first two, then perking up at the third.

"That one?" Poly made a quick, positive trill. Vamir slid the heavy book free, careful not to disturb the stacks on either side. He passed it down, then selected two thinner volumes, both in poor repair but rich with margin notes and glosses. "Just in case," he said. Poly gave a skeptical squawk, but didn't protest.

Back at the table, Yoren had removed his gloves. His hands were big, yes, but Vamir now noticed how the callouses had given way to patches of raw skin. He didn't seem like a man easily broken, but he looked tired in a way that had nothing to do with sleep.

"Here you go," Vamir said, setting the books down with care. "These are the most detailed accounts we have. The last is translated from Old Mistral, so it may be unreliable. Most people who claim to speak the language are fooling themselves, I think."

Yoren flipped open the top volume, scanning the first few pages with a speed that suggested he was more literate than he let on. "Thank you," he said, the phrase awkward and abrupt, as though it were something he hadn't used much in his life.

Poly jumped onto the table and paced around the books, keeping one eye fixed on Yoren at all times. Its movements were slow and deliberate—not curious, as it usually was with customers, but watchful. It completed one circuit of the table, then settled near the edge closest to Vamir and stayed there, utterly still.

Vamir noticed. In fourteen years of working alongside Poly, he could count on one hand the times the creature had stationed itself like that—planted, alert, refusing to be charmed by the transaction at hand. He glanced at Yoren, who was already absorbed in the volume, and felt the quiet pull of something unresolved.

He busied himself with shelving the volumes that had settled on the front desk overnight, giving the man space—and himself time to think. He could not have named what troubled him about Yoren. The man was polite. His request was legitimate. He had paid good coin for books that might genuinely help him. And yet.

And yet Poly sat like a stone sentinel, and Vamir's hands kept finding reasons to stay in the aisle near the back table.

Eventually, Yoren closed the last book and pushed it forward. "I need to buy these. How much?"

Vamir hesitated, waiting for the shop's nudge. "Two silvers, but I can offer one back if you bring them back in one piece. Some of these are irreplaceable."

Yoren nodded, fished a small pouch from inside his coat, and poured six silver coins into his palm. The metal was dull, but old—minted in a style Vamir hadn't seen in decades. "If I don't bring the books back, someone else will."

Vamir took the coins, weighing them thoughtfully. "If you don't come back, should I worry?"

Yoren's eyes flashed, not with malice but with a strange, bone-deep resolve. "Worry about whoever comes looking for me."

Vamir nodded, understanding perfectly.

Yoren gathered the books, stacking them with more care than Vamir expected. He rose, gave Poly a lingering look—Poly returned it without blinking—and strode out of the shop, the bell's single ring marking his departure.

For a long moment, the bookshop was silent.

Vamir stood in the aisle, Poly now on his shoulder, the creature's small heart beating faster than usual against the side of his neck. He watched the empty doorway. He could follow. He could ask Sam to keep an eye on where Yoren went next. He could find Jen and mention the old coins, the raw hands, the way Poly had sat.

He did none of these things. He held very still, and let the moment pass, and listened to the shop settle around him.

Whatever Yoren was carrying into the mountains, it was Yoren's to carry. That was the shape of things. That was how it worked.

Poly chirped, once, softly. It was not approval exactly, and it was not reproach. It was the sound the creature made when it was waiting to see what happened next.

"I know," Vamir said. "Me too."

He returned to the counter, pocketed the old coins, and stared out the window at the empty street.

It wasn't long before the gloom that Yoren left behind was swept out by a gust of laughter and the tap-tap of quick, light feet.

three

. . .

THE BROKEN CLAW looked different in the evenings, as it always did: same room, same scarred bar, but transformed by the crowd and the hush of dusk. Light from the front windows slanted gold through the taproom, highlighting the dust motes and turning the worn table-tops to mirrors. The old stove at the far end cast a reddish pulse over the floor, so the whole pub glowed with warmth and the scents of yeast, caramelizing onions, and smoked fish. Vamir lingered a moment at the threshold, cataloguing the subtle changes—the tables shuffled closer, the benches more crowded than at lunch, the steady murmur of voices much thicker and more urgent than in the slow times.

Sam manned the bar, her face impassive as she polished a row of mugs with swift, sure hands. Her hair was bound tonight, pulled back in a warrior's tail, and her scar caught the light, brightening to a thin silver streak across her cheek. Vamir knew she liked the evenings best, when she could stand sentry over her little fiefdom and every regular was an ally, every stranger a minor puzzle. Susan sat in the shadowed corner, a mug and a battered deck of cards in front of her. Beside her, Dardrad Pebbleblade nursed an ale with the sullen determination of a man who found the world both insufficient and impossible to ignore.

At two tables near the back, six travelers occupied the field. The first table hosted three men—one lanky and pale, one squat and thick-necked, one a scrawny youth with a mustache like a strip of lichen. They huddled over a battered map, the lines and notations visible even from across the room. The other table claimed three women: the oldest in battered leathers, another with her hair cropped close and dyed a sickly yellow, the third so small she seemed more spirit than person, wrapped in layers of brown wool. The travelers all drank as if they needed it to fortify their nerve, and their conversation rose and fell in sharp, fevered waves. Vamir caught phrases as he moved through the room: "the Enchantress is older than any of us," "they say she's got the bones of the mountain in her blood," "if you go up there, you never come back the same."

Dardrad's gaze found Vamir as he approached, and the dwarf's mouth twisted in a faint, contemptuous smile. "You hear this?" he muttered, nodding toward the travelers. "Sennight after sennight, they come. Never with a real plan. Always with stories." Dardrad's dwarfish accent thickened when he was annoyed, vowels flattening like dough under a rolling pin. "I tell you, some folk just want to die in the snow."

Susan sipped her drink, one eyebrow arched. "You'd think this Enchantress would be full up by now, with all the souls she's supposed to have eaten."

"Or bored," Dardrad grumbled.

Vamir set a hand on the dwarf's shoulder, gentle enough not to jostle. "You sound as if you'd rather be up there yourself."

Dardrad snorted. "I'd rather take a slow death in a cask of ale, if it's all the same. But these fools make for good stories." He nodded at the group. "Go listen, if you want. They're about to outdo themselves."

Vamir caught Susan's eye. She gave him a small, amused smile, then slid a card across the table toward him—a silent invitation to join, later, if he wished. For now, Vamir threaded his way to the bar.

Sam tracked his progress with one sharp blue eye, then set down her cloth and leaned in as he arrived. "You look like you want the good stuff," she said.

"Do I?" Vamir replied, feigning surprise. "I thought I wore the air of a man content with the usual."

"You don't," Sam said, and poured a finger of clear, sharp-smelling spirit into a small tumbler. She slid it across the bar, her hands steady even as the room jostled around her. "You hear what they're saying?"

"I do," Vamir said, keeping his voice low. "Is there anything to it?"

Sam's face flickered through several unreadable expressions, then settled into a resigned calm. "There's always something to it, with questers. But this is different. I felt it when they walked in." She tapped her temple with two fingers. "The gift says 'real,' even if my head says 'reckless.'" Then her eyes flicked to the clock-like decoration above the pub's door. "And that says they've a destiny to meet."

Vamir nodded. He trusted Sam's intuition more than his own, especially on matters of quests and the odd rules that governed the flow of travelers through North Pointe. He took a careful sip of the spirit, let it burn its way down, then set the glass aside. "Do you think they'll go through with it?"

"They always do," Sam said. "But I've never seen two groups at once, not for the same thing. That's new." She glanced at the travelers, then back at Vamir. "I half wonder if they should be making appointments."

Vamir's curiosity spiked, but he kept his expression bland. "I suppose I'd better ask, then."

Sam's lips quirked up. "That's what you do, isn't it?"

"Sometimes," he agreed, and turned from the bar.

He approached the first table—the three men, all strangers, their clothes marked with dust from the old trade roads. The leader was the pale, long-limbed one, with a voice that seemed to skate across the surface of his teeth. Vamir waited for a pause, then inserted himself with practiced deference.

"Excuse me," he said, bowing his head. "I'm the bookseller in town. If you're headed to the Mistrals, you might want more than rumors to guide you."

The men eyed him with a mix of suspicion and hope, but the leader smiled thinly and gestured for Vamir to sit. "You know the stories, then?"

"I know a few," Vamir said, "and I know how they tend to change with each retelling. What's the truth, as you've heard it?"

The pale man leaned in, dropping his voice to just above a whisper. "They say the Enchantress lives in the highest keep of the old Mistral people. She's not human. Not even close. Cold as stone, but she knows things—answers, secrets, the way to make even the worst problems go away. For a price."

"You're from the east, originally?" Their accent gave them away, and Vamir wondered if they'd passed through North Pointe during the previous year's exodus.

"Aye." The pale man shook his head. "Might have just stayed east, weathered it out. But so many villages were put to the torch."

Vamir nodded. "And so now you're looking for answers?"

The squat man grunted. "We're looking for survival. Our villages are dying. Something's driving the goblins, and winter was too harsh for us to build proper defenses. We lost a whole village last winter, just gone in a night." His voice cracked. "We heard the Enchantress could help."

The third man, the boy, fidgeted with the map. "Or at least she'd kill us quick, instead of leaving us for the goblins."

Vamir regarded them each in turn, weighing their fear against their resolve. "And you believe she'll listen?"

The leader spread his hands. "What else do we have?"

Before Vamir could respond, the smallest woman from the second table appeared beside him, moving so quietly he almost jumped. Her brown woolen layers muffled her shape, but her voice was brisk and clear. "You're wrong about the goblins," she said, addressing the men. "It's not the goblins. Something's scaring them, too. They're running."

The first group fell silent, eyes narrowing. The woman took a seat without asking and looked directly at Vamir. "You're the only one in town who might know, so I'm telling you: the Enchantress isn't a legend. She's real, and she's awake now because the old gods are shifting."

Vamir raised an eyebrow, intrigued despite himself. "And how do you know that?"

"Because I saw her once," the woman said. "Years ago. I was a child, and she was already old. She doesn't age. She just waits, and when the time's right, she sends for people. For questers." The woman's eyes flickered. "Or maybe for sacrifices."

The leader of the men scoffed, but not convincingly. "You expect us to believe you just walked away from her?"

"I didn't say I walked away," the woman replied, gaze steady. "But I'm here, aren't I?"

The yellow-haired woman at her table called over. "Cira doesn't lie, not about this. If she says the Enchantress is calling, then she is."

Now the conversation drew in half the pub. Susan and Dardrad stopped their game. The man at the stove pretended not to listen, but leaned into the warmth in a way that suggested every word was a secret worth hearing. Even Sam paused, cloth dangling from her hand, eyes bright and fixed on the scene.

Vamir cleared his throat. "What is it that you want from her, exactly?"

The pale man shrugged. "Anything. If she can turn the goblins, or freeze the rivers, or just tell us how to survive another winter—we'd pay any price."

The brown-clad woman, Cira, shook her head. "It's not that simple. She doesn't bargain in normal things. She wants memories, or favors, or years from your life. Or worse. But she always gives what she promises."

Dardrad finally spoke up, his voice like gravel on the flagstones. "Last I heard, the Enchantress got herself chained up in a tower, centuries back. She only gets free if you're fool enough to ask for her help."

Vamir suppressed a grin. He recognized the challenge in Dardrad's tone—the dwarf was just making up tales, now, to see if the others would buy in.

The yellow-haired woman gave a lopsided smile. "Maybe it's time for fools, then."

Dardrad grunted and went back to his ale.

The tension around the tables thickened, every quester and regular alike suddenly invested in the outcome. The second group of women joined the table, chairs scraping as they made room for themselves.

Their leader, the one in battered leather, glanced at Vamir with a seasoned air. "If you're the bookseller, you'd know—what's the way up the Mistrals, these days? We heard the east ridge is closed."

Vamir considered. "There's a new landslide above Mossgate, but the old smuggler's pass is clear as far as the high shelf. If you're light on your feet and careful at night, you could skirt the patrols. But the cold is worse up there. Takes the unprepared every year. We do have an excellent mapmaker in town. Guaranteed up to date."

The woman grinned. "We're not unprepared. But thank you."

The conversation dissolved into argument: which route, what supplies, who had the best luck with bribes at the last outpost. The men and women traded stories and warnings, old rumors colliding and recombining in real time. Vamir sat back, watching the information swirl and contradict itself, making a mental ledger of every inconsistency.

Some said the Enchantress was a ghost, others a bloodline passed down through dozens of identical daughters. Some claimed she could change her shape, turning into mist or crows or a blizzard itself. Others swore she was just a clever woman who'd mastered enough magic to scare the world into obedience. The only point of agreement was that no one returned the same—if they returned at all.

Vamir felt the familiar itch of unsolved mystery, the desire to dig into records and root out the truth beneath the layers of myth. He glanced over at Sam, who met his gaze and gave a tiny, knowing nod. Her gift said "real," and his instincts agreed: this was no ordinary legend.

After a time, the travelers realized they were being watched by half the room and grew quieter, returning to their maps and calculations. Vamir stood, bowed his head in respect, and excused himself. As he passed Susan and Dardrad, the latter barked a laugh.

"You collect these stories like stamps, don't you?" the dwarf said.

"I prefer to think of it as archiving," Vamir replied.

Susan leaned in, voice low. "If you find out the truth, will you tell us? Or is that bad for business?"

"I'll tell you," Vamir promised. "And then you can tell me if it's worth writing down."

Susan raised her mug in salute. Dardrad did the same, albeit with a touch of mockery.

At the bar, Sam refilled Vamir's glass without being asked. "What do you make of it?" she said, voice pitched low for him alone.

"I make it a dozen conflicting tales, none of which match what's in the town records," Vamir said. "Which means it's either brand new, or very old and very well hidden."

Sam's expression didn't change, but her eyes sharpened. "I've never felt it like this before," she said. "It feels fresh."

"I know," Vamir said. "And I think it's important." He drank, savoring the sharpness. Around them, the warmth and the noise built up again, the travelers already trading new rumors and dares.

He was almost at the door when Sam spoke again, just loud enough to reach him over the noise. "Can I ask you something?"

He turned. Her expression was the one she used when she'd been thinking about something for a while and had finally decided to say it —not hostile, but settled.

"That man this morning," she said. "The one who came to your shop before I was up. Yoren."

Vamir went still. "You heard about him."

She grinned. "Makota's kits see hear everything." She set her cloth down and leaned on the bar with both forearms. "She said Poly was upset the whole time he was in your shop. That you noticed. And that you let him walk out with the books anyway, and didn't say a word to anyone."

"I told him to come back if he could."

"That's not what I mean." She studied him for a moment. "Are you all right? Or is there something about him I should know?"

Vamir considered how to answer this. He could say that Yoren was probably fine, that Poly was occasionally wrong, that there was nothing specific to report. All of this was technically true.

"There's nothing I could point to," he said finally. "Only a feeling. Poly's feeling, mostly."

Sam's eyes didn't move from his face. "And if it had been more than a feeling? If you'd known for certain he was carrying something dangerous into those mountains—would you have done anything differently?"

The question landed cleanly, the way Sam's questions tended to.

"I don't know," Vamir said. Which was honest.

Sam seemed to have expected something else. She tilted her head slightly. "You're not being modest."

"No."

She was quiet for a moment, turning that over. "Most people, when they see something wrong, they act. Or they feel bad about not acting. You don't seem to feel bad about it."

"I do, a little," Vamir said. "But not in the way you mean."

"Then explain the way you mean."

He took a breath. Outside, the travelers had lapsed into quieter, more private conversation. The regulars had drifted back to their own tables. The pub had become what it always became at this time of day —a room of people minding their own stories.

"I was an archivist," he said. "With my people. Before I came here." He paused. "That's not quite right—I was born to it. It's a lineage, among Forest Elves of a certain kind. You watch. You record. You hold the memory of what happened so that other people can know it happened." He looked at his glass. "You don't steer. To steer is to put yourself in the story. And if you're in the story, you can't hold the story."

Sam said nothing.

"I know how that sounds," Vamir said.

"It sounds like something a person could use to avoid a great deal of inconvenience," Sam said, not unkindly.

Vamir smiled, because it was fair. "You're probably right that they've become indistinguishable in me. The belief and the preference. I can't fully separate them anymore." He looked at her. "But I'll tell you what I told myself when Yoren left. Someone has to hold the record. If everyone acts on every uneasy feeling, the world becomes a series of interventions and nobody knows what actually happened or why. Someone has to stay back and watch and remember. Otherwise the story gets lost."

Sam considered this for a long moment. The fire shifted in the grate. Somewhere at the back of the pub, Dardrad said something that made Susan laugh.

"I hear what you're saying," Sam said at last. "I just want you to know I don't fully believe it."

"I know," Vamir said. "I'm not sure I fully believe it either."

That seemed to satisfy her in some way that full agreement wouldn't have. She picked up her cloth again. "Well. If Poly's feeling ever becomes a certainty, you'll tell me."

"I will," Vamir said. And meant it.

He left the Broken Claw with the night pressing in around him, and the conversation still turning in his mind. The question Sam had asked—*would you have done anything differently*—was not the kind that resolved itself on the walk home. He suspected it was not the kind that resolved itself at all. It was the kind you carried, and looked at from different angles, and never quite put down.

He went home, fed Poly the last of the seedcake, and sat for a while in the quiet of the shop before bed, listening to the old building settle around him. Whatever the Enchantress was—new legend or old power or something the mountain had decided to make—he would find no answers tonight in the upstairs shelves. He had looked before, in other late-night searches, and always come up empty. If the answer existed anywhere in this building, it was not up here.

He looked at the shelves for a long time. Then he went to bed.

four

· · ·

IT WAS EARLY, even for North Pointe, and the sky above the square was the lavender-pale that lasted only a few minutes before the sun gave up its pretense of restraint and flooded everything in gold. Vamir always considered these the rarest mornings, the ones you could almost believe had been set aside for you alone. The tea shop— Galhani's—was one of the only places in the square open this early, but Vamir wasn't the only one drawn by the scent of herbs and the promise of the first pot brewed.

Inside, the warmth hit immediately, soft and slightly damp, infused with the wild tangle of steeped things: lemon balm, rosehip, some sharper, spicier green Vamir couldn't name. Light came in sharp, milky bands through the lace curtains, throwing little prisms over the mismatched tables and chairs. Galhani herself balanced on a footstool behind the counter, arms already deep in the day's work, her voice trilling as she measured out dried petals into a pot. There were already four cups set on the big round table by the window, each one different: a blue-rimmed cup that had clearly survived a few close calls with gravity, a cracked porcelain rose that looked too delicate to touch, a mug painted with birds, and an oversized gnomeware stein better suited for soup than tea.

Vamir hovered near the entry, feeling the chill on his back from the receding night and the pleasant prickle of anticipation on his front. He was not first—Jen was already at the table, back straight as a ruler, fingers drumming the handle of her cup with the restless precision of someone accustomed to keeping order even among friends. She'd left her constable's badge somewhere, but you didn't need it to know who she was. Jen nodded at Vamir, then returned to her inspection of the square beyond the lace.

"Your turn to bring the sweets, Vamir," said Makota, emerging from the kitchen with a tray balanced on her shoulder and a towel slung like a sash across her chest. The tray bore a pyramid of tiny, iced biscuits, each dusted with something glittery and gold.

"I thought I'd let the experts handle it," Vamir said, settling into the chair next to Jen. He accepted a biscuit and took an exaggeratedly delicate nibble, earning a snort from the constable.

"See? He does remember the rules." Makota slid the tray into the center of the table and began filling cups with Galhani's latest blend.

Galhani arrived a beat later, hair in a messy braid and hands already stained with berry juice. She hopped onto her chair—boosted by a small stack of dictionaries Vamir recognized from his own shop— and poured herself a generous measure of tea. "No sugar for me," she announced, before anyone could offer. "Lara says I'm sweet enough to rot my own teeth out."

They all sipped in silence for a moment, the air full of the first, tentative birdsong from the eaves and the occasional distant clack of a wagon somewhere beyond the square. It was the sort of silence that comes easy to people who've known each other long enough that every word means something, and none of them need to rush.

It was Jen who broke it, as she always did. "They're already lining up outside the stables. The travelers. Another batch with nothing but winter coats and too much hope."

Makota made a face. "Didn't we just get rid of the last lot?"

"Two nights ago," Galhani said, wriggling in her chair. "That's when the moon was full and the kits kept everyone up with their yelling."

Vamir cradled his tea, letting the steam sting his nose. "The quests are coming closer together. Or the stories are getting louder."

Galhani snickered. "Both, maybe. Or the travelers are just getting lazier, and this is the only town with decent beds."

"That's slanderous," Makota said. "Our beds are the finest between here and Ogrehame. That's just science." She grinned, flashing a few pointed teeth.

Jen sipped her tea, considering. "It used to be every few sennights. Now it's every three, four days. And not just the usual types—there's been more variety. A pair of twins last sennight, then a scholar with a half-melted hat, now a woman who looks like she's never walked further than the end of her own garden path."

Galhani gestured with her spoon. "Maybe she's a spy. Or a very bored noble."

Vamir shrugged. "There are worse reasons to walk the world."

Makota set her tea down with a decisive thunk. "If it's the Enchantress they're after, they're in for a surprise." She plucked a biscuit and snapped it in half, crumbs scattering over her lap. "Every group I've seen looks less prepared than the last."

"Who's to say she doesn't already run a queue system?" Vamir said. "First come, first served. One wish per supplicant."

"Do you think she makes them fill out forms?" said Galhani, delighted. "Name, age, desired outcome, last known address."

Jen's mouth twitched, threatening to turn up at the edges. "If the forms are anything like the ones for the town censuses down South, most will just forge their answers anyway."

"That's why she eats them," Makota replied, deadly serious. "Forgery is her only real crime. She's a stickler for paperwork."

The laughter that followed was gentle, but it made the tea taste better and the morning feel warmer. Vamir caught himself smiling, the tension of the previous night drifting away for a few blessed minutes —the conversation with Sam, Yoren's old coins, Poly's watchful stillness. He topped up everyone's cup, then leaned back in his chair, letting his gaze wander to the small, irregular shadow cast by Polyocular perched atop the curtain rod.

It was Galhani who sobered first, tracing a circle in the condensation on her cup. "But there's a lot of talk lately, isn't there? Not just about the Enchantress. People are getting desperate, and desperate people believe whatever makes them feel safer." She looked at each of them in turn. "If something really does change, will we be able to see it coming?"

Vamir nodded, suddenly serious. "We always have before."

"But what if it's not something we can fix?" Jen said, voice low. "What if this is the sort of story that doesn't end with a clever plan or a lucky break?"

Makota shrugged, but her tail twitched behind her. "Then we do what we always do. Keep the town safe, bake extra, and hope someone else deals with it first."

"Not a bad plan," Vamir said. "Though I'm starting to think I should update the emergency manual in the shop."

"You have an emergency manual?" Galhani looked surprised, then delighted. "Is there a section on evil sorceresses?"

"There's a section on just about everything," Vamir said. "But I may need to add a few chapters."

They lapsed into companionable silence again, each turning the thought over in their own way. Makota rose first, brushing the crumbs from her lap and straightening her apron with practiced efficiency. "I'd better get back. The kits are probably eating the profits."

Jen set her cup down with a little clink. "I'll do a walk through the square. There are three travelers already peering in the windows at the inn."

Galhani poured herself a last cup, holding it between both hands. "I'll wait for Lara, then open the shop proper."

"I'll swing by for a taste after lessons," Vamir promised.

Jen lingered a moment as the others filed out. She watched Makota cross the square, her gait purposeful and efficient, then turned to Vamir. "You really think it's new? The Enchantress?"

"I do," he said. "And that worries me."

Jen nodded, then tipped her head as if listening to something only she could hear. "The travelers just passed the west gate. You'll have your hands full in a few minutes." She gave a little smile, then turned and slipped out, leaving only the faintest echo of her presence behind.

Vamir took a deep breath, savoring the silence. The sun, higher now, had melted the dew, and the air outside shimmered with the promise of a perfect spring day. He stood, helped Galhani clear the cups and saucers, then made his way toward the bookshop.

Whatever came next, he knew, would be worth remembering.

———

Evening at the Broken Claw started slow, like a kettle set on the back of the stove: the heat crept in beneath notice, the room changed color and tone, and then all at once it was alive with voices and a glow like nothing else in town. Vamir arrived early enough to claim a spot by the wall, midway between the bar and the fireplace. The fire was already burning, Sam's work, and it gave the place its familiar scent—oak, a little sweet, and the fainter hint of roasted fish from the kitchen next door. A few regulars occupied their usual positions: Susan, the card sharp, nursing a small beer and building a card house; Dardrad, already three mugs in and arguing quietly with himself; and a pair of local traders with their heads bent together over a half-played game of dominos.

But it was the travelers who caught Vamir's eye. Not because they were loud or clumsy—if anything, they did their best to blend in, shrinking into the woodwork and keeping their words low—but because the room seemed to orient itself around them, the way the surface of a pond makes space for every tossed pebble. Tonight there were two groups, each staked out at opposite ends of the room. One was a trio of men, hard-worn, their clothes mismatched and patched. The other was a pair, a woman and a boy, both with the taut, watchful look of people who'd learned to expect trouble at every turn. All five sat hunched over their drinks, eyes on the door or the fire, barely speaking even among themselves.

Sam worked the bar, her arms bare and scar bright against her cheek. She moved with a careful steadiness, filling and cleaning as if the bar top were a battlefield and every glass a potential weapon. She glanced at the travelers, then at Vamir, then at the traders, her expression unchanged.

Vamir set his book on the table and watched. Polyocular was with him, perched on the edge of the banquette, tail feathers dusting the seat. The little creature was alert, all three eyes open and moving.

He was watching the three men when he caught the oddity: a single traveler, sitting alone at the far end of the bar. Not odd in the usual sense—single travelers came through every few days, sometimes looking for a party, sometimes for work, sometimes just for a bed and a morning without rain. But this one was different. She was older, easily past sixty, with silver hair braided back and pinned with wooden sticks. Her dress was plain but clean, and she wore a heavy wool shawl over her shoulders. The woman's face was broad and kind, creased at the eyes, with a dimple that appeared whenever she smiled—which she did, often, despite the fact that no one seemed to be talking to her.

She looked nothing like the other questers. She looked like someone's grandmother, misplaced from a bigger, busier city and now making the best of it. She sipped her tea—tea, in the pub—and watched the crowd, every now and then offering a little nod or a smile to anyone who glanced her way.

Vamir tried to place her, but he was sure she hadn't come through his shop, or the tea shop, or the bakery. He would have remembered.

A moment later, the front door banged open, letting in a cold breath of spring and a flurry of noise. Galhani swept in, cheeks flushed and arms full of parcels. Behind her, Lara—her partner, taller and more reserved—carried a sack of dried beans and a set of folding stools. They made straight for Vamir, dropping their cargo at his feet with twin sighs.

"Evening, V," said Galhani, climbing up onto the bench and pulling Lara along with her. "Hope you don't mind. We heard the new shipment from the southern groves was in, and I wanted to try it before the regulars drink it all."

"I'd never deny you a seat, Gal," Vamir said. "Or you, Lara."

Lara gave a polite nod and turned to scan the menu chalked above the bar, then leaned in to speak softly with Galhani. It was a well-practiced routine: Galhani would handle the people, Lara the logistics.

Between the two, they ran the tea and herb shop as efficiently as any army.

Vamir poured a measure from the little carafe on the table and gestured for Galhani to help herself. She did, and the three of them sat in companionable near-silence for a few moments, content to watch the pub fill up.

It was Galhani, as ever, who broke the spell. "Do you know her?" she whispered, tipping her chin toward the silver-haired woman at the bar.

"I do not," Vamir said. "But I intend to. She's the only person here not looking over her shoulder."

Lara said, "She was in the square earlier. Gave Makota's boy a piece of licorice and called him 'dearie.' He's still talking about it."

"I'm going to talk to her," Galhani declared. And before Vamir could protest, she slid off the bench and crossed the room, pulling Lara in her wake.

Vamir waited, watching the travelers at their separate tables, then turned to Polyocular. "Who do you think she is?" he asked softly.

Poly's middle eye blinked in the slow, measured way it always did when considering a question. It offered no opinion.

Across the room, Galhani reached the bar and greeted the woman with a bright, "Hello! Is it your first time in town?" The woman's face split into a broad, genuine smile.

"Not the first, but it's been a long while," she replied. Her voice was soft, but had a clear note that carried even over the noise.

Galhani made the introductions, loud enough for Vamir to hear: "I'm Galhani, this is my partner Lara, and that's Vamir, bookseller and most patient man in North Pointe." She jerked a thumb toward Vamir's table. The woman laughed, a round, pleasant sound.

"Lovely to meet you all. I'm Elspeth. Elspeth Riverpine." She stuck out her hand, shaking first with Galhani, then with Lara. "This is a nice place. Warmer than the last pub I tried."

Galhani said, "You look like you could use a friend. Want to join us?"

Elspeth considered, then nodded. "I'd like that, thank you."

It took a moment to gather cups and shuffle benches, but soon

Elspeth was seated at the table with Vamir and the others. Up close, she was even more formidable—her hands were broad and lined with years of kneading, weaving, or perhaps just living. Her eyes sparkled with amusement, as if she was in on some cosmic joke and happy to share it with you if you just asked.

"Passing through?" Vamir inquired, as politely as he could.

Elspeth took a measured sip. "I suppose you could say that. Been a widow twenty-odd years now. Raised my children, saw them off. Decided I should see the world, or at least a bit of it. Why let the young folk have all the fun?"

"Are you questing?" Galhani asked, eyes shining.

Elspeth laughed. "What would I quest for? Youth? Lost love? I'm more interested in good company and seeing places that look different from my own front yard." She swept a hand around the pub. "And this—this is different. I like it."

Lara said, "You picked a good sennight. Most of the dangerous types are still north of the pass. Only the lost and the lonely left here tonight." Her tone was gentle, not a trace of mockery.

Elspeth's eyes twinkled. "Well, that suits me fine. If I get bored, I'll just start a fight." She said it so matter-of-fact that Vamir nearly spit his drink.

The conversation carried on, light and easy. Elspeth asked about the town—its history, its best bakeries, what made the tea shop different from the others in the valley. She listened with real interest, never once looking past the speaker or glancing at the door. She was, as Vamir decided after half a mark, utterly at home no matter where she was.

Eventually, Galhani asked, "Where are you staying tonight? If you need a place, we can make up the guest room—"

Elspeth waved the offer away, smiling. "I'm planning to ask at the inn, if they've got a room with a view of the square. Or failing that, a cot near the window so I can see the sunrise."

Vamir gestured to Sam, who had been following the conversation from the bar with subtle interest. "Sam, does Minnie have a room for our friend here?"

Sam nodded. "Two, in fact, unless someone's taken them in the last candlemark, which I doubt. Take your pick, friend. First drink's on the house for newcomers."

Elspeth beamed. "You're all so kind. It's no wonder your town is famous for hospitality."

Jen had come in sometime during the conversation and now hovered near the hearth, arms crossed, watching the room with her usual wary poise. But when she heard Elspeth's voice—its warmth, its sincerity—her expression softened. She drifted over and joined the table, squeezing in between Vamir and Lara.

Sam arrived with a round of drinks, expertly balanced. She set a dark beer in front of Elspeth, who accepted it with a nod, and refilled the others.

"Good evening, Elspeth," Jen said. "I'm the constable. If you need anything, or if anyone gives you trouble, just let me know."

Elspeth lifted her beer in salute. "Thank you, dear. But I haven't had trouble since our old alderman tried to fine me for selling cider without a permit. And I beat him at cards, so he had to let it go."

The table exploded in laughter, even Sam cracking a grin as she returned to the bar. The travelers at their distant tables looked over, some with open curiosity, others with envy. A few minutes later, one of the men stood and crossed to the bar, ordering a round for his group and watching the locals with the shy hunger of someone who'd lost their own sense of home long ago.

As the night deepened, the line between locals and visitors blurred. The regulars told stories of wild harvests and strange storms; the travelers spoke of places farther west, where the rivers ran red and the mountains were haunted by more than snow. Elspeth, for her part, listened and responded with just the right mix of disbelief and delight. She told a story of a town where the cows learned to open the gates and had to be bribed with sugar cubes to stay in the pastures. Another about a tea shop with a secret menu—if you ordered the right thing, they'd tell your fortune, but only in haiku. The stories got wilder, the drinks stronger, and by the time Sam started clearing tables for the night, the Broken Claw felt like the happiest, noisiest living room in all the northern valleys.

Polyocular had, at some point, migrated onto Elspeth's shoulder, where it preened and nuzzled her hair, purring like a very contented kettle. Elspeth seemed not to mind, even stroking its feathers as she spoke.

When the first notes of a song drifted up—one of the traders at the domino table, quietly humming an old marching tune—it was Elspeth who picked it up, her voice clear and sweet. Others joined in, then more, and soon the whole pub sang together, the melody rising and falling like the wind over the hills. They sang through three choruses before someone requested a second song, this one with a little more bite to it. And then, perhaps emboldened by the warmth and the beer, Elspeth led the room in a gently bawdy tune about a miller's daughter and the lengths she'd go for a fresh loaf of bread.

The pub roared with laughter. Even Jen, who rarely sang above a murmur, joined in for the refrain.

As the song wound down, the fire burned low and the room settled into a quiet contentment. People paired off, or retreated to their corners, or dozed where they sat. Sam polished glasses at the bar, watching with the air of a woman who'd seen it all and approved.

Vamir caught Elspeth's eye and raised his glass. "Thank you, Elspeth. You made this a better night."

She smiled, soft and full of secrets. "That's all any of us can hope to do, isn't it?"

———

The Broken Claw lingered in a comfortable afterglow long after most of the customers had drifted off to bed. Sam moved through the bar with her usual efficiency, gathering empty mugs and wiping tables. Here and there, a candle guttered out or a chair scraped the floor as someone gathered their things, but mostly it was quiet: a good, rich quiet, made from the sediment of stories and song.

Vamir stayed at his table with Galhani and Elspeth, the three of them basking in the warmth that remained. The fire was little more than embers now, but it threw shifting patterns across the low-beamed ceiling and the scuffed wooden floor. Polyocular had retreated to Vamir's lap, where it slept curled like a particularly feathery glove. Lara had gone home earlier, promising to see them in the morning; Jen had left, too, walking her last circuit of the square before retiring.

It was Elspeth who finally broke the spell, her voice soft in the hush. "I haven't had a night like this in years," she said. "Not since my Henry was alive. We used to go down to the Red Lantern, back home, and he'd always get me to sing, even though I said I wouldn't."

"You're a natural," said Galhani, pouring a little more from the dregs of the carafe. "I'd pay to hear you sing every night."

Elspeth's cheeks colored. "You say that, but you haven't heard my 'River Queen Lament.' It's enough to sour the beer."

"Impossible," Vamir said. "Sam's beer is unsourable. It's a point of local pride."

Sam, who was sweeping nearby, snorted and kept moving, but Vamir caught her smile as she bent to pick up a stray coaster.

They sipped in companionable silence for a few minutes. Outside, the wind had picked up, rattling the pub's windows in their frames. Vamir glanced toward the door, wondering if the rain would come tonight or hold off until morning.

Elspeth caught the gesture and said, "I'll have to be up early, if I want to make the first stage out to the pass. I hate to leave such good company, but I promised myself I'd see the next sunrise from the ridge."

Galhani set her cup down with a little tap. "Then you have to stop by the tea shop first. I'll make you a travel blend—something to keep your hands warm and your spirits up."

Elspeth's eyes crinkled at the corners. "That would be lovely, dear. I do like a good cup, and it makes the walking easier."

Vamir nodded agreement. "It can be sharp in the mornings, even in spring. Especially if the clouds roll in."

Elspeth patted his hand, the gesture light and practiced. "Thank you, Vamir. For making me feel like I belonged here, even for a night."

Vamir smiled. "That's what towns like this are for, Elspeth. A place to rest, and to be remembered."

At that, Sam returned with a small ring of keys, her businesslike manner belying the warmth in her voice. "Whenever you're ready,

Elspeth, I'll show you to your room. It's just upstairs and to the left. Sheets are clean, window looks out on the square."

Elspeth finished her drink, stood, and straightened her shawl. "Thank you, Sam. I hope you'll wake me if I oversleep. I'd hate to miss the sunrise."

Sam gave a little salute. "I'll send Sora with a mug of hot milk at dawn. She's better than any alarm clock."

Elspeth's laugh was quiet but carried. She turned to Galhani and Vamir and gave each a firm, fond hug. "You two take care of each other. The world's better with both of you in it."

Vamir felt something knot in his chest at the words, but he only nodded and said, "Travel safe, Elspeth. And don't let any questers talk you into saving the world unless there's a good meal at the end of it."

"Noted," she said, and with a final wave, followed Sam toward the stair.

Galhani lingered a little longer, watching the fire shrink and settle. She leaned over and whispered, "I hope I have her spirit when I'm old."

"You already do," Vamir said. "You just hide it under sugar and lemon zest."

Galhani squeezed his arm, then got up to gather her things. "I'll see you in the morning, V. Save me a good book—something with a happy ending."

"Always," Vamir said.

When the pub had finally emptied, and Sam had locked the door behind the last straggler, Vamir waited by the dying fire a moment more, savoring the feeling of being exactly where he was supposed to be. Outside, the lanterns on the square swayed in the wind, painting slow, dancing shadows across the glass.

He carried Polyocular home in the crook of his arm, and as he crossed the silent square, he glanced up at the inn window where a soft glow now burned. For a moment, he imagined Elspeth awake, watching the lamplight, thinking her own quiet thoughts. Something about her nagged at him pleasantly, the way a half-remembered song does — not troubling, just present, waiting to resolve.

He let the thought go, and walked on.

five

. . .

THE BOOKSHOP after dark had a personality wholly its own. Gone were the bright pools of sunlight, the bustle of children or gossips or questers. In their place: a hush thick enough to hear the bones of the building settling, the faintest breath of wood smoke through the chimney, the way the shelves loomed in the lantern-light as if they might grow arms and wrap you in a padded embrace. The only light came from a brace of candles on the main desk and the lantern Vamir carried, its glow spilling over the carpet of ancient, well-oiled boards.

Polyocular was asleep, curled into a compact orb atop the "Lost Histories" section, its breathing deep and slow. It did not stir when Vamir entered, nor when he hung his cloak and set down his bag with a soft thump. He left the creature to its rest. What he needed tonight, he suspected he could find himself.

He started methodically, the way he always did: local legends first, working outward. He pulled the three volumes he knew best — the valley histories, the compendium of northern folklore, the annotated collection of Mistral-adjacent myths that a travelling scholar had left as payment two summers ago. He carried them to the back table, spread them open, and read.

A candlemark passed, and he candle continued to shorten.

He found references to mountain spirits, to cold-weather omens, to a half-dozen variations on the theme of the dangerous woman in the high place — the ice witch, the storm bride, the keeper of the passes. But these were old stories, worn smooth by retelling, their origins traceable to specific famines or floods or the particular anxieties of particular generations. None of them matched the Enchantress as the travelers described her. None of them were *new*.

He restacked the volumes and moved to the next section. Mythology, regional. Then comparative folklore. Then the shelf he thought of privately as the catch-all — books that had arrived without clear category and been shelved by instinct rather than system. He pulled anything that looked promising, carried it to the table, skimmed. Set it aside.

The pile of rejected books grew.

Poly stirred somewhere in the dark, made a small sound, and was quiet again.

Vamir rubbed the bridge of his nose and looked at what remained on the shelf. He'd covered the obvious ground twice over. In fourteen years of keeping this shop, he had never failed to find what a customer needed — the shop had never failed to produce it, whether by Poly's instincts or by the quiet rearranging of the shelves that happened when no one was watching. Travelers arrived asking for books he'd never heard of, and somehow the books were always there. A magistrate's apprentice needing obscure clan histories. A scholar wanting a translated text he hadn't known existed. The shop provided. That was its nature. That was its gift.

But tonight, for the first time he could remember, it was not providing.

He stood in the middle of the aisle, lantern in hand, and had the peculiar sensation that the shop knew it. The hush felt different than the usual late-night quiet — not restful but expectant, like the held breath before a door opens. The shadows between the shelves seemed to lean in slightly, attentive. Even the familiar smell of paper and old glue seemed sharper, as though the building had become more itself while he wasn't looking.

I need this, he thought, not quite addressing anyone. *Not for a traveler. For me.*

It was the first time he had made that distinction aloud, even in his own mind.

As if in answer, Polyocular woke.

Not gradually, the way the creature usually surfaced from sleep in a slow unfurling of feathers and a sequence of blinks. It woke all at once, every eye open simultaneously, upright on its perch with a focus that Vamir had never seen in it before. It looked at him directly — not with the sideways curiosity it used when tracking an interesting customer, but straight on, all three eyes aligned, as though it were seeing him clearly for the first time and finding the view significant.

Then it dropped from its shelf and flew, not with its usual looping investigation of the room, but in a straight line to the southernmost end of the shop. It landed on the lowest shelf of a case Vamir had always thought of as the miscellany — the books that didn't belong anywhere else, that had accumulated over years into a quiet, unexamined row. It walked along the shelf with deliberate steps, tail feathers fanned, and stopped at the far end.

It looked back at him.

Vamir crossed the room, lantern swinging. "What have you found?"

Poly stepped aside. Its wing-tip rested lightly on the spine of a slim blue volume at the end of the row.

His grandfather's book.

Vamir stopped. He had shelved it there years ago — more than a decade, perhaps — because he hadn't known where else to put it. It wasn't a reference work or a history or a legend compendium. It was a personal volume, hand-written, in the cramped Forest Elf script his grandfather had used for everything. He had read it once, long ago, and understood perhaps a third of it. He had never thought to reach for it in a search.

He looked at Poly. "That's not—"

Poly pressed its wing to the spine more firmly.

Vamir reached down and picked it up. The cover was worn smooth with handling, the boards slightly warped at the corners, the pages foxed at the edges. It felt exactly as it always had — familiar, slightly melancholy, the weight of a life he had not lived pressing gently through the binding.

He pulled it from the shelf.

The wall clicked.

Vamir did not move for a long moment. He looked at the shelf, then at the wall behind it, then at his own hand holding the book. The click had been definitive, mechanical — not a sound the building made when settling, not a mouse in the wainscoting. Something had engaged. Something had been waiting for exactly this.

Poly made a sound he had never heard from it before: low, resonant, almost ceremonial.

Vamir set the lantern on the floor and pressed his free hand to the back wall of the shelf. Where there had always been solid plaster, he found a seam — barely perceptible, running in a rectangle roughly the height of a door. He traced it with his fingertips, feeling the faint groove, and then the wall shifted. Not dramatically. Just a fraction of an inch, the way a door moves when the latch releases and gravity begins its work.

He stood back. The section of wall swung inward on hinges so well-balanced it made no sound, revealing a darkness and a set of narrow wooden steps descending into it.

Cold air rose from below, carrying a scent so unexpected that Vamir stood very still and simply breathed it: parchment, old and dense and absolutely dry. Not the comfortable shabbiness of the upstairs shelves — something older, more concentrated. The smell of preservation. Of things kept.

He thought of the shop's gift — its insistence on always having what was needed, its quiet management of arrivals and departures, the way it had served every traveler who had crossed its threshold for however many years before him, and however many before that. He had always understood it as a gift for *them*. The travelers. The questers. The people passing through with needs the shop was equipped to meet.

He looked at the steps. He looked at the book still in his hand.

It has been waiting for you to need something, he thought. *It has been waiting for you.*

He wasn't sure if that was a comforting thought or a frightening one.

Poly had already slipped past him and descended the first three steps, its blue plumage faintly luminous in the dark below. It looked back up at him with all three eyes.

Vamir picked up the lantern, tucked his grandfather's book under his arm, and followed.

———

The steps were narrow, each one slightly concave from use — which meant, Vamir registered distantly, that they had been used. Many times, by many people, over a very long span of time. The walls of the passage were stone and mortar, irregular, older than anything he'd encountered in the building above. The floor sloped gently downward. The cold deepened with each step, clean and mineral, nothing like the damp chill of a cellar. It was the cold of deep places that had never known weather.

He paused at the first landing to catch his breath and take stock. Above him, the secret door was still open, a pale rectangle of candle-light. Below, Poly moved ahead, the third eye casting a faint blue ring on the walls. He was, he realized, not frightened. He was something else — the feeling he got when he opened a book to a random page and found exactly the sentence he needed. The feeling of having been anticipated.

At the midpoint of the stair, the passage opened slightly into a shallow alcove on the left side. Vamir raised his lantern.

A small altar had been carved into the stone — not added later, but built into the wall as part of the original construction. The surface was basalt, worn smooth at the center by the pressure of hands laid flat over many years. Two sigils were carved into the face: the first he recognized immediately, the pinched-glass shape and cragged peaks of Nimarith, the Mountain God. The second he did not recognize — an open eye surrounded by curling lines that suggested both flame and the particular fluid curve of ink letters. Beneath the sigils, the remnants of ancient offerings: a stub of candle so petrified it had become mineral rather than wax, a few desiccated berries, a single feather bound in red thread that crumbled slightly when the draft of his passing touched it.

He stood before the altar for a long moment, feeling that quality of attention again — the sense of being observed by something patient and specific. Then he continued down.

The last few steps opened abruptly into the archive proper, and Vamir's first coherent thought was that the geometry was wrong.

He had mapped this building in his mind a hundred times — its footprint, its proportions, the relationship between the shop floor and the rooms above and the shallow cellar beneath. None of that mapping accounted for what he was looking at. The chamber before him was vast. Shelves ran in long curving rows, rising higher than his lantern could illuminate and extending laterally into a darkness that the lantern could not begin to address. Laddered walkways spanned gaps between platforms. Stairs rose to balconies stacked above balconies. The architecture was not impossible — each element, taken alone, was comprehensible — but the aggregate was larger than the world above could contain it.

And then the ambient light began to rise.

It came from nowhere specific — not from torches or windows or any source he could identify — a slow, steady illumination like the sky brightening before dawn. It was cool and white and cast no shadows, and as it grew it revealed the shelves in their full extent: thousands of books, scrolls, folios, manuscript bundles, leather cases closed with brass clasps. Some volumes were chained to their shelves. Some seemed to glow faintly from within, their titles swimming across their covers in scripts he could not read. Some were so enormous they rested on dedicated lecterns. Some were so small they would have been invisible without the strange sourceless light to catch their spines.

Vamir stood at the threshold and understood, all at once, why the upstairs shop had been unable to help him tonight.

The upstairs shop was for travelers. It provided what they needed from its own resources, and it was very good at that, and it had never once failed in fourteen years, and he had been grateful for it without ever asking why. But travelers needed particular books — specific, findable things. An annotated clan history. A translated myth collection. Items.

What Vamir needed tonight was not an item. It was the deep record. The pattern beneath the patterns. The memory of the valley going back further than any book he owned upstairs could reach.

He was not a traveler in this building. He had never been a traveler. He was something else — had always been something else, had known it without naming it — and this place, this impossible archive built beneath a bookshop on a trade road in a small northern valley, had been built for exactly that something else.

His grandfather's book was still in his hand. He held it carefully, aware of it in a new way.

Poly glided ahead into the archive, its third eye blazing, and looked back at him with an expression that Vamir could only describe as patient.

"All right," Vamir said. His voice sounded strange in the space — not swallowed by it, as he'd expected, but held by it, returned to him clearly. "Let's see what you have."

He stepped forward, and the archive — warm now, purposeful, attentive in the way that living things are attentive — began to answer.

———

He did not find the Enchantress that night. That is to say, he did not find her origin, her precedent, the account he'd been looking for when Poly had led him to the grandfather's book and the wall had opened. The archive was vast and he was a single evening into it, and it quickly became clear that the question he'd arrived with was a great deal smaller than the resource he'd been given access to. He was like a man who came to a river to fill a cup and found an ocean.

What he found instead was the shape of the question. He pulled books at Poly's guidance — old, many of them, in scripts he could read only partially, in languages he recognized but didn't fully command — and they told him, in fragments and cross-references and marginalia and illustrations, that the valley had a history he had not known. A deep history. A history that had been kept somewhere, carefully, by someone, against the day it would be needed.

The Enchantress had no direct precedent in what he read that night. No name, no exact analogue. But around the edges of a dozen different texts, he began to see the outline of something: a pattern of disruption, cyclical, spanning generations. Not her, specifically. Something that became her, in this particular season, in this particular form.

It was not an answer. It was the first intimation that an answer existed.

He read until the ambient light shifted subtly — he couldn't have said how he knew, but the quality of it changed, like a room brightening toward morning — and Poly began to circle his feet with the particular persistence that meant, unambiguously, *enough for tonight.* He stacked the books he'd been using with care, noting their positions for his return. He gathered the lantern, which had burned very low.

At the altar on the way back up, he paused. He looked at the two sigils — the god he knew and the one he didn't — and felt, for the first time, that the not-knowing was intentional. Not a gap in his education. A space being kept open. A name to be learned.

He climbed the rest of the stairs, stepped through into the shop, and held his grandfather's book for a moment before returning it to its place on the shelf. His hand rested on it briefly after he let go.

The wall closed behind him, silent, the seam invisible.

He replaced the displaced books, doused the low-burned candles, and stood in the ordinary dark of the ordinary shop. Outside, through the stained glass, the first grey suggestion of morning was beginning in the east.

He had not found what he came for. He had found what he needed. He was beginning to understand that these were, in this building, never the same thing.

He went upstairs to sleep.

six

. . .

HE SLEPT FOUR MARKS, which was enough. He lay for the remaining two with his eyes open, listening to the building around him.

He was listening, he admitted to himself, for sounds from below. A rustling. The particular silence of a large space that is not empty. He heard nothing, which proved nothing, and eventually the sky beyond the warped glass of his bedroom window went from black to grey to the tentative gold of early morning, and he rose, dressed, and went downstairs.

The shop was as he had left it. The books were on their shelves. The grandfather's blue volume sat at the end of its row, flush with its neighbors, unremarkable. The wall behind it was a wall.

Vamir made tea, stood at the window with the cup warming both hands, and did not cross to the southernmost shelf.

It was not that he doubted what had happened. He doubted very little — his memory was precise, and the cold mineral smell still lived faintly in the back of his throat, and there was a quality to the tiredness in his legs that was not the tiredness of a late night at the desk but of stairs descended and climbed. It had happened. The archive was real and it was below him and it was full of things he had not read yet, and the restraint required to not go back down immediately was considerable.

But he had learned, over a long life with books, that the impulse to consume was not always the same as the readiness to receive. He had rushed at texts before, in his younger years, in the forest — arrived at a manuscript with his questions already formed and found only the answers he'd expected, missing the deeper thing the text had been trying to tell him because he hadn't been quiet enough to hear it. The archive had been there, presumably, for longer than he had been alive. It would still be there this afternoon. It would be there tomorrow.

More importantly: he was not sure, yet, what his presence in that space meant. He had a sense of it — the two-tier logic he'd felt at the threshold, the understanding that the lower archive was not for travelers but for him, for the keeper — but a sense was not a knowledge, and he did not act on senses alone. Especially not in matters that touched the town.

Because that was the thing he kept returning to, standing at the window with his tea going cold.

The town had been part of a story before. Less than a year ago, the fire cult, the loss of the magic, the icosagon broken and the gifts gone dark. It had recovered. It always recovered; that was part of its nature, maybe the most essential part. But recovery was not immunity, and the fact that it had happened once meant Vamir could no longer maintain the comfortable assumption that North Pointe Common Towne was the stage on which stories played out rather than a participant in them.

If the town could become the story, then he could too. He, the keeper. He, the archivist. The one whose function depended on remaining outside.

He did not care for that thought. He turned it over several times, looking for the angle at which it became less true, and couldn't find one.

Polyocular dropped from the rafters and landed on his shoulder, apparently having slept better than Vamir had. It pressed its beak briefly to his cheek, which was as close as it came to sympathy, and then fixed its attention on the square outside with the alert satisfaction of a creature that had done its job and was now prepared for whatever came next.

"You're very pleased with yourself," Vamir told it.

Poly made a sound that did not dispute this.

———

He forced himself out of the shop before the morning settled into the particular quality of stillness that made it easy to stay. He locked the door, turned the sign — OPEN, though he would not be immediately behind the counter — and crossed the square to Galhani's, where the smell of the first steeping reached him half a block away.

The tea shop at this time was a different creature than the bakery. Where Makota's was warm and loud and faintly industrial, Galhani's was close and aromatic and meditative, the kind of place that asked you, gently, to slow down. The shelves were crowded with jars, the walls hung with drying bundles, the light filtered through glass of various colors to produce an effect somewhere between a greenhouse and a chapel.

Galhani was behind the counter, standing on her footstool, engaged in what appeared to be a careful negotiation with a small ceramic pot that was either boiling over or threatening to. She had both hands on the lid and an expression of intense concentration.

"One moment," she said, without looking up.

"Take your time," Vamir said, and settled onto a stool.

The pot was convinced to behave. Galhani set it aside with a look of mild reproach and turned to him. "You look like you read all night."

"Most of it."

"Find what you were looking for?"

"Not exactly." He considered how much to say. "I found the shape of it. That's something."

Galhani poured without asking — a green blend he didn't recognize, brighter than the usual morning offering. She watched him taste it with the candid interest of a craftsperson checking their work.

"New?" he asked.

"Very. Lara found the base herb at the market in Wrenfeld. I've been trying to work out what it wants to be paired with for three sennights." She tilted her head. "Well?"

"Something citrus," Vamir said. "But not sharp. Something that's been in the sun."

Galhani pointed at him. "That is exactly what I thought. I tried bergamot, which was wrong, and dried apricot, which was almost right but too sweet." She leaned on the counter. "I'll find it."

"I don't doubt it."

She refilled his cup before it was empty, a habit he'd long since stopped remarking on. "You're thinking about the Enchantress."

"I find I'm often thinking about the Enchantress."

"You're thinking about her *differently* this morning." Galhani had an uncomfortable accuracy about people's interiors, which she deployed without malice but without much restraint either. "You got that look. Like you're sorting something."

"I'm trying to place her," Vamir said. This was true, and it was the part he didn't mind saying aloud. "She fits too many patterns at once, which is its own kind of problem."

Galhani propped her chin on her hand. "Tell me."

He set the cup down and looked at the window, where the square was coming to life in its morning stages — first the deliveries, then the early errand-runners, then the slow accumulation of the day's ordinary business. "When a new story appears in a place that has old stories, it usually comes from somewhere. It's a variant. A local adaptation of something that's been told before. The Snow Witch becomes the Enchantress; the Mountain Hermit becomes the Wise Recluse. The costume changes but the underlying shape is stable. You can trace it."

"But you can't trace her."

"I've tried. And the trouble isn't that she has no precedents — the trouble is that she has too many. The all-knowing oracle. The dangerous woman in the tower. The price-charger, the wish-granter, the test-setter. She contains at least a dozen distinct archetypes, all at once, without clearly belonging to any of them." He picked up the cup again. "When a story fits every mold simultaneously, it either means the story is very old — so old that it predates the molds — or it means the story is very new, and it hasn't settled yet. Hasn't decided what it is."

"Can't it be both?" Galhani asked.

Vamir looked at her. "That's the uncomfortable possibility, yes."

Galhani seemed pleased to have arrived at the uncomfortable possibility. She straightened up and went to check on something simmering at the back of the counter, speaking over her shoulder. "And that's bad because—?"

"Because stories that are both very old and very new tend to be important," Vamir said. "The old ones have weight — they've been told so many times they've worn grooves in the world. The new ones have momentum — they're still forming, still gathering mass. Something that's both at once is—" He paused, searching for the right word.

"Dangerous?" Galhani offered.

"I was going to say *consequential*. But perhaps both."

Galhani returned with a small dish of something — sliced dried fruit, the apricot she'd mentioned, he assumed — and set it between them. "And what does that mean for us? Specifically."

There it was. Vamir took a piece of the fruit, not because he was hungry but because it gave him a moment. "It means North Pointe may not be just the place where the story passes through," he said. "It may be part of the story. Which has happened before." He looked at her directly. "Which has happened very recently, in fact."

The reference didn't need explaining. Galhani's expression changed — not to fear, but to a kind of careful attention, the look she wore when she was measuring something precisely.

"But the town recovered," she said.

"The town always recovers," Vamir agreed. "That's part of its nature. But recovery is—" He stopped.

"Recovery is not nothing," Galhani said quietly.

"No," Vamir said. "It's not nothing."

They sat with that for a moment. Outside, one of Makota's kits raced across the square with a basket twice her size, pigtails streaming. The ordinary morning continued its ordinary business, indifferent to the conversations happening inside it.

"Well," Galhani said finally, in the tone she used when she'd decided to set a worry aside without dismissing it, "you'll figure it out. You always do, eventually." She picked up the apricot dish, reconsidered it, and put it back. "And in the meantime, we keep the tea warm and the doors open."

"The founding philosophy of North Pointe," Vamir said.

"I prefer to think of it as good sense." She smiled. "More tea?"

"Please."

———

He spent the morning in the shop, doing the work the shop required. There was a delivery to catalog — two crates, arrived at dawn, containing a mixed lot that included three duplicate copies of a history he already had, a set of broadsides that were almost certainly seditious somewhere, and one volume that he could not identify at all, its cover blank, its pages filled with a script he didn't recognize in an ink that was slightly too dark to be ordinary. He set that one aside on the corner of the desk, meaning to examine it later, and when he looked up a candlemark afterward it was gone. He checked the shelf where he'd taken it from, then the floor around the desk, then gave up and wrote "one unidentified volume, contents unknown, currently unknown location" in the ledger in the resigned tone of a man who had long since made peace with this particular kind of inventory discrepancy.

Poly, monitoring from its usual perch, offered no information.

Travelers came and went in the way of spring, which was to say constantly and with a quality of urgency that varied from the genuine to the performative. A young woman needed maps of the eastern passes and got them. A pair of older men, traveling together with the comfortable silences of long partnership, spent half a mark browsing without buying and left with a novel apiece, both of them looking slightly surprised at themselves. A child, apparently unaccompanied, came in, stared at the shelves for five minutes with the gravity of a scholar, accepted the small illustrated bestiary that Poly deposited at her feet, and left without speaking. Vamir added it to the running total of small transactions the shop conducted on its own initiative and recorded in no ledger.

Between customers he found himself at the window, or in the aisles, or behind the counter with the ledger open and the pen not moving. Thinking about the Enchantress, yes — the problem of her was persistent and he turned it over methodically, approaching it from different angles the way you work a knot, trying different pressures and directions. But also thinking about the archive.

He was aware of it, now, in the way you become aware of a room in your house that you've never entered. It was not that he had forgotten it was there. He simply knew it *was there,* specifically and weightfully, in a way that made the floor between him and it feel slightly different than ordinary floor.

The restraint continued to require effort.

You have been an archivist for a long time, he told himself, sometime around midday, in a tone he recognized as the one he used when reminding himself of things he already knew and was temporarily forgetting. *Patience is the whole of the work. If you arrive before you're ready, you will read what you expected to find and miss what's actually there.*

This was true. He believed it.

He went back to the ledger.

———

Late afternoon brought the children, which was both a relief and a productive distraction. Vamir had taught the town's young people for years — reading and sums, mostly, but also the habit of asking questions and the associated skill of sitting with questions that didn't resolve quickly. They arrived in their usual loose formation, dumping bags and arguing over seats, and filled the shop with the particular chaos that made it temporarily impossible to think about anything except managing the chaos.

He taught for two marks. They covered addition and its discontents, a brief skirmish over whether a story could have more than one ending, and an impromptu geography lesson prompted by a boy called

Tannos who had been told by a traveler that there was a sea made entirely of sand three sennights east of North Pointe, and who needed to know if this was true before he could think about anything else.

It was, mostly. Vamir showed him on the oldest map, traced the route, explained that "sea" was perhaps ambitious but "very large expanse of sand that behaves somewhat like water at certain times of year" was accurate.

Tannos seemed satisfied. The lesson continued.

He thought about the Enchantress once during the lesson — not deliberately, but in the way that problems surface when you're focused on something else. It came while he was watching a girl called Ailie explain to a younger child why numbers didn't change when you looked away from them: *they stay the same because that's what they're for,* she said, with the authority of someone who had recently and conclusively solved this question for herself, *they stay the same so you can trust them.* And Vamir found himself thinking that this was exactly what the Enchantress did not do — she was not a number but a variable, shifting between the oracle and the predator and the test-setter depending on who was telling the story, and the reason she was hard to categorize was not that she was mysterious but that she was, deliberately or not, different things to different people.

Which meant she was not a fixed point. Which meant the story around her would not have a fixed shape.

He filed this away and returned his attention to Tannos, who had found something new to be concerned about.

———

After the children left, the shop was quiet in the way that follows useful noise — a clean quiet, earned. Vamir swept the chalk dust from the floor, stacked the slates, replaced the books that had migrated from the shelves in the natural way books migrated when children were present. Poly tidied in its own manner, which involved inspecting every surface at beak-height and periodically relocating small objects for reasons it did not explain.

The evening was coming in. The light through the stained glass had shifted from gold to the long amber of late afternoon, and the square outside was doing the thing it did at this time — condensing, drawing inward, people finishing their business and heading toward the warmth of home or pub.

Vamir stood in the middle of the shop and allowed himself, finally, to think about the archive directly. Not the question of what it contained or what it meant or what his presence in it signified. Just the simple fact of it. The steps. The cold air. The altar at the midpoint with its two sigils, one known and one not. The ambient light rising to meet him. The scale of the shelves resolving out of darkness as the light grew.

It had been there all day, under his feet, patient.

He was not ready yet. He thought he might be ready this evening. He was willing to sit with the uncertainty of *might be* for a few more marks, through supper and whatever the evening brought, and then reassess.

He was, after all, an archivist. Patience was the whole of the work.

He went to put the kettle on.

seven

. . .

HE MEANT to go to the archive that evening.

He had the kettle on and his coat off and was in the process of convincing himself that the particular quality of readiness he felt — settled, unhurried, curious in the clean way rather than the anxious way — was the right state in which to descend, when he looked out the window at the square and saw the light in Barnaba's shop.

This was not unusual. Barnaba kept an irregular schedule, which was a polite way of saying she spent the time the work required and gave no particular thought to what a candle said about it. But there was a quality to the light tonight — the warm amber of a lamp turned high, moving slightly as though being carried from surface to surface — that suggested she was working rather than simply present, and that the work had gotten hold of her in the way it sometimes did, when she forgot to eat and forgot the time and would forget to sleep if no one intervened.

Vamir looked at the light for a moment. Then he put his coat back on.

The archive would be there tomorrow. It had, by all available evidence, been there for considerably longer than he had, and it was not going anywhere.

————

Barnaba's shop occupied the narrow building between the weaver's and the empty storefront that had belonged, until recently, to a chandler who had decided the trade road was not, after all, the life for her. It was easy to overlook from the outside — no display window, just a plain door with a small brass plate that read *Barnaba Ashwick, Cartography* in letters so precise they looked engraved by a machine rather than a hand. Inside, it was another matter entirely. Every flat surface held a map, a chart, a survey in progress. The walls were papered three layers deep in some places, older documents visible at the torn edges beneath newer ones. The smell was particular and wonderful: linseed oil, iron-gall ink, the specific dusty sweetness of good drafting paper, and underneath it all something faintly mineral, like river sediment.

Barnaba herself was at the central table when Vamir knocked and entered, bent over a large sheet with a ruling pen in one hand and a straight edge held against the paper by the pressure of her forearm. She had the focused stillness of a person doing delicate work — not frozen but contained, every movement economic and exact.

"One moment," she said, without looking up.

Vamir closed the door quietly and waited. He used the time to examine the nearest wall, which held a series of overlapping surveys of the Mistral range at different scales. The oldest was hand-colored, the mountains rendered in the slightly fanciful style of a previous century, all dramatic shadow and symbolic crags. The newest was precise to the point of severity, every elevation noted, every pass marked with seasonal accessibility ratings in Barnaba's tiny, legible hand.

"There," Barnaba said, setting the ruling pen down. She straightened and turned, and the expression that crossed her face when she saw him was the one he had come to recognize as her version of genuine pleasure — not effusive, but immediate. "I thought you'd gone to bed."

"I thought so too," Vamir said. "Your light was on."

"My light is always on."

"I know. But tonight it had that quality."

Barnaba looked at him with the slight narrowing that meant she knew exactly what quality he meant and was deciding whether to be amused or resigned by being so legible. She settled on amused. "Sit down. There's tea."

There was, on the low table by the window: a pot, two cups — though she had been alone — and a plate of the hard, flat biscuits she preferred because they didn't leave crumbs on the drafting table. Vamir sat and poured for both of them, and for a few minutes they were quiet in the way of people who have, without quite discussing it, decided that they are friends.

It was a relatively recent development, the friendship. They had been acquaintances since Barnaba had arrived a few seasons back — the town's bookseller and the town's mapmaker, natural allies, occasional collaborators when a traveler needed both a chart and a text. But friendship, the kind that could sit in comfortable silence and reach for the tea and not feel the need to fill the air, had come on faster than either of them had expected. Vamir suspected this was because Barnaba had no patience for performances of friendliness and he had no particular gift for them, which meant there was nothing to get through on the way to the actual thing.

"You've been thinking today," Barnaba said. It was not a question.

"Is it visible?"

"You have a particular stillness when you're working through something. Less movement than usual. Like you're trying not to disturb whatever's in your head." She picked up her cup. "The Enchantress?"

"Partly." He looked at the wall of Mistral surveys. "Can I ask you something professionally?"

Barnaba gestured: go ahead.

"When you draw a map — a new survey, a first charting of something — do you think of it as recording what's there, or making something that wasn't there before?"

Barnaba was quiet for a moment, in the way of someone who takes questions seriously. "Both," she said. "But not equally."

"Tell me."

She set her cup down and turned slightly toward the nearest wall, where the oldest Mistral survey hung. "When I'm working from survey data — elevation measurements, compass bearings, physical observations — I'm recording. The mountain is the mountain. My job is to make it legible. I don't flatter myself that I'm doing anything more than translating what exists into a form that people can use."

"But," Vamir said.

"But." She turned back to him. "A map is also an argument. Every map is. The moment you decide what to include and what to leave out, what to name and what to leave unnamed, where to draw the boundary of one thing and the beginning of another — you've made choices that aren't neutral. And those choices have consequences." She paused. "I had a commission once, early in my career. A local landowner wanted a survey of a disputed area — land that two families had been arguing over for three generations. The line could reasonably have been drawn three different ways. He wanted it drawn the way that favored him."

"Did you?"

"I drew it the way the physical evidence supported. Which was not entirely in his favor, but not entirely against him either." She folded her hands. "Twenty years later, that map is the document both families cite in their continued argument. The line I drew — which I believed to be accurate, which I still believe to be accurate — has become the reality around which other realities have organized themselves." She looked at him steadily. "So. Recording or making?"

"Both," Vamir said. "But not equally."

Barnaba smiled, briefly. "You see the problem."

She was quiet for a moment, turning the cup in her hands. The lamp on the drafting table threw a long shadow across her face, and in the shadow, or perhaps in the light, something in the angle of her jaw looked different than it had a fortnight ago. He filed this without examining it.

"There's another version of it," she said, and her tone had changed slightly — more careful, the way it got when she was approaching something she hadn't quite decided to say. "When you redraw a map because the territory has genuinely changed. A river shifts its course. A border becomes contested and then is resolved. The map follows the reality." She set the cup down. "But sometimes it goes the other way. Sometimes the map changes first, and the reality follows, because people stop questioning the map." She paused. "And sometimes the thing that changes first is inside. The internal map. And then you have to wait to see whether the external one follows."

Vamir looked at her. "Are we still talking about cartography?"

Barnaba gave him a look that was equal parts amusement and rueful acknowledgment. "Briefly, yes. Then we were talking about something else." She reached for a biscuit, held it without eating it. "I should tell you something. Not because it's urgent. Because you're the right person to tell and it's been sitting in my chest for a few sennights and I'd like it to sit somewhere else for a while."

"Tell me," Vamir said.

"I'm Everkin," she said. Simply, the way she stated things she'd thought about long enough that the drama had been worn off them. "My people change. Not metaphorically — physically. Form, appearance, sometimes presentation. Every decade or two, depending on the person. It's called the Change, and it's—" She stopped. "It's not a bad thing. It's not a sickness. It's just what we are. What I am."

Vamir was quiet, holding the information with the attention it deserved.

"And you think yours is coming," he said.

"I think mine is already happening." She looked at her hands, spread them on the table. "The hands are always last. Everything else shifts first — the way I sleep, the way food tastes, the way I feel about the work. Then the face. Then, eventually, the hands." She looked up at him. "I'm not worried about it. I've done it before, though I was young enough that I don't remember the first one well. My mother told me it was like waking up in a house you've always lived in and finding all the furniture rearranged. Disorienting, but you learn the new layout."

"And does the new layout—" He searched for the right word. "Fit? In the same places?"

She was quiet long enough that he understood the answer before she gave it. "That's the part I'm still working out," she said, and there was something in the precision of it — the careful boundaries of the statement, the thing it was not quite saying — that he recognized as someone who was being as honest as they currently could.

He wanted to ask more. He didn't. She had shown him the edge of it, and he understood from the quality of her silence that the edge was as far as they were going tonight, and that this was not a failure of trust but a respect for her own pace.

"Thank you for telling me," he said. Which was true, and was also everything.

Barnaba nodded, once, and then did what he suspected she had been half-planning: she picked up her tea, looked at the wall of Mistral surveys, and said, "But you came here about the Enchantress."

It was not quite a change of subject. It was a door held open.

"I did," Vamir said, and walked through it with her.

"I see a problem. My problem is slightly different." He turned the cup in his hands. "A map can be wrong. Can be challenged, revised, redrawn. The mountain can be resurveyed."

"Yes."

"What about a story?"

Barnaba considered this with the same seriousness she gave the previous question. "A story is a map of something that doesn't hold still," she said slowly. "So in some ways it's harder. In some ways easier — people are more forgiving of imprecision in a story than in a chart. If I'm wrong about an elevation by twenty feet, someone might fall off a cliff. If a story gets a detail wrong—"

"The story adjusts," Vamir said. "The next teller corrects it."

"Or the next teller makes it worse. Or the next teller changes it for reasons that have nothing to do with accuracy." She reached for a biscuit. "I'll tell you what I believe, and you can argue with it."

"I expect I will."

"I believe that drawing a boundary — or telling a story — is an act of creation as much as an act of recording. I believe that if you draw a political line in a place that's genuinely contested, and you draw it with enough authority, and it goes into enough hands, and nobody challenges it — that line becomes real. Not because the ground changed. Because the consensus changed. And consensus is how humans make reality." She looked at him. "A story about the Enchantress, told enough times, believed by enough people, becomes the Enchantress. Not metaphorically. Actually."

Vamir was quiet for a moment. "Then you believe the archivist creates by archiving."

"I believe the archivist is not as neutral as the archivist thinks."

It was said without challenge, without the edge Sam's observation had carried. Barnaba was not trying to destabilize him. She was, in her precise and direct way, offering him the most honest version of her view, because she thought he deserved it and could handle it.

He thought about it genuinely. He gave it the time it deserved, which was more than he usually gave to things he disagreed with.

"I understand the argument," he said at last. "I think it's a good argument. I think it's even partly right — the observer affects the observed, always, and anyone who believes otherwise is fooling them-selves." He set the cup down. "But I think there's a difference between affecting and authoring. Between the shadow a person casts and the object they're standing next to. Yes, my records are not neutral. Yes, the act of writing something down gives it a certain weight it might not otherwise have. But the thing I'm writing down was there before I wrote it. The Enchantress — whatever she is — exists independently of my record of her. The mountain doesn't need my map to be a mountain."

"No," Barnaba agreed. "But the people crossing it need the map."

"Yes. And that's where the responsibility lives — in the quality of the translation. In the accuracy. In the discipline of keeping yourself out of what you're recording as much as any human being can." He paused. "If I start believing that my record creates the thing, I'll start making choices about what to include and what to leave out based on what story I want to tell. And then I'm not an archivist. I'm something else. Something I don't know how to be."

Barnaba looked at him for a long moment. Her expression had the quality of careful evaluation, the look she wore when she was checking whether a line she'd drawn was straight.

"That's a real conviction," she said. Not conceding. Acknowledging.

"It's the only one I've got," Vamir said. "I've been carrying it long enough that I'm not sure anymore where it ends and I begin."

"I know that feeling," Barnaba said quietly. She looked at the wall of maps. "I think I draw boundaries because I need them. The world is very large and very uncertain and a line on a page is — not certain, exactly. But stable. It gives the uncertainty a shape." She was quiet for a moment. "What gives you the same thing? The archiving, or the thing you're archiving?"

It was a good question. Vamir thought about it honestly.

"The act," he said. "The watching, and the writing down. The sense that the thing is being held. That it won't be lost, even if I can't change it." He glanced at her. "Does that sound like cowardice?"

"It sounds like a vocation," Barnaba said, with a precision that settled the question more cleanly than any reassurance could have. "Which is different."

She reached for the pot and refilled both cups, and they sat in a silence that was different from the earlier silence — fuller, somehow, the way a room feels after a real conversation has happened in it. More than one real conversation, in fact. The lamp threw its warm light across the drafting table, across the half-finished survey, across Barnaba's face, which held what it held without apology or announcement.

After a while, Barnaba turned back to her drafting table, not dismissively but with the natural gravity of someone whose work had been waiting patiently and was being returned to rather than escaped to. Vamir watched her pick up the ruling pen and find the line she'd been drawing when he arrived, resettling into her working stillness.

"The maps you draw for what might be," he said. "The speculative ones. The boundaries that don't exist yet."

"What about them?"

"Do you believe those, when you draw them?"

Barnaba didn't look up. "I believe they're possible," she said. "That's enough to draw them."

Vamir nodded, though she wasn't looking at him. "I think that might be the difference," he said. "You believe in the possible. I believe in the actual. And the town is large enough for both."

Barnaba's ruling pen moved in a long, steady line. "Yes," she said. "I think it probably is."

Vamir finished his tea, said goodnight, and let himself out.

———

The square was cold and quiet, the last of the evening's foot traffic gone, the lanterns doing their patient work against the dark. Vamir stood for a moment on the walkway, hands in his pockets, feeling the night air clear the warmth of the map shop from his lungs.

He was, he noticed, not unsettled. He had expected to be — Barnaba's argument was not easily dismissed, and he had not dismissed it, and the distinction he'd drawn between affecting and authoring was genuine but not airtight, and he knew it. But the conversation had not loosened anything in him that he needed to stay tightened. It had, if anything, done the opposite: the act of articulating the conviction to someone who genuinely challenged it had made the conviction more present to him, more clearly his, more understood rather than merely held.

He was what he was. Barnaba was what she was. Both were useful. Both were true, in the way that parallel lines are both true without ever meeting.

And Barnaba was Everkin, and the Change was coming, and he had been told this in the careful way of someone who was not yet ready to say what it would mean, and he had received it in the careful way of someone who understood that the meaning would arrive in its own time.

He crossed the square, unlocked the shop, went inside.

He stood for a moment in the dark, listening to the building around him. The particular quality of the silence — attended, expectant, the silence of a space that knows you — was unmistakable now that he knew how to hear it.

He was ready. Not because he could wait no longer, but because he was settled, and settled was the right state for the work. Not anxious, not consuming, not arriving with his conclusions already formed. Ready to receive what was actually there.

He crossed to the southernmost shelf. He did not hesitate.

He lifted the blue volume, and the wall opened, and he descended.

eight

. . .

THE STEPS FELT different on the second descent.

Not physically — the stone was the same, the cold the same, the slight concavity of each tread worn by the same generations of unknown feet. But Vamir was different, and the steps knew it the way a path knows the difference between a person passing through and a person who has decided to return. He moved without hesitation, without the first-time alertness that had made him catalog every detail on the way down. He was not a visitor tonight. He was not sure yet what he was, exactly, but it was something closer to resident than visitor, and the distinction felt significant.

Poly went ahead, its third eye open and steady, casting its faint blue light on the walls. The creature had a different quality of movement down here than it had upstairs — less the shopkeeper's assistant, alert for customer needs, and more something older and more purposeful, as though the archive activated a part of it that the bookshop above didn't require. Vamir watched it move and thought, not for the first time, that he did not fully know what Poly was. He knew what it did. He knew how it behaved. He had never asked what it was, in the way you don't ask certain questions about things you depend on, because the answer might change the depending.

He paused at the altar.

Tonight he looked at it with different eyes than he'd had on the first descent, when the discovery of everything that followed had made it a detail to be noted and passed. He crouched before it now, lantern held close, and examined it properly.

The basalt was old — older than the building above, older than the town, possibly older than the trade road that had drawn the town into existence. The surface had been worked by someone who knew what they were doing: the two sigils were not decorative but precise, the lines of each carved with the confidence of a person who had made this symbol many times before and understood what it meant. The Nimarith sigil he knew well — the mountain god's mark appeared in a dozen of the oldest texts in his upstairs collection, rendered in various styles across various centuries but always carrying the same essential geometry: the compressed peak, the radiating lines suggesting both elevation and authority, the particular asymmetry that distinguished it from merely decorative mountain imagery.

The second sigil — the open eye above the stylized quill — he had not found in any of his upstairs texts, but he recognized it now with the partial recognition of someone who has seen a face in a photograph and then met the person. He had seen this mark last night, in the archive, in the margins of several volumes. Small, unobtrusive, the way a printer's mark appears at the foot of a page: present for those who know to look, invisible to those who don't.

Patron of the archive. Patron of — what, exactly, he did not yet know. But the altar had not been built by Nimarith's people alone. Someone else had been here, someone who kept records and considered the keeping of records important enough to carve their god's mark into the foundation of a place where records were kept.

He pressed his palm flat to the altar, the way he had seen done at shrines of this age — not prayer, exactly, but acknowledgment. *I see you. I'm paying attention.*

The stone was fractionally warmer than the ambient temperature, which it had no physical reason to be. He noted this and stood and continued down.

———

The archive received him.

He understood this more clearly on the second visit than he had on the first, when he'd been too stunned by the scale of the place to register its quality. The first visit had been visual — the impossible geometry, the shelves extending beyond the reach of any light, the ambient illumination rising to meet him. Tonight he noticed the other thing: the atmosphere of the space. It was attentive in the way that a very good library is attentive — not because anything moves or speaks, but because the arrangement of everything in it suggests that someone has thought carefully about what you might need and placed it within reach.

The ambient light was warmer tonight than it had been. Not dramatically — not a welcoming blaze, nothing so performative — but the quality had shifted from the cool white of the first visit to something with more gold in it, the color of late afternoon rather than pre-dawn. Vamir noticed this the way you notice when a room you've entered before has been cleaned: not from any single changed detail but from the aggregate impression.

He also noticed, on the table nearest the foot of the stairs, a cup of tea.

He stopped and looked at it. It was in a plain ceramic cup, brown with a small chip at the rim, the kind of cup that has been used so many times it has become invisible through familiarity. Steam rose from it in an unhurried thread. He looked around the archive — the nearest shelves, the shadowed aisles beyond, the galleries above — and saw nothing. Heard nothing. The absolute silence of a space that had been quiet for a very long time.

He picked up the cup and drank. The tea was exactly as he took it: strong, slightly bitter, with the particular edge of a morning blend he'd been buying from Galhani for eleven years.

He set the cup back down.

"Thank you," he said, to no one visible.

Somewhere deeper in the archive, at the edge of audibility, something rustled. Not the settling of old paper. Something with intention to it — a brief flurry, purposeful, gone before he could locate it.

He looked at Poly, who was watching the direction of the sound with calm interest.

"How long has that been going on?" Vamir asked.

Poly blinked. Its expression suggested the question was slightly beside the point.

Vamir picked up his lantern, though the archive's own light made it less necessary with every visit, and went to work.

———

He had arrived, as he had told Galhani that morning, with too many patterns and not enough specificity. The Enchantress fit every archetype simultaneously and therefore fit none decisively, and what he needed was not more examples of the type but the thing that preceded the type — the underlying principle, the structural reason why stories of this shape appeared in this place at this time.

He began with what he knew, which was the correct place to begin. He found a table deep in the main gallery — the archive had, he was discovering, a loose organizational logic to its spaces, the way a city has neighborhoods without strict borders — and spread his notes from the previous night, supplemented by the observations he'd accumulated through the day. The archive had provided a fresh sheet of paper and a pen without his asking for them. He noted this and wrote without remarking on it further.

He wrote:

She appears suddenly, with no traceable origin in local legend. She is: all-knowing, or appears to be. She sets tests. She charges prices that are non-monetary. She grants what is asked for, or something adjacent to it. She does not age. She is not seen directly. She communicates through dreams. She is dangerous, or appears to be. She is specifically described as old — ancient — by people who have not seen her and cannot know this. She is located in the Mistral range, in a structure that may or may not be the old Mistral keeps.

He looked at this list for a while.

What she is not: traceable. Motivated by ordinary desires. Limited to what can be physically explained. New — or she behaves as though she is not new, and others have absorbed this behavior and reflected it back as fact.

He underlined the last observation. *Others have absorbed this behavior and reflected it back as fact.* This was the thing that had been nagging at him since Galhani's question that morning. The Enchantress's antiquity was asserted by people who had no means of knowing it. She was ancient because the story said she was ancient, and the story said she was ancient because that was the shape ancient-powerful-woman stories took, and the shape was being applied to something that might be — that Sam's gift said was — real.

Which meant the story and the thing were not the same. Which meant, somewhere beneath the accumulated archetype, there was an actual woman, or an actual force, that the story had been mapped onto.

Barnaba's voice: *the map precedes the territory, in time.*

He pushed the thought aside — not dismissing it, filing it — and went looking.

———

The archive's organization rewarded a particular kind of searching, which was not the kind Vamir was accustomed to. In his upstairs shop, and in every library he had used before, the correct approach was directed: you knew the category, you found the shelf, you worked through the relevant section. The archive resisted this. Not obstructively — it was not a maze and it did not mislead — but it seemed to understand that the question you arrived with was rarely the question you actually needed answered, and it organized itself around the latter.

This meant that when Vamir went looking for the Enchantress, he found the town.

He did not find it immediately or all at once. He found it the way you find a large thing in low light: first a detail, then another detail, then the moment when the details resolve into a shape and the shape is larger than expected.

The first detail was a small volume, no larger than his hand, bound in a dark red that had faded at the spine to the color of old roses. Poly had led him to it — he was beginning to understand that Poly's guidance in the archive was different from its guidance upstairs, less a nose for what was needed and more a sense of what was ready to be found — and he'd opened it expecting something about mountain topography or Mistral clan history. Instead, the first page bore a title in a script that mixed Old Elvish with two other languages he recognized but rarely read: *On the Planting of Waypoints: A Practical Account of the Establishment of Service Stations Along the Great Routes.*

Vamir stopped.

He read the first page standing up, the way you read something that won't let you set it down.

The volume was old — genuinely old, the kind of age that didn't express itself in yellowed pages so much as in the quality of the thinking, which had a confidence and a practicality that suggested it had been written when the ideas in it were not theoretical but operational. It was written by someone who had done this before, who was recording a process they had refined through repetition. The tone was almost bureaucratic: a professional account of how to establish a waypoint, which the author defined as *a place of consistent service on a trade route, designed to support the passage of travelers engaged in significant journeys, providing material, informational, and restorative resources to those who require them.*

Vamir read the list of requirements for a properly functioning waypoint.

He read it again.

He sat down.

The requirements included: a source of provisions; a source of tools and equipment; a source of information (defined as *maps, records, and local knowledge*); a source of physical restoration (*lodging and sustenance*); a source of *spiritual restoration* (the author's term, defined in a footnote as *the renewal of purpose and resolve through encounter with genuine human community*); and — the detail that made him sit down — *a mechanism of conflict-avoidance, ensuring that the waypoint remains accessible to all travelers regardless of affiliation, allegiance, or history.*

Serve all who come in peace. Stay in peace. Leave in peace.

He looked at the words for a long time.

———

He did not read quickly through what followed. He read carefully, the way you read something you want to understand rather than merely know. The archive seemed to sense this and arranged itself accordingly: when he needed to cross-reference something in the small red volume, a larger text appeared at his elbow — he did not see it arrive, did not hear it arrive, but when he looked up it was there, opened to the relevant section. When he needed more light to examine an illustration, the ambient illumination in his corner of the gallery brightened by precisely the degree required. Once, when he was deep in a passage and the cup of tea had gone cold, he reached for it without looking and found it warm.

He did not remark on any of this. It was, he was beginning to understand, simply how the archive worked. The trappings of what some scholar somewhere would call a magical library — the responsive light, the conveniently placed texts, the refreshed tea — were to the archive what Galhani's excellent sourcing was to her tea shop: not the point, but the evidence of something that cared about doing its work well.

Somewhere in the deeper stacks, the rustling happened again. Brief, deliberate, receding.

He did not look up.

———

The town's history, as the archive held it, was older than anything in his upstairs collection by several orders of magnitude. The founding documents he knew — the civic records, the early census, the account of the first permanent buildings — dated back three hundred years, give or take. The archive held records from before that, and before that, and before that again, going back to a time when the trade road itself was being established and the question of where to locate the waypoints was being actively debated by people whose names did not survive in any other record Vamir had ever seen.

North Pointe had not been chosen randomly. The site had been surveyed, evaluated, and selected with the same deliberateness that Barnaba applied to her own work. The valley's position on the major east-west route, the lake's proximity providing water and a secondary transport option, the shelter of the Mistral range to the north providing protection from the worst of the winter weather — all of this had been considered and recorded. The decision had been made by a committee whose composition the archive preserved in fragmentary form: at least one mountain elf, at least two humans, and someone described only as *the Walker*, whose species and origin were not recorded but whose observations about foot traffic patterns were cited repeatedly as authoritative.

What the town was for had been established before the town existed.

And what it was for, stated plainly in the earliest documents and restated in variant forms across centuries of records, was this: *to serve the passage.* Not to be the destination. Not to shape the journey or influence its outcome. To be the place where the journey paused, refueled, and resumed. A place that was, by design and by deep intention, a stage rather than an actor.

Vamir sat with this for a long time.

He thought about the conversation with Sam — *someone has to hold the record, someone has to stay back and watch* — and about the conversation with Barnaba — *the map and the territory are not the same thing* — and about the fear he had been carrying since the morning, the fear that the town might become part of the story the way it had during the fire cult, the way it might again with the Enchantress.

The archive had not answered that fear directly. It had done something more useful: it had shown him that the fear was based on a misunderstanding. The town did not become part of stories accidentally or against its nature. Its nature was to be part of stories — to be the indispensable hinge point, the place where the traveler's journey acquired what it needed to continue. The stage was not a lesser thing than the play. The stage was what made the play possible.

Which meant the question was not whether the Enchantress's story would touch North Pointe. Of course it would. Everything touched North Pointe. Everything had always touched North Pointe. The question was whether North Pointe would hold its nature in the touching — would remain the waypoint, the restorative pause, the place of service — or would be pulled into the story as something more than that.

The creed is not just a rule, he thought. *It's a load-bearing wall.*

He wrote this down, because it was the kind of thing that needed writing.

———

There was more. There was always more — the archive had the quality of a deep subject, which is that every answer opened onto more questions, and the more questions were more interesting than the fewer questions you'd arrived with, and you could keep going indefinitely if you forgot that the world above had a claim on you.

He found a section of the archive that held what appeared to be records of the waypoint's operations across its history — not the civic records he knew, but something more granular and less official. Logs, in various hands across various centuries. Accounts of travelers who had passed through, of the resources they'd required, of the outcomes of their journeys as reported by those who returned or by messengers who brought news afterward. The record was not complete — there were gaps, some of them spanning decades — but what it held was extraordinary: a longitudinal account of what the waypoint had been *for*, evidenced not by intention but by result.

The results were consistent in a way that he found, when he considered it, both humbling and clarifying. In the records he read, North Pointe appeared again and again as a place where journeys changed — not because the town had done anything dramatic, but because the pause had allowed the traveler to become ready. The provisions had sustained them. The information had redirected them. The community had, in the author of the original documents' phrase, *renewed their purpose and resolve.* And then they had gone on, and the outcomes were — not always good, but more often good than the baseline of unresupplied journeys, and almost always more good than the outcome would have been without the pause.

The town had not made them heroes. It had made them capable of becoming heroes on their own.

The stage doesn't act, Vamir thought. *It holds the space in which acting becomes possible.*

He wrote this down too. Then he looked at what he'd written and crossed out *doesn't act* and wrote *chooses not to act* instead. The distinction mattered. A stage that couldn't act was a floor. A stage that chose not to act was a philosophy.

His philosophy. His town's philosophy.

He thought about the fire cult, and the loss of the icosagon's magic, and the long slow recovery. He had understood it at the time as an aberration — something that had never happened before and should not have happened and must not happen again. The archive suggested a different frame: it had happened before. Not often, not easily, but the record held accounts of times when the waypoint had been disrupted — by conquest, by abandonment, by the creeping erosion of the creed — and what the record showed was that the disruptions were always temporary, and the recovery was always the same: a return to function, to service, to the fundamental purpose for which the site had been selected and built.

North Pointe was not fragile. It was *resilient* — but resilient in the specific sense of a thing that knows what it is and returns to it.

He sat back from the table and breathed.

The fear had not gone away. But it had changed shape. It was no longer the fear of something happening to the town. It was the fear of not being adequate to the town's nature — of failing, in some crucial moment, to hold the function that the town required its keepers to hold. Of becoming part of the story when the story needed him to be the stage.

This was a better fear. A more useful fear. You could do something with a fear like this.

———

He had lost track of time entirely when Poly landed on the table beside his notes and looked at him with the patient authority it reserved for situations where it had been asking him to stop for a while and he hadn't been listening.

He looked up. The archive's ambient light had shifted again — cooler, more silver, the quality he was beginning to associate with the approach of early morning.

"Yes," he said. "All right."

He spent a few minutes organizing his notes, writing a final summary entry in the margin of the last page: *Town's nature: waypoint by design. Creed is structural, not decorative. Stage, not actor — but stage by choice. Return to function is the pattern of recovery. Enchantress: still unresolved. But the frame for understanding her is clearer. She is, by town's nature, passing through. The question is what she needs and whether we can provide it.*

He paused over the last sentence for a moment, aware that it was a significant reframe — the Enchantress not as threat to be survived but as traveler to be served — and that he had arrived at it not by reasoning but by reading. The archive had not told him this directly. It had shown him the town's history and trusted him to see it.

He appreciated this about the archive. It did not lecture. It provided.

He gathered his notes. He returned the books he'd used to their places on the shelves, though he suspected they would have found their way back regardless. He drank the last of the tea, which was still warm.

At the table's edge, he noticed a small object that had not been there when he sat down: a single brass button, old, with an unusual pattern pressed into its face — a radial design that might have been a compass rose or might have been a stylized eye. He turned it over in his fingers. It had the feel of something that had been carried a long time.

He set it down carefully, in the center of the table. An offering seemed insufficient and presumptuous in equal measure. He settled for acknowledgment.

"I'll be back," he said. "There's more here than one night holds."

The rustling in the deep stacks, brief and purposeful as ever, did not respond. But the ambient light, as he turned to go, warmed a degree or two.

At the altar on the way up he paused and pressed his palm to the stone again. The warmth was the same as before — steady, non-urgent, the warmth of a presence that had been there a long time and expected to be there a long time more.

He climbed the stairs. The shop received him in its ordinary dark. The stained glass windows held the very first grey of morning in their hundred uneven panes.

He was tired in the way of good work rather than lost sleep.

He went upstairs, lay down, and was asleep before the first bell.

nine

. . .

HE SURFACED from the archive into a shop still dark, the stained glass holding nothing but the flat grey of pre-dawn. His legs ached in the specific way of stairs descended and climbed, and his notebook was dense with the previous night's work — the waypoint documents, the founding records, the long slow revelation of what North Pointe was and had always been. He felt the particular exhaustion of too much understanding arrived at too quickly, the kind that sat behind the eyes and made ordinary objects look slightly provisional.

He made tea without tasting it, stood at the window watching the square resolve out of darkness, and thought about sleep. Decided against it. The morning was already happening without him and he had, he realized, somewhere to be.

———

Barnaba's shop was quiet in the way of places where someone is sleeping — a quality of held stillness, different from empty. Vamir let himself in with the care of long practice, easing the door past the point where the hinges complained, and stood for a moment letting his eyes adjust.

She was on the settee in the far corner, exactly as he might have predicted: still dressed, one hand tucked under her cheek, the drawings she'd been working on spread across the floor around her in a loose radius, as though she'd simply stopped mid-motion and the papers had settled where they fell. The lamp on the drafting table had burned down to a stub. The room smelled of ink and cold coffee and the particular exhaustion of a person who had worked past the point of sense.

He crossed to the settee, careful of the papers, and draped the blanket from the back of it over her legs and shoulders. She stirred slightly — a small adjustment, a breath — and did not wake.

He should have left then. He nearly did. But he paused at the drafting table, as he always did, because the work Barnaba did was the kind that repaid attention.

Tonight's drawings were all the same subject: a keep, rendered from a dozen different angles, the same structure approached and re-approached as though she were trying to catch it from the angle at which it would finally make sense. He had seen this series developing over the past sennights, but tonight something was different about the drawings. The lines were more confident. Less searching. Whatever she had been trying to resolve about the keep's geometry, she had resolved it — or come close enough that the remaining uncertainty was a matter of detail rather than architecture.

He looked at her sleeping face.

The Change, which he had been watching with the careful peripheral attention of someone who doesn't want to be caught staring, had progressed in the night. The sharpness that had always defined her — the angular jaw, the prominent cheekbones, the particular set of her mouth that suggested she was permanently about to make a precise point — had softened and simultaneously strengthened into something different. Not lesser. Not the absence of Barnaba. Something that was becoming its own thing, a face that was arriving rather than departing.

Her hands were the same. He found himself looking at them, the ink-stained fingers, the calluses at the heel of each palm from years of ruling pens and parallel bars. Whatever else was changing, the hands that held the tools remained.

He straightened the drawings she'd knocked to the floor, stacked them loosely on the edge of the table, and let himself out.

———

Back in the shop, the morning had brightened enough to make the lantern unnecessary. Vamir turned the sign to CLOSED — he had learned, in the sennights since the archive's discovery, that the days he descended were not days he could also run a bookshop — and wrote the familiar note in his looping hand: *Closed for Inventory. Please try again tomorrow.*

He gathered what he needed. The notebook, still half-full from last night. Fresh pencils. The biscuits Makota had pressed on him yesterday that he'd forgotten to eat. He moved through the preparation with the settled efficiency of someone who has established a ritual, and recognized, with a slight internal amusement, that this was exactly what it had become. The archive had not lost its quality of strangeness — he suspected it never would — but he was no longer a visitor to it. He was, in the way of a person who has been given a key and used it often enough to stop thinking about the key, someone who belonged there.

Poly watched from the lintel with the alert patience of an animal that has decided its job begins when yours does.

"Ready," Vamir said, and wasn't sure which of them he was addressing.

———

The altar on the way down had acquired a new offering since his last visit — a small bundle of dried herbs, tied with blue thread, set at the base of the carved sigils with the care of someone who knew what they were doing. He crouched and examined it without touching it. The herbs were mountain-grown, something resinous and sharp, and the knot in the thread was not decorative but functional, the kind used in binding-work. Someone else had been here.

He sat with this information for a moment, turning it over. The archive was not, apparently, his alone. This was not alarming — the waypoint records had suggested as much, the town's history being held by the keeper, whatever keeper was current — but it was the first concrete evidence that his predecessor, or predecessors, had been real rather than theoretical. Someone had stood at this altar before him. Many someones, over a very long time, leaving their small acknowledgments in the dark.

He left one of Makota's biscuits beside the herb bundle and continued down.

———

The archive received him with what he was beginning to think of as its morning quality — the ambient light at its clearest, the air carrying the faintest movement, as though the space had been recently tidied. The tea on the table by the stairs was already poured. He had stopped being surprised by this and started being grateful for it, which he suspected was the intended progression.

He settled at the table, opened the notebook, and reviewed what he'd written the previous night. The waypoint material, the founding records, the revelation of the town's designed purpose. He read his own notes with the slight detachment of someone returning to work they did while tired, checking for the mistakes that exhaustion produces. He found none, which he took as confirmation rather than complacency.

Then he turned to the question he'd been carrying since he'd left Barnaba's shop.

He wrote: *Everkin. The Change. Barnaba.*

And then, below it, because the thought had been forming since he'd seen her face in the lamplight: *What does the archive hold about her people?*

He looked up.

Poly was already moving.

———

The bestiary that Poly led him to was not, at first glance, what he expected — not the dry taxonomic volume he'd anticipated but something warmer, more personal, written by someone who had clearly spent significant time among the people they were describing. The Everkin entry was long and carefully observed, and Varmir read it the way he read things that mattered, which was slowly and more than once.

The Change, as the author described it, was less a physical transformation than a fundamental reorientation of self — the body following what the essential person had already decided to become, or had been drawn toward becoming, or had always been and was only now expressing. The language was imprecise in ways the author acknowledged were intentional: the Everkin themselves, she noted, used different words for it in different contexts, and the divergence in vocabulary was not inconsistency but accuracy, because the Change was genuinely different for every individual who underwent it.

What was consistent: the compulsion toward movement that preceded it, the visions, the drawings and mappings and obsessive renderings of places not yet visited. The hands staying the same while the face found its new shape. And then, almost always, the departure — not because the world drove them out, but because the self that emerged from the Change was not the same self that had inhabited the old place, and the old place did not quite fit anymore.

Their new faces are always a stranger's, yet the eyes are always the same, the author had written. *They hold memory as if it were a rare, precious stone — displayed only to those who truly ask.*

He thought of Barnaba's eyes. The precision in them. The measuring quality that had always made him feel, in a good way, seen rather than simply observed.

He set the bestiary aside and reached for the next volume Poly indicated — a slim record of Everkin settlements in the northern valleys, dry and administrative in tone but useful for context. He read through it noting the pattern: communities that had included Everkin tended to describe periods of unusual creative fertility followed by departures, and then a brief settling period, and then the community continued. Sometimes the departing Everkin returned, in new forms, years or decades later. Sometimes they didn't. Both outcomes were, the record implied, equally within the nature of things.

Being allowed to pick my own narrative for once, Barnaba had said to him, in the conversation he'd been turning over since she said it.

He understood this better now than he had then. The Change was not an ending. It was a page turn. The question was what the next page was for.

He closed the slim record and sat for a while, not reading, just thinking about the town and the gap that was coming. Because it was coming — he had no doubt of that now, looking at her face this morning and at the drawings and at the way she'd been sleeping with the completeness of someone who had made a decision and found it restful. He did not know when. He thought probably soon.

The icosagon would be incomplete again. The town would wobble, in its subtle way, as it had when the dryads left and when the chandler closed her shop and moved on. It would recover. It always recovered. He knew this with the certainty of the waypoint records, which showed him recovery after recovery across centuries of departures and arrivals, the town's fundamental resilience expressed again and again as a return to function rather than a resistance to change.

But recovery was not nothing. He had said this to Galhani, and he meant it more now than he had then.

He put the thought away — not dismissing it, filing it — and let Poly lead him to the next thing.

———

The Mage Wars chronicle was not a book that welcomed casual browsing. It announced itself with the weight of it — half again as large as anything else on the shelf, bound in grey leather that had the texture of something that had seen more than ordinary use. Poly regarded it from a careful distance as Vamir carried it to the table, which Vamir took as information.

He started at the middle, the way he did with long histories, letting the shape of the thing establish itself before he committed to a direction. The chronicle was meticulous and unsparing: campaigns, casualties, the specific mechanics of destruction rendered with the precision of someone who wanted the record to be accurate rather than comfortable. He read with the part of his mind that could absorb difficult material without dramatizing it, making notes in his small, careful hand.

Leonard the Weaver appeared early and often.

The name was not unknown to him. Leonard existed in the town's collective memory the way certain things exist — present when referenced, absent otherwise, the kind of history that people know they know without thinking about it much. A battle mage. Significant. Long ago. Changed, eventually, into something else.

The chronicle gave him the specifics that collective memory did not.

The images first: a slight man, consistently slight across decades of portraits, but with a quality of attention in the eyes that made the slight frame irrelevant. Not physically threatening. Precisely, specifically dangerous in the way of someone who understood systems — how they worked, where they failed, how to reach inside them. The hands in the portraits were always depicted with particular care by the artists, as though the hands were the point. Fine-boned, ink-stained at the cuticles. The hands of someone whose work was detailed and patient and who did it for a very long time.

He stopped. Looked at his own notes. Read back.

Ink-stained at the cuticles.

He read the chronicle entry for the Siege of Sevenfold Vale with the focused attention he gave to things he needed to understand precisely. Leonard's spells had been adaptive rather than destructive — designed to entrap, to exhaust, to render opposition unable to continue rather than unable to exist. The Net of Sleep. The Unraveling. The Seamless Night. The names were poetic in the way of things named by people who were trying to make something terrible easier to say. The effects were not poetic.

He read the later entries. The withdrawal from the field. The retreat to the northern archives — *these archives*, he thought, with a small shock of connection — and the years of consultation and teaching that followed. The portraits from this period showed the same slight figure, the same careful hands, but something in the eyes had changed. Not softened exactly. Reoriented. The same precision, aimed at different work.

The appendix entry was brief: *Leonard the Weaver, later known as Leota Harbinger, presumed to have changed form and function after the Great Accord.*

He read it three times.

He knew, of course, that Leota had a history. This was not a secret, exactly — it was the kind of thing that was known without being discussed, present in the way the scar on Sam's face was present, a fact that had been absorbed into the person so thoroughly that remarking on it felt like a failure of attention. He had never asked. She had never offered. The exchange had suited both of them.

What the chronicle gave him was not the fact of the history but its texture. The specific weight of it. He had known Leota as someone who had been a battle mage and had chosen to become something else, and he had understood this in the abstract way you understand things you have not witnessed. Now he understood it in the specific way. The Siege of Sevenfold Vale. The silence so total the survivors never again spoke above a whisper. The withdrawal — *citing exhaustion,* the chronicle said, in a phrase that was doing enormous work — and the long slow reorientation toward repair.

He thought of Leota on the bakery stoop, embroidering a small angry owl and watching the bridal party with dry affection. He thought of the way she deployed her precision now: a word placed exactly right, a silence held exactly as long as needed, the careful management of the distance between herself and the world. The same instrument, rebuilt for different work.

Leota had changed to escape the cycle, he thought. *But now —*

He stopped.

He had been about to complete the thought in the way it wanted to complete itself — *but now the story is writing her back into it* — and he held it at arm's length for a moment, examining it. Because this was the kind of thought that felt like insight but might be imposition. The town was not, as he now understood, a passive stage on which stories played out. It was a waypoint, a designed thing, its purpose served by holding its function in the face of whatever stories passed through it. Leota was part of that function. Her history as Leonard was part of what she brought to it — the knowledge of what destruction looked like from the inside, the hard-won understanding of what repair required.

The story was not writing her back into conflict. The story was — might be — asking her to apply what she knew.

This was not the same thing. The distinction mattered.

He wrote it down, because it was the kind of distinction that needed to be written to be held.

The chronicle gave him one more thing before he closed it: a passage highlighted by an earlier hand, a different ink, someone who had read this before him and found it worth marking. *It is the will of the antagonist that shapes the hero; the greater the resistance, the more refined the response.* And below it, in the same earlier hand, a single marginal note that might have been a question or might have been an answer: *But who shapes the antagonist?*

Vamir looked at this for a long time.

He wrote it in his notebook and underlined it.

Then he closed the chronicle, which was heavy and which he was glad to close, and sat for a while with the tea that had been refreshed at some point while he was reading — he hadn't noticed it happening, which was normal — and let the discoveries settle into the configuration they wanted to take.

The Everkin: Barnaba's people, her Change, her departure approaching. The town's pattern: resilient, designed, returning always to function. Leonard/Leota: history with texture, the precision of a person who had done terrible things and built something careful from the understanding. And the question in the margin, which he could not yet answer and did not intend to pretend he could.

He was not finished here. There was more — there was always more, and he was beginning to understand that the archive's depth was not a challenge to be met but a nature to be respected. You did not finish the archive. You returned to it, and each return found you different, and the difference changed what the archive showed you.

Tonight he had found what tonight could hold. That was enough.

He gathered his notes, left a careful record of what he'd read and where, and began the long walk back toward the stairs.

At the altar, he paused. The herb bundle was still there, his biscuit beside it. He considered the marginal note — *but who shapes the antagonist* — and thought about Nimarith, and the second sigil he still could not fully name, and the relationship between them that the archive was not yet ready to show him.

Not tonight, he thought. *But soon.*

He pressed his palm to the stone, felt the warmth that was always there, and climbed toward morning.

ten

. . .

HE HAD SLEPT PERHAPS three markss when the morning found him, and the morning was not gentle about it. The light through the stained glass arrived with its usual indifference to human schedules, fracturing into its blues and golds and pressing through his eyelids until he gave up the pretense of rest and swung his feet to the floor.

The archive visit sat in him the way substantial work always did — a productive heaviness, the kind that came from having moved through difficult material and come out the other side changed by it. He had the notes. He had the discoveries. He had the question in the margin, underlined, waiting. He also had the specific exhaustion of someone who had spent a night underground by lamplight, and his eyes felt it, and his legs felt it, and the tea he made while standing at the window tasted like the effort required to make it rather than like tea.

He looked out at the square.

Barnaba's shop was dark.

Not unusual, at this time — she was rarely open before nine bells, and on the nights when the work had its teeth in her she sometimes slept past that. But there was a quality to the darkness that was different from the darkness of a shop whose proprietor was sleeping.

It was the darkness of a shop that was simply closed, the shutter drawn and the sign turned and no particular expectation of light forthcoming.

He finished the tea. Made another cup. Stood at the window longer than he meant to.

Then he put his coat on and crossed the square.

———

The brass plate on the door — *Barnaba Ashwick, Cartography* — caught the morning light with its usual precision. The sign in the window read CLOSED in Barnaba's characteristically exact hand, the letters so evenly spaced they might have been typeset. There was no note. No indication of when, or whether, the sign would change.

Vamir pressed his hand flat against the glass, the cold of it immediate through his palm. Inside, as much as he could see through the reflected glare of the morning, the drafting table was clear. The drawings that had carpeted the floor on his last two visits — the keep, rendered and re-rendered from every angle — were gone. The shelves of rolled surveys were there, the wall maps were there, the tools in their neat ranked order along the back bench. But the work-in-progress was absent, and the absence of it was louder than the presence of everything else.

She had taken what mattered and left what could be left.

Polyocular landed on his forearm, its head cocked, all three eyes open. They stayed like that for a moment — Vamir, the bird, the dark shop — as though a different outcome might crystallize from the act of waiting.

It did not.

He lowered his hand. The cold remained on his palm for a while after.

———

He had known it was coming. He had known since the evening in her shop when she'd told him about the Change with the careful precision of someone disclosing something they had thought about from every angle and arrived at a settled relationship with — not easy, but settled. He had known since his morning visit when he'd seen her face in lamplight and understood that the arriving thing had nearly arrived. He had known, and knowing had not made the shuttered window any less final.

This was, he reflected, the reliable inadequacy of preparation. You could understand a thing completely and still be surprised by its weight when it landed.

He turned from the shop and walked, not with any particular destination, simply moving because the square was too still to stand in.

————

Makota's bakery was open and warm and populated in the way it always was at this time, which should have been a comfort and was, but was also a reminder of the wrongness in the air. He could feel it before he crossed the threshold — a faint but unmistakable off-note in the quality of the morning, the way a room feels when something in it has been moved and you can't immediately identify what. The town's magic, which operated below the level of daily notice when it was working correctly, announced itself precisely when it wasn't.

Inside, the bread was baking. The kits were working. The coffee was hot. Everything was as it should have been, and yet Makota, behind the counter, had the particular quality of controlled energy that in a less contained person would have been agitation.

She saw him the moment he walked in.

"You knew," she said. Not an accusation. An observation, made in the flat tone of someone processing information.

"I knew it was coming," Vamir said. "Not today specifically."

Makota absorbed this, her tail moving in a slow, involuntary arc. She reached for a roll, wrapped it in paper, pushed it across the counter. He took it because refusing it would have been wrong.

"The dough's been strange since yesterday evening," she said. "Wouldn't hold its shape. I thought it was the humidity." She glanced at the display case, where the morning's offering was, to all visible appearances, perfectly normal. "It's fine now, mostly. But it's like working with something that isn't sure of itself."

"It'll settle," Vamir said.

"I know." She said it firmly, the way she said things she believed and didn't want to debate. "I know it will. We've been through this before. We'll settle too." She picked up a cloth and wiped down a surface that was already clean. "I just — I liked having her here. She was good for the town. Good for the square." A pause. "Good for you, I think."

"Yes," Vamir said simply.

Makota looked at him. Her expression had the quality of someone choosing not to say the several things they could say, and instead saying the one true thing. "She'll be all right, wherever she ends up."

"She'll be better than all right," Vamir said. "She's Everkin. She knows exactly what she's doing."

Makota nodded, once, and returned to her work. The economy of it — the way she moved back into the rhythm of the bakery, not suppressing the feeling but containing it — was its own kind of wisdom. The kits swirled around her, and the bread baked, and the morning continued.

Vamir ate the roll on the walkway outside, watching the square fill up with its ordinary business, and let the warmth of the bread and the cold of the air exist together without resolving either.

———

He spent the morning moving through the town the way he sometimes did when he needed to think without sitting still — not aimlessly, but without a fixed destination, following the thread of whatever wanted following. He stopped at the fishmonger's, where Pavati's scale was reading everything as exactly one pound, which she was dealing with by the simple expedient of not using it and estimating by hand instead. He stopped at the dry-goods shop, where Alred's ledger had been adding phantom entries — sacks of "moon oats" and "phantom beans" that didn't exist in inventory — and Alred was crossing them out with the resigned efficiency of a man who had seen stranger things. He stopped at the Broken Claw, where Sam was working the taps with her usual exactness but the beer had developed an opinion about when it wanted to pour, which was not always when it was asked.

None of these were disasters. None of them were even, precisely, problems — they were the town slightly out of tune, the icosagon one note short of its full chord, the magic running through nineteen circuits instead of twenty and making do. The town had done this before. The town would do it again.

What struck him, moving shop to shop, was less the wrongness itself than the way each shopkeeper held it — with a particular quality of practical acceptance that was not resignation and was not indifference but was something specific to people who had chosen to live in a magical place and understood that magical places required a certain flexibility of expectation. Nobody was panicking. Nobody was pretending it wasn't happening. They were simply adjusting, and continuing, and trusting that the equilibrium would return when it was ready.

He found this, despite everything, quietly magnificent.

At some point he found himself at Jen's office, which was less an office than a room with a desk and a locked cabinet and the specific austere quality of a space inhabited by someone who did not consider comfort a professional requirement. The door was open. Jen was at the desk, writing in the cramped, precise script she used for official records.

She looked up when he appeared in the doorway. Read his face in the efficient way she had. Looked back down at her writing.

"When?" she said.

"This morning, I think. Sometime in the night."

Jen made a small sound that was not a response to the information so much as a confirmation of receipt. She finished the line she was writing with the deliberateness of someone who will not let grief interrupt good penmanship, then set the pen down and leaned back.

"She left the stock for whoever takes the shop," Vamir said. "She said anyone could have it."

"That's like her." Jen looked at the wall for a moment. "She'll be all right."

"So I've been telling people."

"It's true." Jen's voice was flat and certain in equal measure. "There's no reason it shouldn't be true." She picked up the pen again, set it back down. A small gesture, quickly contained. "She was a good shopkeeper. She'll be a good whatever-she-is-next."

Vamir leaned in the doorway. "Makota is on edge."

"Makota is always on edge. The bakery just usually absorbs it." Jen looked at him directly. "You should open the shop. People will need things today, and you being visible will help."

It was practical and it was also, coming from Jen, a form of comfort. He recognized it as both.

"Yes," he said. "You're right."

He left her to her records and crossed the square to the bookshop, turned the sign to OPEN, and stood behind the counter and let the day's first customers find him.

The afternoon brought the wedding party.

Vamir was on the stoop of Leota's house when it started, having been drawn there by the particular quality of noise emanating from Prudence's tailor shop — a noise that occupied the precise register between comedy and catastrophe and demanded an audience. Leota herself was already installed on the upper step, embroidery hoop in hand, watching the proceedings with the expression of someone who has decided to find this entertaining rather than annoying and is succeeding by a narrow margin.

"How long has this been going on?" Vamir asked, settling beside her.

"Since just after second bell," Leota said, without looking up from the hoop. "The eldest one cried for twenty minutes about the sleeves. The youngest one started it, I think, on purpose."

Across the green, Prudence's display window had been thrown open to the mild day, and through it played a scene of escalating textile drama: three young women in progressive states of undress and repair, popping in and out with the velocity of something clockwork and badly calibrated. Each emergence brought a fresh torrent of fabric and opinion. A length of white gauze became a point of principle. The question of ankle visibility was apparently a matter of some moral significance.

Polyocular, perched between them, watched with three-eyed equanimity.

"Prudence will survive it," Vamir said.

"Prudence has survived worse. She was a war seamstress for six years. Three wedding parties is nothing." Leota's needle moved through the hoop — the small angry owl was gaining detail, its expression increasingly specific. "It's good, actually. The square needed something to look at today."

He knew what she meant. The energy of the morning — the muted quality of it, the careful adjustments, the shop-to-shop wrongness — had lifted somewhat as the day progressed, replaced by the kind of watchful normality that follows a disruption and is not quite the same as ordinary normality but is closer to it than the disruption was. The wedding party helped. It was impossible to maintain a mood of subdued loss while watching someone's youngest sister launch herself off a tailor's stoop and pirouette across the grass shrieking about freedom.

The girl landed in a heap of petticoats at the bottom of the slope, apparently unharmed, and received the scattered applause of everyone within sight with a theatrical series of bows.

"She's a natural," Vamir said.

"She's something," Leota said, in a different tone.

He looked at her. She had stilled, the needle hovering above the hoop, her attention focused not on the spectacle but on the girl specifically — with the quality of precise attention she reserved for things that warranted it.

The girl had straightened, finished her bows, and was now looking back across the square. Not at the audience generally. At Leota particularly. Watching, with the careful peripheral awareness of someone who was trying to appear not to be watching.

"She's been glancing at me for the last five minutes," Leota said quietly. "Testing, watching. Pretending not to notice, but tracking every movement." Her mouth pressed thin. "That's the look of a hedge-witch. Or something close to it."

"Maybe she's just clever," Vamir said. "Lots of clever girls in the world."

Leota's laugh was soft, almost sad. "Maybe. Or maybe it's something else." She looked at him sidelong. "Don't you think it odd — all these stories about the Enchantress, and suddenly there's a girl in town who acts like she's been cast in the lead?"

The girl made a small gesture — two fingers raised, then three, then two again, a pattern that might have meant nothing or might have meant something specific to someone who knew the language — and then turned back to her sisters as though nothing had happened.

Leota looked back at her embroidery. The needle resumed its work.

Vamir watched the girl for a while longer, filling in the image of her without appearing to do so, the way he catalogued everything — carefully, peripherally, without announcing the attention. Young, perhaps sixteen. Considerable self-possession for someone performing bridal chaos. The gesture might have been nothing. The way Leota had responded to it was not nothing.

He stored it, said nothing, and let the afternoon continue.

The wedding party eventually achieved coherence — Prudence emerging to issue a single inaudible command that returned all three sisters to the solemnity of nuns filing into chapel — and the square settled back into its ordinary rhythms. The girls departed a mark before dusk, ribbons in their hair and dresses apparently resolved, waving thanks to every shop they passed. In their wake the square felt both emptier and more itself, the comedy having done its work.

Leota packed up her embroidery without comment. Vamir stayed on the stoop until the last of the late-afternoon light had gone, thinking about hedge-witches and Enchantresses and the way the story kept throwing candidates at the wall to see what would stick.

———

Evening drew the town inward, as it always did — closing down the square's public life and funneling everything toward warmth and company. The Broken Claw that night was what it was at its best: belonging to the locals, the travelers' beds empty for once, the fire burning with the steady domestic quality of a fire that knows it has nowhere to be. Sam had the taps running clean again, by whatever negotiation she conducted with the beer, and the air was doing the right things with the smell of yeast and woodsmoke.

Vamir arrived to find Galhani and Makota already at the corner table, with the particular quality of occupation that suggested they had been there long enough to have one conversation and be partway through a second. He settled in beside them, accepted the glass that materialized as though Sam had seen him coming — she had, because she always did — and let the warmth of the place absorb the day.

Jen arrived later, as she usually did, having completed whatever final circuits the evening required of a constable. She shed her coat, took a stool at the bar rather than the table, and drank with the contained efficiency that was her default social mode. But she had positioned herself within earshot of the table, which was, for Jen, a form of participation.

For a while they simply let the evening be what it was. Makota recounted a small kitchen catastrophe involving a kit, an ill-advised experiment with new spicing, and a batch of rolls that had needed to be categorized as a learning experience rather than a product. Galhani had three new tea theories she needed to test on willing subjects. Polyocular made a bid for the bread basket and was redirected with moderate success.

It was the kind of conversation that was doing the thing conversations do when a group of people are not quite ready to talk about the thing they're all thinking about — building warmth, establishing ground, getting the kindling going before the larger log. Vamir recognized it and let it run its course.

It was Makota who said it, eventually, in the direct way she said things that cost her something.

"I keep thinking about who takes the shop." She turned her glass between her palms. "Not because I want someone to take it — not yet.

I just keep thinking about it. Like my head won't let me leave it empty."

"The town fills its own gaps," Galhani said. "It always has. That's part of how it works."

"I know that." Makota's tail moved, that slow involuntary arc. "I know the town will be fine. I just — Barnaba was good to have around. She was sharp, and she knew things, and she made good maps." A pause. "We recruited her. Specifically. To fill the gap we had. And now there's a gap again." Her voice stayed steady through this, which cost her something; Vamir could see it in the set of her jaw.

"We'll find someone," Galhani said, and then, more honestly: "Or someone will find us."

"That's not the point." Makota set the glass down with a quiet precision that indicated she was managing herself carefully. "The point is that the someone who was here is gone. And I know it's the right thing for her. I understand that. It doesn't make the gap feel smaller."

From the bar, without turning around, Jen said: "She's not gone."

They looked at her. She was still facing the taps, both hands around her glass.

"She's Everkin," Jen said. "The Change is what it is. She becomes someone new in a place that fits the new person. That's not leaving — it's arriving." She took a drink. "She was always going to be somewhere. She's still going to be somewhere. Just not here." A beat. "The gap isn't her absence. It's the space she made while she was here. That doesn't go away."

Silence at the table. Not the uncomfortable kind — the kind that follows something that has been said correctly and needs a moment to settle.

Galhani said, quietly, "That's — yes. That's right."

Makota was quiet for longer. Her tail had stilled. "I know that," she said finally. "I know it up here." She touched her temple. "It just takes the rest of me a while to catch up."

"That's what tonight is for," Sam said, from behind the bar. She had been listening, in the way Sam listened to everything that happened in her pub, which was completely and without making it obvious. "Catching up."

She brought the pitcher around and refilled without asking, which was as close as Sam got to a benediction.

Vamir held his glass and felt the conversation land in him along-side everything else the day had given him. He thought about Barnaba at her drafting table, the ruling pen finding its line, the absolute speci-ficity of her engagement with whatever work was in front of her. He thought about the way she had told him about the Change — *it's not a bad thing, it's not a sickness, it's just what we are* — and the way she had said it with the completeness of someone who had made a decision about how to carry this particular truth and was carrying it well.

She was writing herself. That was the thing. The Change was not happening to her — she was, in some essential sense, doing it, becoming the next version of the person she'd always been in the direction she'd always been going. She had told him: *sometimes the internal map changes first, and then you wait to see whether the external one follows.* She had been talking about cartography and she had been talking about herself and both had been true simultaneously.

He thought about his own self, which did not change in that way and would not. He was what he was and would remain it. The archivist, the witness, the keeper of the record. He had articulated this conviction to Sam and to Barnaba both, had held it under genuine pressure, had come out the other side more certain of it rather than less. He was in the right place for the person he was, and the person he was was not a person who underwent changes of that kind.

And yet.

There was something in Barnaba's capacity for fundamental trans-formation that he could not be entirely indifferent to. Not envy, exactly — he did not want to be someone else, did not want the vertigo of becoming, did not want to wake in the middle of a Change and find the furniture of himself rearranged. But something adjacent to envy. The recognition that she possessed a freedom he did not, a freedom that was simply not available to him by nature, and that he could admire it without pretending the admiration was uncomplicated.

She could write her own story, change its direction, become a new teller of it. He could not. His story was the holding of other people's stories, and the holding was everything, and he had chosen it and would choose it again. But choosing it again did not make the admiration smaller. It just made it honest.

She writes her own story, he thought. *I hold everyone else's. Both are necessary. Neither is lesser.*

He believed this. He had believed it for a long time, and today had tested it, and he still believed it.

He raised his glass slightly — not to the table, not to anyone who could see it — and let the gesture be what it was.

It was Galhani who started the singing, because it was always Galhani. She launched into the old marching tune from the valley without preamble, in the reckless way of someone who knows the tune will catch whether it wants to or not, and it caught, as it always did. Sam joined on the second verse, low and steady. Makota came in on the chorus with an alto that was sharp and clever and slightly louder than the room required, which was exactly right. Even Jen, at the bar, could be heard in the refrain if you knew how to listen for her — a low, contained contribution, present and gone before you could be sure you'd heard it.

Polyocular contributed something that was either a harmony or an editorial opinion and was possibly both.

When the song wound down, the room had a different quality than it had when it started — the grief not gone, not resolved, but shared out among enough people and enough warmth that no single person had to carry all of it. The evening continued. The fire burned. Sam kept the glasses full.

Vamir let himself be present in it — not cataloguing, not archiving, not watching from a careful distance. Just in it. For tonight, that was the right thing to hold.

Later, walking home across the dark square with Polyocular tucked warm against his neck, he looked up at the window of the mapmaker's shop. Dark. Closed. The brass plate on the door catching a slant of lamplight, the letters precise and even, as everything Barnaba had made was precise and even.

Barnaba Ashwick, Cartography.

She had changed her external map before she left, he realized. She had decided what to take and what to leave. She had sorted her own record with the same care she'd given every commission, every survey, every speculative line drawn in the belief that the possible was enough to draw.

He stood for a moment, just looking.

Then he went home, and the night was cold and quiet, and somewhere in the mountains the story was still moving.

eleven

. . .

THE WAGON that rolled into the square on Thursday morning was not the kind of wagon that arrived quietly.

It was not large, exactly — not a merchant's heavy-laden conveyance, not a traveling theater's painted behemoth — but it had the quality of something that took up more space than its physical dimensions accounted for. The lacquerwork was deep red, chased with gold at the corners. The horses were matched greys, which in Vamir's experience indicated either genuine wealth or the very committed performance of it. A driver sat up top with the expression of someone who had been doing this for a long time and had made his peace with it, and behind the curtained windows there were shapes suggesting passengers who had not yet seen fit to emerge.

Vamir watched from the bookshop window with the particular attention he gave to arrivals that didn't fit the usual categories.

The wagon stopped in the center of the square with the deliberateness of something that intended to be looked at. The driver descended and opened the door with a small ceremony. Two attendants — a young woman and a young man, both wearing the slightly dazzled expression of people in proximity to something they found genuinely extraordinary — stepped out first and arranged themselves on either side of the door.

Then Madame Armfeldt emerged.

She was perhaps seventy, or perhaps considerably more, in the way of certain people for whom age had become less a biological fact and more an aesthetic choice. She was dressed in layers of deep purple and forest green that should not have worked together and did, magnificently. Her hair was white and elaborately pinned. She wore rings on every finger that caught the morning light with the enthusiasm of things that had been bought specifically for that purpose. She surveyed the square with the expression of someone who had surveyed many squares and was prepared to find this one adequate at best.

Then her expression shifted, slightly, to something more interested.

"Yes," she said, to no one in particular, in a voice that carried across the square without apparent effort. "I think this will do."

Poly, on Vamir's shoulder, made a sound he could not immediately categorize. Not the alert attention it gave to genuine questers. Not the dismissive quiet it reserved for people passing through without needing anything. Something in between, uncertain in a way it rarely was, which he noted as information and filed without yet knowing what to do with it.

———

She went to the bakery first, which was where everyone went first, and which would ordinarily have told her nothing she was not supposed to know. The bakery's gift was subtle — the bread was extraordinary, yes, but more than that, Makota had a quality of knowing what people needed to eat, which sometimes produced items that hadn't been on offer until the specific person who needed them walked through the door. The gift was reliable. The gift was, currently, running on nineteen circuits instead of twenty, and Vamir wondered, watching from across the square, whether it would tell Makota anything useful about the woman in purple and green.

He crossed the square at a pace that put him at the bakery window approximately two minutes after Madame Armfeldt entered it. He was not hurrying. He was simply choosing a route that happened to pass the bakery window at a relevant moment.

Through the glass he could see the scene with the clarity of the morning light: Madame Armfeldt at the counter, Makota behind it, Sora hovering at the edge of the back room with the expression she had when something was happening that she was too young to interrupt and too curious to miss. Madame Armfeldt's two attendants — he would learn their names were Perri and Theo — had positioned themselves just inside the door with the practiced efficiency of people whose job was partly logistical and partly ambient, providing the appropriate atmosphere of significance.

He couldn't hear through the glass. He went inside.

"— and the crust," Madame Armfeldt was saying, turning the heel of a loaf in her ringed hands with the critical attention of a professional examining raw material. "The crust is correct. Most bakers don't understand the crust. They think it's a container. It isn't."

"It's part of the bread," Makota said, in the tone of someone who has held this view for twenty years and is mildly surprised to encounter it stated correctly by a stranger.

"It's the argument," Madame Armfeldt said. "The crumb makes the promise. The crust delivers the verdict." She set the heel down. "Your verdict is — " she paused, as though genuinely considering — "honest. Which is rarer than you might think."

Makota's ears moved in the way they did when she was receiving a compliment she hadn't expected and was deciding whether to be pleased or suspicious. "We try," she said.

"You succeed," Madame Armfeldt said, without excessive warmth — a statement of assessment rather than flattery. She looked around the bakery with the inventory look, her gaze moving across the shelves, the display cases, the careful arrangement of the morning's offerings. "You've been doing this a long time."

"Twenty-three years," Makota said.

"No." Madame Armfeldt looked at her with the directness of someone who had decided to say a thing. "The shop has been doing this a long time. You are — newer than the shop." She paused. "The shop has a quality of — accumulated purpose. As though it has been waiting to be used correctly, and you are using it correctly, but the purpose is older than you are."

Makota went very still in the way she went still when her gift was trying to tell her something and wasn't quite getting through. Vamir watched from near the door and thought about the icosagon running on nineteen circuits, and the bakery's gift slightly muffled, and the specific quality of Madame Armfeldt's observation, which was either the parlor trick of a skilled cold-reader or something more particular.

"That's — an interesting thing to say," Makota said carefully.

"I say interesting things," Madame Armfeldt agreed, without apparent arrogance. "It is, unfortunately, my nature." She looked at the display case. "The small ones. The seeded ones. Three, please, and whatever you think should accompany them."

Makota reached for the seeded rolls with the automatic professional movement and then paused, hand hovering, with the expression she had when the gift was and wasn't working simultaneously. She selected three seeded rolls and then, after a moment, added a fourth — a small, honey-glazed round that she hadn't apparently planned to add and seemed slightly surprised to find herself adding.

Madame Armfeldt looked at the fourth roll and then at Makota, and something in her expression suggested she had expected exactly this and found it confirming.

"Thank you," she said. She took the bag, paid without negotiating, and moved toward the door. She paused beside Vamir, who had been standing near the entrance trying to look as though he had come for a roll.

"You're the bookseller," she said. Not a question.

"Yes," he said.

She looked at him with the full attention she had been parceling out across the bakery, and it was, he had to admit, a considerable amount of attention. He felt the quality of being assessed by someone who was genuinely good at it, which was a different feeling from most assessments.

"Come and find me later," she said. "I have a feeling your shop is also older than you are."

She went out. Theo held the door.

Vamir looked at Makota, who was looking at the space where the fourth roll had been with the expression of someone reviewing a decision they didn't fully remember making.

"Well," Makota said.

"Yes," Vamir said.

———

The tea shop was next, which Vamir anticipated before it happened. The logical progression of a person making a tour of the square's significant offerings would proceed from the bakery to the tea shop, and Madame Armfeldt gave every impression of being a person who proceeded logically in matters she considered worth her attention.

He followed at a distance that was either respectful or cowardly, depending on how one framed it, and arrived at Galhani's door just as Madame Armfeldt was settling onto the high stool at the counter with the ease of someone who had sat on many high stools and found them all comprehensible.

Galhani was behind the counter with her usual morning energy, which was considerable even on ordinary days, and was currently occupied with the citrus-blend experiment — the same blend that had been almost-right for weeks, the same blend that would not fully resolve itself until Barnaba came home and the icosagon was whole. She was measuring dried petals into a pot with the focused attention of a craftsperson mid-problem, and she looked up at Madame Armfeldt with the warm curiosity she brought to everyone who came through her door.

"Morning," she said. "You're the one with the wagon."

"I am," Madame Armfeldt said. "The wagon is — a necessary tool."

"For what?" Galhani asked, beginning to arrange cups.

Madame Armfeldt considered this with what appeared to be genuine thoughtfulness. "For the work," she said. "The work requires movement, and movement requires a wagon, and the wagon requires matching horses, because there are some aesthetic standards that are not negotiable even in service of practicality." She looked at the jars and bundles covering every surface of the tea shop with the inventory look. "You have a lot of things."

"I have a lot of what I need," Galhani said, with mild precision. "They're not the same category."

Madame Armfeldt looked at her with the same quality of attention she had brought to the bakery, and Galhani, Vamir noted from his position just inside the door, went slightly still in a way she usually didn't — the specific stillness of someone whose gift was not quite giving them the information they expected it to give.

"What is it today?" Madame Armfeldt asked, nodding at the pot.

"A blend I've been working on," Galhani said. "It's almost right. It's been almost right for a while. It needs—" She paused. "Something. I know what quality I'm looking for and I keep finding the wrong sources of it."

Madame Armfeldt reached across the counter without asking and picked up the jar of dried petals Galhani had been measuring from, opened it, smelled it with the focused attention of a trained nose. "Yes," she said. "This is close. The base note is correct. You need something that's been in direct sun for the full growing season — not dried in shade, not dried quickly. Something that has absorbed as much of the season as it's possible to absorb." She replaced the lid. "The eastern valleys, two ranges over, have an herb that does exactly this. I've had it in a blend in the lowland markets. If you have a trade connection in that direction—"

"I have a connection in Mossgate," Galhani said, slowly, with the quality of someone following a thread to see where it went.

"Mossgate will know who goes east," Madame Armfeldt said. "It's a small chain, but it exists." She looked at the pot. "May I?"

Galhani, who was not a person who typically allowed strangers to interact with her work-in-progress, said "yes" before she had apparently finished deciding whether to.

Madame Armfeldt took the pot, added a small pinch from a tin she produced from somewhere in the layers of purple and green, and returned it. "A bridge," she said. "Not the solution — I don't have the full herb — but enough to tell you if the direction is right."

Galhani looked at the pot for a long moment. Then she finished setting up the blend, waited the appropriate time, poured a cup, and drank it.

She set the cup down very carefully.

"That's the direction," she said.

"Yes," Madame Armfeldt said.

Galhani looked at her with the expression she had when she was rapidly revising an assessment. "What are you?" she said, with the directness she used when she had decided that conventional politeness was taking too long.

Madame Armfeldt accepted a cup of tea from Galhani — who had poured it apparently on instinct — and held it with the ease of someone who had been drinking tea in various establishments for a very long time. "I am a woman of considerable experience," she said, "and some particular gifts, which I have spent many years developing and which I offer to those who are ready to receive them." She paused. "For a small fee."

"For a small fee," Galhani repeated, and the two words contained several things simultaneously.

"Expenses," Madame Armfeldt said. "The matching horses are not inexpensive."

Galhani looked at her for a moment longer with the not-quite-working gift and the information the tin had provided and the specific quality of a person who could not entirely dismiss what was in front of them. "What kind of particular gifts?" she said.

"Perception," Madame Armfeldt said. "The ability to see what a thing is and what a thing needs, which are frequently different questions." She drank the tea with evident appreciation. "Your blend, for instance. You knew what it needed. You simply didn't know where to find it."

"And you did," Galhani said.

"I've been to a great many places," Madame Armfeldt said. "It confers a broad catalog." She set down the cup. "My residence is in the mountains." She gestured, with the vagueness she apparently brought to all geographic specificity, upward and northward. "Those who seek me out find that the journey itself is—" She paused, with the timing of someone who had done this speech before and knew where the pauses were. "Educational."

Vamir, from his position near the door, looked at the Mistral range visible above the roofline and then at Madame Armfeldt and then at Galhani, who had the expression of someone doing several calculations at once.

"For a small fee," Galhani said again.

"For a small fee," Madame Armfeldt confirmed. She stood, straightened her layers with the practiced movement of someone for whom this was a regular operation, and produced from somewhere about her person a small ivory card. "Perri can discuss the arrangements." She placed the card on the counter. "Thank you for the tea. And for the direction — I've been looking for a source of that base note in a more accessible location. Mossgate may serve us both."

She went out. Theo held the door.

Galhani picked up the card, read it — *Madame Armfeldt. Wisdom. Transformation. By Appointment.* — and looked at Vamir.

"She knew about the tea," Galhani said.

"She has a good nose," Vamir said carefully. "And trade knowledge. She's traveled widely."

"She knew about the direction," Galhani said. "Not just the ingredient. The direction."

Vamir thought about the archive's trickster taxonomy. He thought about the genuine perceptiveness that lived underneath Madame Armfeldt's performance, the real gift that the performance was built around. He thought about Dardrad's observation, which he had not yet heard but would hear tonight: *the real ones don't need to tell you they're real.*

"She's perceptive," he said. "Genuinely. The castle may be another matter."

Galhani looked at the card again. "She fixed my tea," she said, in the tone of someone presenting evidence.

"She pointed you toward a source," he said. "The tea is yours. It was always going to be yours."

Galhani set the card down, but she didn't throw it away, and Vamir noted this too.

———

He did not follow her to Prudence's window. He stood in the square and watched from a distance, which was the right distance for that particular encounter.

Madame Armfeldt stood outside the tailor's shop for perhaps five minutes, looking at the display with the focused attention of a professional examining a colleague's work. Through the window Vamir could see Prudence see her — the way Prudence's body shifted, the subtle repositioning that put her back to the wall and face to the door, the specific management of herself that had become so habitual it was probably invisible to anyone who hadn't been watching for it.

Madame Armfeldt's expression as she looked at the window was not the theatrical assessment she had brought to the bakery and the tea shop. It was quieter. More specific.

After a while she produced another ivory card and slipped it into the frame of the window display — not prominently, not as an advertisement, but as a thing left for someone who might look closely enough to find it.

Then she moved on.

Vamir looked at the card in the window frame, too small to read from where he stood, and thought about Prudence in her dark dresses in the dark shop, managing herself carefully, the Holdkin women's bench now empty but the memory of it still present in the way memories of particular pressures left their marks.

He thought about Madame Armfeldt's real gift: *the ability to see what a thing is and what a thing needs.* He thought about what she might have seen in the window display and whether she had left the card as a kindness or a solicitation or something that was both at once.

He did not go to retrieve the card. It was not his card to retrieve.

He went to find Leota instead, which was what he did when the morning had given him things to hold that needed a particular kind of holding.

———

Leota was on her bench, which he had expected, and she had her embroidery, which he had also expected. She looked up when he arrived and made the small movement that indicated he should sit, which he did.

"The woman with the wagon," Leota said.

"She's been to the bakery and the tea shop," Vamir said. "She's perceptive. Genuinely." He paused. "She knows about bread. She knew the direction of Galhani's blend problem."

"That could be knowledge," Leota said. "Wide travel, broad catalog."

"Yes," Vamir said. "It could."

Leota set a stitch. "But?"

"The bakery's gift gave Makota a fourth roll," Vamir said. "Unprompted. Unrequested. Madame Armfeldt looked at it the way you look at something that has confirmed an expectation."

Leota's needle paused. "The gift is running below capacity."

"Yes," Vamir said.

"So it might be misfiring," Leota said. "Giving information it wouldn't ordinarily give to someone it wouldn't ordinarily give it to."

"Or," Vamir said, "it's giving accurate information about a person whose nature is genuinely ambiguous."

They sat with this in the good morning light.

"Poly?" Leota said.

"Uncertain," Vamir said. "Which is unusual."

"Yes," Leota said. "That is unusual." She looked at the square, where Madame Armfeldt had now reached the outfitter's and was engaged in what appeared to be a thorough examination of the window display. "What does she want?"

"She offers wisdom and transformation," Vamir said. "From a residence in the mountains. For a small fee." He paused. "She gestures vaguely northward when asked to be specific."

Leota made a sound that contained several things. "Has she said the mountains?"

"She has said the mountains," Vamir said. "She has not said the Mistrals specifically. She has gestured in a direction that includes the Mistrals and approximately half of the known northern range."

Leota looked at him. "That's either very coy or very honest about the fact that she doesn't actually have a castle in the mountains."

"Yes," Vamir said. "Those are the two options."

"And Poly can't tell you which."

"Poly is uncertain," he said again. "Which, as I said, is unusual."

They sat for another moment. In the square, Madame Armfeldt had entered the outfitter's. Through the window they could see Tyran's expression, which was the expression of a very large person encountering a force of nature of a different but comparable scale.

"I want to see what happens at the Broken Claw tonight," Vamir said.

Leota looked at him with the expression she used when she was acknowledging that he was doing something that was technically consistent with his stated values and was also clearly serving his own curiosity. "Of course you do," she said.

"She'll go," he said. "She's been to the bakery and the tea shop and the outfitter's. She's leaving cards. She'll go to the Broken Claw this evening and hold court and we'll learn more from watching her in that room than from anything else."

"And in the meantime you're going to do what?" Leota said.

Vamir stood. "She told me to come and find her at the bookshop," he said. "She said she had a feeling my shop was also older than I am."

Leota looked at him for a moment. "Is that concerning?" she said.

"I don't know yet," he said honestly. "That's what makes it interesting."

———

She arrived at the bookshop at half past eleven, as he had expected.

"The bookseller," she said, at the door, in a tone that made it sound like she had been told to expect one and was reserving judgment.

"The same," Vamir said. "Come in. Tea?"

She came in, took the stool at the counter as though it had been provided for her specifically, and accepted the tea with the gracious efficiency of someone who had accepted a great many things graciously over a great many years.

Vamir waited.

She looked at the shelves with the inventory look — not Makota's practical assessment or Leota's precise attention, but the look of someone accustomed to evaluating collections and forming conclusions about the people who had assembled them. She looked at Poly, who looked back with the three-eyed consideration he had been bringing to her since the moment she'd entered the square, that persistent uncertainty still unresolved.

Then she did something he had not quite expected: she was quiet. She sat with her tea and she was quiet, and the quality of her quiet was different from the quality of her performance in the square — less theatrical, more present. As though in the bookshop she had decided to set something down.

"You know about books," she said, finally.

"Occupational requirement," he said.

"No," she said. "I mean you know about books the way some people know about bread or tea. The way — " She looked at the shelves. "The way some people understand what a thing is for, beyond what it does." She looked at him. "This shop has been here a long time."

"I've been here fourteen years," he said.

"The shop has been here longer," she said. It was not a question.

"Yes," he said.

She nodded, as though this confirmed something. "I'm sensitive to it," she said. "Accumulated purpose. Places that have been doing the same thing for a very long time acquire a quality — a weight, perhaps. A specificity." She looked at the grandfather's blue volume on its shelf without knowing what she was looking at. "This shop has considerable weight."

Vamir held his expression steady and said nothing.

She looked at him with the full attention, the quality of assessment that had been stopping people in their tracks all morning. "You're not going to tell me anything," she said. Not accusatory. Observational.

"I'm listening with great interest," he said.

A smile crossed her face — the real one, not the performance smile, briefer and less constructed. "Yes," she said. "I imagine you are." She drank her tea. "I am what I say I am," she said. "I want you to know that. I do have gifts. I have spent a very long time developing them and they are real and they produce real results for people who are ready to receive them." She paused. "The castle is perhaps—" She stopped.

"An embellishment?" Vamir offered.

She looked at him sharply. "A framing device," she said, with dignity. "People need ceremony. People need the sense that they are making a journey toward something significant. If I sat in a room in a town and offered wisdom for a small fee, I would have — " She paused. "Fewer takers. The ceremony is not the wisdom. But it enables the wisdom to be received."

"That's honest," Vamir said.

"I am honest," she said, with slight surprise, as though this was a conclusion she had not expected him to reach.

"The advice you gave in the bakery," he said. "About Makota's shop being older than she is. About accumulated purpose." He looked at her steadily. "That was accurate."

She looked back at him. The performance had gone entirely now, in the quiet of the bookshop. She was simply a woman of considerable age and genuine perceptiveness, sitting with her tea, in a shop she could feel was something she didn't fully understand.

"I know you know something," she said. "About this town. About what it is."

"I know quite a bit," he agreed pleasantly.

"Are you going to tell me?"

"No," he said. "But I will tell you that your advice — the genuine parts, beneath the ceremony — is sound. The man with the hesitation. The woman with the expectations. You read them correctly."

She looked at him for a long moment. Then she said: "The real one. Up there." She gestured northward, vaguely. "She exists."

"Yes," he said.

"I am not her," she said.

"No," he agreed. "You're not."

"But I am—" She paused. "Something."

"You're perceptive," he said. "Genuinely. And you use that perception in service of people, which matters." He paused. "The ceremony has gotten somewhat ahead of the substance. But the substance is real."

She looked at her tea. Something in her expression shifted — not diminished, but recalibrated, the expression of someone receiving an honest assessment from a source they respect and finding it, on balance, useful.

"Can I show you our mythology section?" he said. "We have several excellent volumes on the trickster tradition."

Madame Armfeldt looked at him. She looked at him for a long moment with the sharp intelligence she kept below the performance. Then, with the specific dignity of someone choosing grace over resentment: "How kind," she said.

She bought two books. Poly selected them with the specific satisfaction of a creature that had been uncertain all morning and had finally found something it was certain about — these were exactly the right books for this particular person, and the certainty of it seemed to relax something in the small creature's bearing.

She paid without negotiating the price.

At the door she paused. "The advice was sound," she said. "I want you to know that I know that."

"I do know that," Vamir said. "So do the people you gave it to."

She held his gaze for a moment with the eyes of someone who had spent a long time being underestimated and had learned to recognize when it was not happening.

"Thank you," she said. Simply.

Then she went out into the square, and Theo held the door, and she was back in the performance again — the rings catching the light, the purple and green magnificent, the matched greys waiting — and Vamir stood in the doorway and watched and held it all in the careful way he held everything.

———

By evening, the square had opinions.

Vamir heard them accumulating in the way the square's opinions always accumulated — through Makota, who had heard from Kene, who had heard from three travelers Madame Armfeldt had approached with her ivory cards. He heard them from Galhani, who had spent the afternoon thinking about the tea direction and the tin and had arrived at a position that was approximately half convinced. He heard them from Tyran, who had described Madame Armfeldt's critique of the outfitter's window display as "like being assessed by a very well-dressed mountain," which Vamir thought was one of the better descriptions he'd encountered.

What he heard, in all of these, was the specific quality of a town whose discernment was slightly blunted — running on nineteen circuits, the gifts muffled just enough that their usual function of telling people what they needed to know about strangers was producing static rather than signal. Nobody was certain. Nobody was dismissing. Everyone was occupying the particular uncomfortable middle ground of people who had been given genuine things by a person they could not fully read.

The grain merchant had received accurate advice about his hesitation and was thinking about it. The weaver had received accurate advice about expectations and had gone quiet in the way of someone sitting with something true. The fourth roll at the bakery had not been explained to anyone's satisfaction.

"She's something," Makota said, in the bakery, to Vamir, which was Makota's way of saying she had no further information but the available evidence pointed in a specific direction.

"Yes," Vamir said. "She is something."

"You know what kind of something," Makota said.

"I have a theory," Vamir said.

"Are you going to tell me?"

"I want to see what happens at the Broken Claw tonight."

Makota's ears went back. "You're terrible," she said.

"I'm an observer," he said.

———

The Broken Claw that evening had the quality it had when something was going to happen in it and everyone could feel it building. The regulars were in their usual spots with an unusual quality of alertness. The travelers who had received Madame Armfeldt's card were there, identifiable by the way they kept glancing at the door. Sam was behind the bar with the contained attention of someone whose gift was also, tonight, giving her something between a clear signal and silence.

Madame Armfeldt arrived at half past eight with the timing of someone who understood entrances.

She was wearing different layers — tonight's combination was midnight blue and deep gold, which was if anything more effective than the morning's purple and green. Perri and Theo arranged themselves at a table near the fireplace with the practiced efficiency of people who had done this before in many rooms. Madame Armfeldt stood in the center of the pub and looked around with the measuring quality she brought to all spaces, and then she smiled, and the smile had in it a warmth that was entirely genuine.

"What a lovely room," she said, in the carrying voice. "What lovely people."

Sam, behind the bar, watched this with the expression she used when she was being professionally neutral and finding it requiring effort.

Madame Armfeldt made her way to the bar with the unhurried certainty of a person who moved through crowds by treating them as audiences. She ordered wine — "something local, something with character" — and settled onto the stool and began, with the ease of long practice, to hold the room.

She was, Vamir had to admit, excellent at it. The stories she told were good stories — well-structured, sufficiently vague in their geography to be unverifiable, featuring transformations and revelations and the specific satisfaction of people who had been lost and found direction. She had the gift of making every listener feel that the story was specifically applicable to their situation.

Dardrad, to Vamir's considerable entertainment, was listening from his stool with the expression of deep professional evaluation.

"She's good," Dardrad said, low, to Vamir.

"Yes," Vamir agreed.

"Not real," Dardrad said. "But good."

"How can you tell?" Vamir asked.

Dardrad considered. "The real ones don't need to tell you they're real. They just are, and you know it, and it's uncomfortable." He picked up his mug. "She's comfortable. She's very comfortable. She wants to be comfortable." He paused. "The real ones don't particularly care whether you're comfortable."

Vamir thought about Elspeth in the bookshop, the matter-of-fact delivery of *I'm the Enchantress, in case that wasn't clear.* He thought about four days on a mountain, paths that didn't go where they seemed to go, a man on a wet rock deciding he was done pretending.

"That's accurate," he said.

At the center of the room, Madame Armfeldt had reached the part of the evening where she was dispensing specific observations about specific people. The man from the grain merchants was told his hesitation came from a fear of his own potential. The woman from the weavers' guild was told she was carrying someone else's expectations. The young boy with the bad haircut was told his future was not what he imagined, and that she could show him a better one, and the boy looked at her with the expression of someone being told something true by someone they're not sure they believe, which was an uncomfortable place to be and also exactly the right place to be.

The advice was accurate. Vamir checked it against what he knew of each person and found it accurate.

Sam caught his eye from behind the bar, and the look she gave him had in it the specific quality of *I see what you're doing and I'm choosing not to intervene because this is also interesting to me.*

Madame Armfeldt held court until nearly midnight, at which point she rose with the theatricality of a curtain call, thanked the room for its company, indicated that those interested in the journey to her mountain residence should speak to Perri in the morning, and swept out.

The room sat in her wake.

"Well," Galhani said.

"Yes," said several people simultaneously.

Vamir finished his drink and went home, carrying the evening's accumulated evidence in the careful way he carried everything, turning it over in his mind, checking it against the archive's taxonomy of tricksters and the specific quality of genuine adversarial figures and the particular blunted state of the icosagon's collective discernment.

He had his conclusion. He would wait until morning to see if the morning confirmed it.

———

The daughter arrived at breakfast.

She came on foot, which distinguished her immediately from her mother, and she had the traveling clothes of someone who had been covering ground quickly and with purpose. She was perhaps forty-five, with her mother's white hair thirty years earlier and her mother's bearing without her mother's theater, and she had the expression of someone who had done this before and was resigned to doing it again.

She went to the inn first. She emerged ten minutes later with Madame Armfeldt, who had the expression of someone being collected against their will and intending to make it known.

The exchange on the inn's front step was conducted at a volume that carried across the square without apparent effort, which Vamir suspected was not accidental on either party's part. He watched from the bookshop window with his morning tea.

"Mother," the daughter said, in the tone of someone deploying a word that contained several years of accumulated experience. "We talked about this."

"We talked about Aldermoor," Madame Armfeldt said. "This is not Aldermoor."

"We talked about all of it. The castle in the clouds and the cards and the fee for expenses—"

"People need guidance," Madame Armfeldt said, with the dignity of someone making a principled stand. "I have guidance to give. It would be selfish not to share it."

"It would be legal not to share it," the daughter said. "We discussed legal."

Galhani appeared at the tea shop doorway. Makota appeared at the bakery doorway. Across the square, Vamir was aware of Leota's window opening and closing in the way it opened and closed when Leota had heard something and was making a note of it.

"The journey to my residence is genuinely transformative," Madame Armfeldt said. "Perri will tell you—"

"Perri is twenty-two and impressionable," the daughter said. "Theo is twenty and more impressionable. Mother, you cannot keep—"

"I have helped people," Madame Armfeldt said, and the dignity in it was genuine. "The man with the hesitation. The woman and her expectations. I saw them truly and I told them truly and they will carry that with them."

"Which is lovely," the daughter said. "And which you could do for free. Without the cards and the castle and the—"

"Atmosphere," Madame Armfeldt said. "The atmosphere enables the receiving."

"The atmosphere," the daughter said, with the precision of someone who had heard this argument before and had prepared a response, "cost us forty sovereigns in matched horse fees last month alone."

A pause.

"They are very well-matched," Madame Armfeldt said.

"Mother."

"The crest on the harness was perhaps excessive," Madame Armfeldt conceded.

"The carriage is at the east gate," the daughter said, in the tone of someone who has won and is not crowing about it. "We're leaving in an hour. Say your goodbyes."

She went back into the inn to collect Perri and Theo and the luggage, and Madame Armfeldt stood on the front step with the expression of someone who had been defeated in a fair fight and was framing it as a strategic retreat.

She looked across the square and found Vamir at his window, which he had not been trying to prevent.

She crossed to the bookshop.

He opened the door.

"You knew," she said.

"I had thoughts," he said.

"From when?"

He considered. "The fourth roll," he said. "The gift was muffled. It shouldn't have responded to you the way it did if you were simply a perceptive woman with good trade knowledge." He paused. "But it also shouldn't have responded to you the way it would respond to something genuinely significant. It gave you a fourth roll. Which is — in the middle. Which is where you are."

She looked at him steadily. "In the middle," she said.

"You're real," he said. "The gift is real. The perception is real. The advice is real." He met her eyes. "The castle is a story you tell in service of the real things. Which is not nothing. But it is also not a castle."

She was quiet for a moment. The matched greys were visible at the edge of the square, and the daughter was emerging from the inn with Perri and Theo behind her, laden with luggage.

"The real one," she said. "Does she — " She stopped.

"Does she know about you?" Vamir said.

"Does she mind," Madame Armfeldt said. "What I do. What I claim."

"I think," he said carefully, "that if she exists, she would mind the castle less than she would mind the advice being given to people who weren't ready to receive it. And she would not mind at all that people have been helped." He paused. "She would know her function. Her function requires that the genuinely significant be difficult to reach. She would not want it confused with something more accessible. But she would not begrudge you the perception or the guidance."

Madame Armfeldt looked at him for a long moment with the full intelligence she kept below the performance. "You are," she said, "a very unusual bookseller."

"Books contain a great deal," he said.

She almost smiled. Then she squared her shoulders, arranged her rings, and turned toward the east gate with the specific dignity of a person who intended to make a graceful exit regardless of the circumstances.

At the edge of the square she paused and called back, without turning: "The advice was sound."

"I know," he said. "So do they."

She went. Makota appeared beside him, as she had the previous morning, having materialized from the bakery without apparent transit.

"You knew," Makota said.

"I had thoughts," Vamir said. "I wanted to see the whole shape of it."

Makota was quiet for a moment. "The fourth roll," she said.

"Yes."

"I didn't decide to give her that," Makota said. "It just — happened."

"The gift was muffled," Vamir said. "It was responding to the genuine thing in her — the real perception, the real gift for under-standing what something needs — without being able to distinguish it clearly from other kinds of significance." He paused. "It will be back to normal soon." He thought of Bartram, coming from the west, the bench already at the right height. "When the shop is complete again, these things will resolve more cleanly."

Makota looked at the east gate, where the red and gold wagon was just visible. "She helped Galhani," she said. "With the tea."

"Yes," Vamir said. "She did."

"And she was right about my shop," Makota said. "About it being older than me. About the accumulated purpose."

"Also yes," Vamir said.

Makota absorbed this. "So she was real," she said. "Just not—"

"Not that kind of real," Vamir said. "A different kind."

Makota nodded, once, with the slow decisiveness of someone filing a complicated thing in the correct location. "I'm going to make the redpeach twists," she said. "We're nearly out and there's a full morning ahead."

"That sounds right," Vamir said.

She went back to the bakery. He went back to the bookshop. The square continued its business, the morning moving through its stages, and somewhere on the eastern road a red and gold wagon was carrying a woman of genuine perception and elaborate ceremony toward whatever came next, and the grain merchant was sitting with a true thing, and the weaver was considering her expectations, and Galhani had a direction for her tea, and the town was still slightly off-key but not for much longer.

He went to open the ledger, and Poly settled on its shelf, and the morning was what it was.

twelve

. . .

THE MORNING after was gentler than it had any right to be. The square came to life in its usual stages — deliveries first, then the early errand-runners, then the slow accumulation of the day's ordinary commerce — and if there was a quality of deliberateness to it, a sense of the town reasserting its own rhythm against the silence of the shuttered mapmaker's shop, nobody mentioned it. The scale read wrong at Pavati's. Alred's ledger was still inventing entries. The beer at the Broken Claw had recovered its willingness to be poured, but only just.

Vamir opened the bookshop at the usual time, stood behind the counter, and let the day's first customers find him. They did, because they always did. A traveling scholar needed a concordance he'd left at the last waypoint and never recovered. A pair of young women, sisters by the look of them, wanted something frightening but not too frightening for a long coach journey. A farmer's boy, sent on an errand, arrived with a list in his pocket and the slightly stunned look of someone encountering a bookshop for the first time and finding it larger than expected.

Poly handled each with its usual efficiency, the third eye working in the quiet way that suggested the archive below was lending some fraction of its attention to the shop above. Or perhaps that was Vamir's imagination. He had learned, in the sennights since the discovery, that the boundary between the two was less a line than a gradient, and that the shop's gift and the archive's gift were aspects of the same thing rather than separate operations.

He was between customers, sorting the morning's returns, when a brisk, metallic rattle reached him through the open door — the sound of tools in a well-organized case, jostling in time with a wagon's progress over the square's uneven stone. He looked up.

A wagon rolled in from the trade road, small and painted a deep rich brown, its brass corners catching the late-morning light. The man who climbed down from it moved with the particular economy of someone whose work had made every gesture precise — no wasted motion, each step placed with the unconscious deliberateness of a craftsman. He wore a tunic the color of new parchment, sleeves already rolled, and the flat splayed pouches at his belt were the kind only a person who had learned the hard way about losing tools would ever use.

He stood in the square for exactly two seconds, surveying it with the assessing look of someone who does this in every new place — cataloguing exits, resources, the quality of the stone underfoot — and then nodded once to himself, as though the square had passed some private inspection, and began to unload.

Vamir watched through the window as the man set out his display with the reverence of a person who understands that the way a thing is presented is part of what the thing is: a case of samples, a set of miniature lasts, a small bench with a cushioned seat, all arranged with the same care a jeweler gives to a window. The wagon's side panel read *Bartram Lastmaker* in plain letters.

Poly landed on Vamir's shoulder and made a sound he had come to think of as the archive's equivalent of a cleared throat — not urgent, but pointed.

He understood. He removed his apron, told the shop he would be back shortly in the way he'd developed of communicating with it, and crossed the square.

———

The cobbler was crouching beside his wagon when Vamir arrived, checking the fit of a boot on a wooden last with the focused attention of a surgeon. He looked up without apparent surprise, as though he'd been expecting someone to come and simply hadn't known who yet.

"Morning," Vamir said. "Welcome to North Pointe Common Towne. I'm the bookseller."

Bartram straightened, wiped his hands on a cloth tucked in his belt, and extended one. "Bartram Lastmaker." The grip was firm but careful — the grip of someone who understood that hands were tools and treated them accordingly. "You always greet newcomers yourself, or am I a special case?"

"The town has a way of letting me know when someone's worth greeting," Vamir said, which was true enough to not be a deflection.

Bartram's eyes moved to Poly, who was regarding the cobbler with the frank, unblinking assessment it reserved for people it hadn't decided about yet. "Interesting creature."

"He has opinions," Vamir said. "When he forms one about you, you'll know."

Bartram accepted this without asking what the opinions tended to look like, which Vamir noted as a mark in his favor. "I was planning to stay a day, see if there was work. But—" He looked around the square, and something in his expression shifted — the assessment replaced by something quieter, more personal. "It feels different here. I've stopped in a lot of towns."

"We hear that often," Vamir said. "Would you like a tour?"

———

They started at the bakery, because the bakery was where everything started.

Makota was behind the counter when they entered, and she looked up with the automatic calculation she applied to every new face — potential customer, probable interest, likely duration of stay. Whatever she saw in Bartram must have satisfied at least two of these criteria, because her ears came forward and her tail made a single decisive sweep.

"Morning," she said. "You smell like good leather and honest work. Have a roll."

Bartram accepted the roll she produced with the ease of someone who understood that refusing food in a bakery was a social error. He bit into it, and his expression did the thing that Makota's bread reliably produced in people who encountered it for the first time — a brief, involuntary stillness, as the flavor registered and the body decided it wanted to pay full attention.

"That," he said, after a moment, "is remarkable."

Makota's ears moved again, pleased but unsurprised. "I know. Try the peach twist."

While Bartram ate, Vamir watched Makota watch Bartram, and saw in her expression something he hadn't seen since the previous morning's grief had settled over her — a lightness, brief but genuine, the particular pleasure of a craftsperson encountering someone who recognizes craft. The dough had been strange. The display case latch had been unreliable. But the bread itself had remained what it was, and here was a man who tasted it and was stopped in his tracks by it, and Makota was, despite everything, quietly delighted.

It was a small thing. He filed it.

They moved on — the tea shop, where Galhani appeared from behind a curtain of drying herbs and immediately began questioning Bartram about his travels with the focused curiosity she applied to all new sources of information; the outfitter's, where Tyran boomed a welcome that rattled the hanging lanterns and then proceeded to spend twenty minutes in the particular mode of intense professional discussion that two craftspeople enter when they realize they've each solved problems the other has been thinking about; Dardrad at the butcher's, who gave Bartram a thirty-second assessment and then launched into an extremely specific discussion of dwarvish boot-making traditions that clearly delighted both of them.

At each stop, Vamir watched the town in its slightly-off-key state and watched Bartram move through it, and noticed the particular way the cobbler engaged — never performing, always genuinely interested, asking the kind of questions that showed he'd been listening rather than waiting to speak. He was, Vamir thought, the sort of person who made other people feel more themselves. The bakery's dough had been stubborn this morning and Makota had been managing it by willpower; by the time they left, she was already at the back with a new batch, and the set of her shoulders was different. At the tea shop, Galhani's three new tea theories had acquired a willing test subject, and her usual electric energy had a direction to go. At the outfitter's, Tyran had remembered where he'd put the mountaineering stock.

None of this was dramatic. All of it was real.

By the time they reached the smithy, Warren was already at his anvil with the quality of focus he got when the work was going right — the hammer falling with the satisfying regularity of something that had found its rhythm. He looked up when they entered, registered Bartram with the slow assessment of a man who measured everything in terms of structural integrity, and offered a grin that made the cobbler take a half-step back before he caught himself.

"The cobbler," Warren said, setting the hammer down. "Good. I've been doing a thing with iron lasts — not sure it works, but I think the theory is sound." He reached under the worktable and produced a sketch. "Tell me what you think."

What followed was fifteen minutes of the most concentrated professional conversation Vamir had ever witnessed, conducted in a technical dialect that he could follow perhaps half of. Bartram and Warren bent over the sketch with the mutual absorption of two people who have been working on adjacent problems for years without knowing the other existed. The sketch acquired annotations. A new sketch was produced. Warren's forge, which had been running slightly cool all morning — one of the subtler effects of the icosagon's incompleteness — had, by the time they left, returned to its proper temperature. Vamir noticed this because Warren noticed it, the ogre pausing mid-sentence to look at the coals with an expression of satisfaction he quickly suppressed.

"Good man," Warren said, at the door. To Bartram, but Vamir felt the remark applied to the morning more broadly.

———

By the time they returned to the square, the afternoon had established itself fully, and the light had the particular quality of a spring day that had decided to take its responsibilities seriously. The square felt different than it had in the morning — not fixed exactly, but in the process of fixing, the way a room feels when the window has been opened and the air is beginning to move.

Bartram stood at the edge of the green and looked around at the shops, the old stone, the children racing something along the gutter that might have been a stick or might have been a small determined animal.

"I'd like to stay," he said. Not asking exactly. Stating a position and seeing if it held.

"There's a shop available," Vamir said. "The mapmaker's. She left recently — the stock is there for whoever takes the space. It may not be the right layout for a cobbler, but the town has a way of adjusting."

Bartram looked at him. "The town has a way of adjusting," he repeated, not quite a question.

"It does," Vamir said. "You might find, if you go look at the shop, that it's more suitable than you'd expect."

Something in Bartram's expression suggested he understood that more was being communicated than the words contained, and that he was choosing to accept the more without requiring it to be explained. He nodded once, and set off across the square toward the mapmaker's shop.

Vamir watched him go. Poly shifted on his shoulder, and the quality of the shift was one he associated with satisfaction — not completion, but the recognition that something was moving in the right direction.

He went back to the bookshop.

————

Jen found him there a mark later, standing behind the counter with the ledger open and the pen not moving, which she correctly identified as thinking rather than writing.

"The cobbler went to look at the shop," she said, from the doorway.

"I know. I sent him."

Jen came in, which she did rarely enough that it always felt like a statement. She looked at the shelves with the expression she wore when she was deciding whether to say a thing, then said it. "The scale at Pavati's is reading correctly."

Vamir set the pen down. "Since when?"

"About a candlemark ago. And Alred's ledger stopped adding entries. And the clock on the town hall is keeping time again." She paused. "I went and checked the icosagon."

He waited.

"Not restored," she said. "But — less wrong. Like something's settled." Another pause. "The shop isn't his yet. He hasn't committed. But the town seems to have already decided."

Vamir thought about the waypoint records in the archive — the town's resilience expressed again and again not as resistance to change but as the speed with which it returned to function. The stage preparing itself for the next act before the actor had formally accepted the role.

"It usually does," he said.

Jen made a sound that was not quite agreement and not quite skepticism but acknowledged both as reasonable positions. Then she said, in the tone she used for things she'd decided to say once and not repeat: "It was a good morning. Whatever you did to bring him here."

"I walked across the square," Vamir said.

"I know," said Jen. "That's what I mean."

She left. Poly watched her go, then returned its attention to the shelves, already cataloguing the afternoon's likely requirements.

———

Bartram came to the bookshop as the afternoon was tipping toward evening, carrying the slightly dazed expression of someone who had expected a room and found something larger.

"The shop," he said, by way of greeting.

"Yes," Vamir said.

"There's a workbench. A proper one — the right height, the right angle on the surface. There's a rack for drying leather that I would have specified if I'd been asked. There's—" He stopped. Started again. "I had a dream last night, in the inn. A shop with a blue sign and a cat in the window. I didn't think much of it, the way you don't think much of dreams." He looked at Vamir with the expression of a practical man being asked to revise his understanding of what practical meant. "The sign on the shop is blue."

"It is," Vamir agreed.

"There's a cat."

"There are several cats in this town. They go where they like."

Bartram was quiet for a moment. "Is there something I should know about this place before I commit to it?"

Vamir considered how to answer this. The honest answer was long and would take more than one conversation. The useful answer was shorter.

"The town has a creed," he said. "Serve all who come in peace, stay in peace, leave in peace. All who follow it, regardless of who they are or where they've come from. No exceptions." He let that settle. "In exchange, the shops have gifts. The bakery's bread is extraordinary and the harvest never fails. The inn sends useful dreams. The pub tells Sam what travelers need to hear. My shop always has the book someone needs." He paused. "Your shop will find its own gift, once you're properly in it."

Bartram absorbed this with the focused attention he gave to everything. "And the blue sign? The dream?"

"The inn knows when someone is coming before they do," Vamir said. "Or before they know it themselves. It prepares you."

"For what?"

"For staying," Vamir said simply.

Bartram looked out the window at the square, at the last of the afternoon's light doing what it always did to the old stone at this time, turning everything slightly gold. He looked at it for a long time.

"I'd like to stay," he said. "If that's — I'd like to formally say so. To whoever needs to hear it."

"I'll let Jen know," Vamir said. "She has the keys. And tomorrow the town will want to welcome you properly, which will involve more food than you'll expect and opinions about your craft from people who've never made a shoe in their lives."

Bartram's face did something that started as a professional expression and ended as something more open. "I think I'd like that."

"You will," Vamir said. "It's their way of saying you're already one of them."

———

The welcome happened the next morning, as Vamir had said it would, with the informal precision the town brought to everything it considered important. It began in the bakery — the natural gathering place, the civic hearth — and expanded outward as word moved through the square in the way word moved in North Pointe, which was quickly and without anyone having to make an announcement.

Makota produced a quantity of food that suggested she had been planning for this, or something like it, for longer than a single night. Galhani arrived with tea in a pot large enough to serve a small army and the particular energy she had when an occasion gave her permission to deploy her full force of sociability. Kene and Sora worked the crowd with the efficiency of people who had been watching their mother do this all their lives and had learned the skill without noticing they were learning it.

Bartram stood in the center of it with the look of a man who had spent a long time being welcomed nowhere in particular and was finding the experience of being welcomed somewhere specifically somewhat larger than he'd been prepared for. Not overwhelmed. Just — taking it in carefully, the way you handle something you don't want to drop.

Dardrad arrived late and handed over a length of waxed thread without comment, which was his version of a speech. Tyran appeared with the iron last they'd discussed the day before, already cast, already cooled — he'd apparently gone straight from the smithy to the forge after their conversation and worked through the night, which was the sort of thing Warren did when the work had its teeth in him, and which struck Vamir as significant. Jen materialized, produced the key to the shop from her coat pocket, and placed it in Bartram's hand with the ceremony of a constable performing an official act, though no official act was technically required.

"One key," she said. "The lock sticks in damp weather. Lift and turn simultaneously."

"Thank you," Bartram said.

Jen nodded once, pocketed her hands, and stepped back into her usual observational position, which was slightly outside whatever circle had formed.

Vamir stood at the edge of it too, watching the town do what it did when it was being most itself — absorbing a new person into its fabric with the practiced ease of a place that had been doing exactly this for longer than anyone currently alive could remember. The morning's light was cleaner than it had been in days. The clock on the town hall was keeping time. Through the bakery window he could see the square, and the mapmaker's shop, which was no longer quite the mapmaker's shop, its sign still reading *Barnaba Ashwick, Cartography* but already beginning to seem like a caption for what the building had been rather than what it was.

Sam appeared beside him with the quiet arrival she had when she wasn't performing a role, just moving through a space. She handed him a cup of tea without comment and looked at the gathering.

"The beer poured clean this morning," she said.

"I heard."

"All the way clean. First pull, no argument."

"The scale at Pavati's has been right since yesterday afternoon," Vamir said.

Sam was quiet for a moment. "Not all the way back. Not yet."

"No," Vamir agreed. "But close."

They stood and watched Bartram accept a hand-painted mug from Lucy the potter with the expression of someone who had been told the rules of a game he'd always wanted to play and was discovering that he'd been good at it all along.

"He'll stay," Sam said.

"Yes," Vamir said.

"Good." She took her tea back to the bar, which was her way of declaring the observation complete.

Galhani detached herself from the crowd long enough to appear at Vamir's elbow, flushed and pleased. "Did you see? He knew about the citrus thing — the tea I've been working on. He'd had something similar at a shop three towns east, and he knew the herb." She grabbed his arm. "He knew the herb, Vamir."

"That's a good sign," Vamir said.

"It's an excellent sign." She pulled him back toward the center of things. "Come on. Stop watching from the edge."

He went, because she was right, and because tonight was not a night for the archive or the ledger or the careful peripheral attention of the archivist. Tonight was for being in it.

The morning stretched on, warm and unhurried, the town arranging itself around its newest member with the ease of something that had been practicing the motion for a very long time. Outside, the trade road carried its usual traffic — travelers passing through, the ordinary business of a waypoint in spring. Inside the bakery and spilling out onto the green, North Pointe was quietly, competently, joyfully doing the thing it had been built to do.

Vamir ate the bread and drank the tea and talked to Bartram about shoes and books and the particular challenges of working in materials that had their own opinions, and let the morning be what it was.

The square was not fully in tune. But it was getting there.

And it was, without question, enough.

thirteen

. . .

THE DAY HAD BEEN ordinary in the way that days were ordinary when something larger was running beneath them. Travelers in and out of the shop, the usual transactions, the ledger updated, the shelves tidied. Bartram's wagon had disappeared from the square and reappeared, lighter each time, as he moved his stock into the old mapmaker's shop in careful stages. Through the window Vamir had watched him work — methodical, unhurried, the movements of a man who understood that the way you moved into a space determined the relationship you'd have with it.

The afternoon lesson with the children had produced, among other things, a spirited debate about whether a map of a place you'd never been was still a true map, which Vamir had let run longer than strictly necessary because it was the most interesting question anyone had asked him all sennight and because Tannos, who had started it, deserved to see where it went. It went, eventually, to the question of whether truth required a witness, which was where Vamir had gently redirected it toward sums.

After the children left he had stood in the quiet shop and felt the evening arrange itself around him — the light shifting, the square condensing toward its closing-time rhythms, the quality of the building's attention changing in the way he had come to recognize as the archive being aware that he was aware of it.

He lifted the blue volume. The wall opened. He descended.

The altar on the way down had a new offering — a small folded square of paper, set precisely at the base of the sigils. Not an old offering. Recent, the fold still crisp. He crouched and looked at it without touching it, noting the weight of the paper, the deliberateness of the fold. Someone was maintaining this altar with regularity and care, someone who was not him and who had been doing it far longer than he had been descending these stairs.

He left a biscuit from his coat pocket — Makota's, the good ones — and continued down.

The archive received him in what he was coming to think of as its working mode: the ambient light at a steady, even temperature, the reading table nearest the stairs already cleared and set with a fresh sheet of paper and two pens. The tea was there, as it always was, and the particular rustling that he associated with the archive's unseen housekeepers had already stilled to the background quiet that meant the space was settled and ready. He had stopped thinking of these things as remarkable. They were the archive's habits, the way the shop above had its own habits — the bell over the door, the way light pooled in certain corners at certain candlemarks. The archive was not performing magic for his benefit. It was simply itself.

He sat, poured a cup, and opened his notebook to the question he'd left underlined.

But who shapes the antagonist?

He looked at it for a moment. Then he wrote below it: *Start with what the archive knows about why they exist.*

Poly landed on the opposite side of the table, third eye already open, and waited.

All right, Vamir thought, in the direction of the shelves. *Show me what you have.*

The first thing the archive showed him was not a text about the Enchantress or about adversarial figures at all. It was a collection of field observations — genuine observations, written in the particular compressed style of someone recording what they'd seen while still in the field, before the mind had time to shape the raw material into narrative. The observer was unnamed; the script was a variant of Old Mountain Elvish that Vamir could read with effort, and the subject was a series of questing parties that had passed through a valley — not this valley, but one with similar geography — over the span of about thirty years.

The observer had recorded each party's composition, their stated purpose, their evident state when they arrived, and — where the information was obtainable — what became of them afterward. The tone was scrupulous and impersonal. The observer noted what they saw and did not speculate about what they didn't. At the end of each entry was a column for outcome, which used a simple notation system: completed, failed, turned back, unknown.

What struck Vamir, reading through twenty or so entries, was the pattern in the failures. The parties that failed were not, in the main, the poorly equipped or the badly led. Some of the most comprehensively prepared expeditions had failed. Some of the most physically capable parties had turned back. What the failures had in common, when the observer noted it at all, was a quality of expectation — a sense that the thing being sought was owed rather than earned, that the journey was a formality preceding an inevitable reward rather than a test with a genuine possibility of an unfavorable outcome.

The parties that succeeded were, without exception, the ones that had been broken and rebuilt by the journey. Not destroyed — rebuilt. The ones that had lost something significant and continued anyway. The ones that had arrived at the threshold of whatever they sought not with the confidence of people who expected to receive but with the exhaustion and steadiness of people who had already given something real.

Vamir read this three times, the compressed field-observation style slowly yielding its full meaning. Then he turned the page and found a second observer, different hand and script, describing a different valley over a different span of years, and the pattern was exactly the same.

He sat back.

The archive was not a library. He had understood this in the abstract since his first descent — the two-tier logic, the distinction between the shop above and the space below — but reading these field observations brought it into specific focus. A library collected texts for the use of readers. An archive collected observations for the use of whoever needed to understand what the observations, in aggregate, meant. These observers had not been writing for an audience. They had been recording what they saw because that was what they did — because they were, like him, people whose function was to stand outside the story and hold the record of it.

He thought of the marginal note, the earlier hand. Someone like him had sat in this space before, reading observations like these, and had written a question in the margin of a chronicle. Had they found an answer? Or had they left the question for whoever came next?

He let Poly lead him further.

The second text was more formal — a treatise rather than a field record, written by someone who had clearly had the benefit of many years and many observations before putting pen to paper. The author identified themselves only by a professional title: the Keeper of the High Pass Record. The title implied an institution, a lineage of people who had held this role before and would hold it after.

The treatise was structured as an argument, proceeding through a series of propositions with the careful logic of someone who antici-pated objections and wanted to preempt them. Vamir read it with the attention such a text deserved, which was considerable.

The central argument was this: that the adversarial figure — the obstacle, the gatekeeper, the thing that stood between the quester and the sought object — was not incidental to the quest but constitutive of it. Without genuine resistance, what was sought could not be genuinely received. Not because the resistance produced virtue in some abstract sense, but because the capacity to receive a significant thing — healing, wisdom, power, whatever the quest was for — had to be developed, and the adversity was the development. You could not pour water into a vessel that had not been made. The adversarial figure was the making.

The author was careful to distinguish between types of resistance. There was obstacle-as-filter: the adversary that separated those who were not ready from those who were, ensuring that what was sought went only to those capable of using it well. There was obstacle-as-forge: the adversary that transformed the quester through the encounter, so that they arrived at the destination as something different — and more capable — than they'd been when they started. And there was obstacle-as-balance: the adversary whose existence ensured that nothing was received without equivalent cost, that the economy of significant things was maintained.

None of these, the author noted with characteristic precision, were mutually exclusive. A single adversarial figure might serve all three functions simultaneously, and the most significant ones tended to.

Vamir wrote this down in his own notation. Then he stared at what he'd written for a while, thinking about the questers who passed through North Pointe — their fear, their resolve, their desperate need for something the Enchantress supposedly possessed. He thought about what it meant that Sam's gift said *real* when she sensed their quests. The gift told Sam what travelers needed to hear, and what Sam heard when these travelers came through was the word *real*, which meant their quests were genuine, which meant whatever they were walking toward existed and had something to offer them.

Which meant the Enchantress, whatever she was, was functioning as an adversarial figure in the specific sense this author described. She was the making.

He added a note: *Not the destination. The threshold. The forge.*

The third text was the one that introduced the complication, and it was also the one that reminded him that he was working in an archive rather than a library — that what he was reading was not a curated collection of arguments but a record of what had actually been observed, including observations that contradicted each other and observations that raised questions without answering them.

It was a compilation, assembled from multiple sources, of the specific *stories* that had accumulated around adversarial figures in various regions and periods. The stories of origin — how the adversary had come to be what they were, how they had come to occupy the threshold position they held.

Vamir read through them with growing attention and growing unease.

They were, without exception, too neat.

The Evil Wizardess who had been denied a rightful inheritance. The Old Hag whose comfortable life had been destroyed by a village that feared her gifts. The Sorceress who had loved badly and been left to her fury. The ancient creature whose grief had curdled over centuries into the specific shape of obstacle and test. Each story had the quality of a thing that explained itself, the satisfying internal logic of a tale that had been told enough times to acquire smooth edges.

The compiler — another unnamed observer, this one with a dry, precise style that Vamir found himself appreciating — had noted this explicitly. After presenting some twenty of these origin stories, each one rendered in the compressed form of something summarized rather than told, the compiler had written a single paragraph that Vamir read three times:

The foregoing accounts have been gathered from field observers across seven regions and four centuries. The compiler notes that the similarity of their structure is not, in the compiler's assessment, evidence of their accuracy. A story that explains the existence of a threshold-guardian in terms of personal grievance or historic injustice is a story that a community tells itself about a phenomenon it does not fully understand. The grievance and the injustice may be genuine. But the threshold-guardian's function does not depend on them, and the compiler has found no reliable mechanism by which personal history of the type described could reliably produce a threshold-guardian of consistent capability and purpose. These stories are what people say when they do not know what to say. The compiler does not know what to say either. This record is offered not as an explanation but as an accounting of the explanations that have been attempted.

Vamir set the text down.

He sat for a while, listening to the archive's deep quiet and the faint purposeful rustling from somewhere far back in the stacks. The tea had been refreshed at some point. He drank it without noticing.

The stories were too neat. The compiler was right. And he had known this, in the way you know something before you have the evidence for it — had felt it in the questers' rumors, in the way each account of the Enchantress's origin was internally consistent and externally incompatible with every other account. She had been wronged. She had always been this way. She had chosen this. She had been appointed. The stories multiplied and contradicted and the only thing they agreed on was that she existed and that she served a function.

He added to his notes: *Origin stories are community narratives. The function precedes the story, not the other way round. Someone or something determines the function. The stories don't explain how.*

He looked at the underlined question.

But who shapes the antagonist?

The archive had shown him what the antagonist was for. It had shown him that the origin stories were insufficient. It had not yet shown him the mechanism — the actual answer to the question. That was still ahead of him, somewhere in the deep stacks, waiting for a visit he wasn't ready for yet.

He recognized this without frustration. The archive did not withhold things arbitrarily. It showed what was ready to be shown, and the fact that the mechanism was not yet available meant he was not yet equipped to understand it. He needed to sit with what he had. He needed to let the observations settle into the configuration they were working toward.

He was, after all, an archivist. He understood the difference between the raw record and the interpretation it eventually supported.

He wrote one more note: *The function is clear. The mechanism is not. Return when you have more of the pattern.*

Then he closed the notebook, stacked the texts he'd used with care, and stretched the stiffness out of his back.

Poly looked at him from across the table.

"I know," Vamir said. "Food."

The square was blue-dark by the time he surfaced, the last of the evening light having made its exit while he was underground. The shops were closed or closing, the square in its late-evening mode — a few figures moving with the purposefulness of people heading some-where specific, the lanterns doing their patient work.

Light from the old mapmaker's shop — Bartram's shop, he was already thinking of it — fell in a warm rectangle across the walkway. Through the window Vamir could see the cobbler at work, bent over something on the new bench, the quality of his attention absolute. There was already a boot-shaped sign above the door that had not been there this morning, plain wood, cleanly lettered.

He had not eaten since the morning's lesson.

The Broken Claw was the obvious answer, and he turned that way, and almost immediately encountered Galhani coming from the oppo-site direction, bundled against the evening chill with a basket on her arm and the particular forward lean of someone who has somewhere to be.

She stopped when she saw him. Looked at him with the accuracy she always brought to these assessments.

"You look like you've been underground," she said.

"I've been working," Vamir said, which was true.

Galhani fell into step beside him, apparently having decided that wherever she was going could wait. "You've been doing this a lot lately. Disappearing." She glanced at him sideways. "We used to see you at the tea shop most mornings. And the lessons aside, you're barely in the bookshop. You've been putting up the inventory sign."

"The inventory takes time," Vamir said.

"Fourteen years of inventory suddenly takes a great deal of time," Galhani said, with the precision she deployed when she had thought something through and was now presenting her conclusions. She was not hostile. She was, as she always was, simply accurate. "Makota noticed too. And Jen." A pause. "Nothing's wrong, is it? With the shop?"

The answer that formed itself — the deflection he'd been in the process of constructing, the version of the inventory explanation that would satisfy without raising further questions — stopped itself before he could deliver it. He was aware of stopping it. The awareness sat with him for a moment, slightly uncomfortable, the way honesty sometimes is when you've been working toward something else.

He did not want to tell Galhani about the archive. Not because he didn't trust her — he trusted her completely, and the trust was not in question. It was something else. The archive was not, he was increasingly certain, a thing to be discussed over tea in the bakery. It was the back room of the shop's gift — the part that served the keeper rather than the customers — and the same logic that kept the shop's upstairs workings quiet and unremarked applied, he thought, to the archive below. It was not a secret. It was simply not a part of the story that the street-level world needed to know about, in the same way the inn's dream-work wasn't announced and Sam's gift wasn't advertised.

He was, he realized, applying the archivist's logic to the archive itself. Holding it outside the record. Keeping himself outside the story.

He noticed this. Filed it. Wasn't sure what it meant yet.

"Nothing's wrong," he said. "I've been doing some research that requires extended quiet. The bookshop after closing is the right space for it." He looked at her. "I should have said something earlier. I didn't want to make it seem more significant than it is."

Galhani studied him with the look she used when she was deciding whether to accept an answer or press further. He met it without elaboration.

"All right," she said, finally. Not entirely satisfied, but satisfied enough. "As long as you're eating. You look like you've been forgetting."

"I'm eating now," he said. "I'm going to the Claw."

"Good." She shifted her basket to the other arm. "Bartram was asking about you, by the way. He wanted to know if there were any books on northern tanning methods. Apparently the leather up here is different from what he's used to."

"I'll find him something," Vamir said. "Tomorrow."

Galhani nodded, said goodnight, and peeled off in the direction she'd originally been heading, already absorbed in whatever was next.

Vamir stood for a moment in the evening air, the conversation settling in him. He had not prevaricated — not exactly. He had withheld, which was different, and he had withheld for reasons that were, he thought, defensible. But the fact that the decision had required thought, and that he had then immediately examined the decision, was information. He was not certain the information meant anything yet. He was, however, certain that it was worth holding.

He went into the Broken Claw.

Bartram was there, in a corner booth with a bowl of something and the look of a man taking a meal seriously after a long day of work. He looked up when Vamir came in, and something in his expression settled — the mild alertness of someone who'd been hoping to see a particular person without being certain they would.

"The bookseller," he said.

"The cobbler," Vamir replied, and took the opposite seat without being asked, because the booth had the look of an invitation.

Sam produced food with the efficiency that meant she'd been expecting him, which she probably had. The evening crowd was the usual assembly — regulars at their regulars' spots, a few travelers who'd made it in before the road closed for the night, Dardrad at the bar nursing something amber and conducting a private argument with the middle distance.

Bartram had, he noticed, the shop's first commission already complete — a small repair job, a buckle reattached to a strap, sitting on the seat beside him wrapped in brown paper. The first work done in a new space always mattered. It established the relationship between the craftsperson and the place.

"How's the bench?" Vamir asked.

"Perfect," Bartram said, and the word had no excess in it — not emphatic, just precise. "I don't know how it's at the right height. I hadn't told anyone my measurements." He looked at Vamir with the expression he'd been wearing since the blue sign and the dream, the one that said he had accepted the terms of the place without fully understanding them yet. "That happens a lot here, I'm noticing."

"Yes," Vamir said.

"Does it stop being surprising?"

Vamir thought about the refreshed tea in the archive, the books that appeared at his elbow, the quality of the light adjusting to whatever he needed. "You stop being surprised by the individual instances," he said. "The general fact of it becomes part of how the town feels. It's harder to explain than that, but I think it's accurate."

Bartram seemed to find this satisfactory. He ate with the methodical thoroughness of someone who treated all tasks equally, and Vamir ate too, and for a while the conversation moved through the easy channels of new acquaintance — where Bartram had been before, what the trade road was like in the south at this season, whether the northern leather really did require different working methods and if so why. Bartram had opinions about leather that were deeply specific and expressed with the confidence of someone who had spent years acquiring them, and Vamir found himself genuinely interested, in the way he was always genuinely interested in the specifics of how a craft worked.

"Galhani said you were asking about tanning texts," Vamir said.

"If you have anything. I don't want to work blind on material I'm not fully familiar with."

"I'll find you something. There's a survey of northern tanneries from about thirty years ago that covers the regional variation. Probably more than you need, but better to have it." He paused. "There may be something older too. I'll look."

Bartram nodded, and then said, with the slight change of register that meant a different kind of question was coming: "What do you do? In the evenings, I mean. When the shop's closed."

Vamir looked at him. "Research, mostly. Reading. The shop has an extensive back catalog that requires regular attention."

"Galhani mentioned you'd been harder to find lately."

"Word travels quickly here."

"It seems to." Bartram was quiet for a moment. "I'm not asking to pry. I'm asking because I've been in a lot of towns, and in a lot of towns the person who runs the bookshop is also the person who knows everything, or at least who everyone assumes knows everything. And you clearly do know a great deal. But you have a quality of — being somewhere else at the same time. Even when you're right here." He looked at his bowl. "I thought maybe the research explained it."

Vamir considered this. It was the most precise description of a thing he'd heard from someone who didn't know the thing they were describing. He felt, again, the pull toward disclosure and the counter-pull toward holding it — the archive's private nature, the keeper's role, the logic of the back room.

"The research does explain some of it," he said. "There are aspects of the town's history that I'm working through. It takes time. It's quiet work." He met Bartram's eyes. "When I know more, I may be able to say more. For now that's the most accurate thing I can offer."

Bartram held his gaze for a moment, then nodded once — the same nod he'd given in the square when Vamir had said *the town has a way of adjusting*. The nod of someone who has accepted more than the words contain.

"Fair enough," he said. "Thank you for the tour yesterday, by the way. I think it made the difference."

"It always does," Vamir said. "For people who are going to stay."

They finished their meals with the comfortable ease of people who have arrived at a mutual understanding without having to formalize it. Sam cleared the table with her usual efficiency. Outside, the trade road was quiet.

———

He descended again after the meal, because the evening was not finished and neither was the work.

The archive was in its night mode — the light slightly cooler, the atmosphere the deep quiet of a place that has been working while you were away and has arrived at a particular patience. The table held fresh paper. The tea was there.

He did not immediately open the notebook. He sat for a while, letting the conversation with Galhani and the conversation with Bartram settle alongside the day's readings, finding the configuration they wanted to take.

He had withheld the archive from Galhani. He had withheld it, in a different register, from Bartram. He had done so for reasons that felt sound — the archive was the back room of the shop's gift, the keeper's resource, not a part of the street-level story — and he had done so instinctively, the way you protect something you understand to be private without having been told it's private.

He thought about this with the honesty he tried to bring to everything he did.

Was it the archive's nature that required discretion? Or was it his own instinct toward the kept record — the archivist's habitual sense that certain things belonged in the back, held rather than displayed, preserved rather than shared? The two had become indistinguishable in him. He had said as much to Sam, moons ago now: *the belief and the preference, I can't fully separate them anymore.*

The archive, he thought, was not secret. It was simply not yet ready to be explained. The moment he tried to describe it to Galhani over morning tea, the description would become the story of the archive, and the story would have its own momentum and its own distortions and would eventually be something other than the thing. Better to hold it until he understood it well enough to hold it accurately.

That was, he recognized, an archivist's reason for silence. It was also, he recognized, a reason that could be used to justify any silence indefinitely.

He sat with the tension of this rather than resolving it, because resolving it prematurely would falsify the record.

Then he opened the notebook to the question he'd left underlined, looked at it for a long moment, and turned to the next clean page.

The function is understood: filter, forge, balance. The origin stories are community narratives and insufficient. The mechanism — who shapes the antagonist, and how — is still ahead. The archive has not yet shown it to me. I am not yet equipped to receive it.

I will be.

He closed the notebook, left the table tidy, and climbed toward morning.

At the altar he paused. The biscuit was gone. The paper fold was still there, crisp and deliberate. He pressed his palm to the stone, felt the warmth, and stood for a moment thinking about the person who had left the paper — their regularity, their care, their presence in this space that predated his own by what might have been decades.

Not alone in this, he thought. *Not the first. Probably not the last.*

He climbed the remaining stairs into the shop, replaced the blue volume on the shelf, and stood in the ordinary dark.

The archive was below. The town was around. The story was moving, as it always was, without him and because of him and in spite of him, in the complicated way that stories moved when they were real.

He went to bed, and slept without difficulty, and dreamed of nothing he could remember in the morning.

fourteen

. . .

THE MISTRESS VALDAINE arrived on a Monday, which Vamir was prepared to accept as simply how Mondays were.

The party came in from the western road, which was unusual — most significant arrivals came from the east, from the direction of the longer trade routes and the larger cities. The western road was shorter and less traveled, and people who came from that direction tended to be either locals from the nearer valleys or people who had made a specific choice about their route, which was itself a kind of information.

There were seven of them: six retinue members and a driver, with the central figure visible only as a shape behind the curtained window of a conveyance that was not quite a carriage and not quite a wagon but something between the two, sleek and dark and well-maintained in the way of things that were used seriously rather than displayed casually.

The retinue was young — early twenties to early thirties, Vamir estimated, a mix of genders and apparent origins — and they had a quality he found interesting: they moved with the attentiveness of people in the proximity of something they considered genuinely significant, not the performed reverence of Perri and Theo but something more specific, more earned. They had been with this person for a while and had not become jaded by it, which said something about the person.

He noted this from the window and watched the party settle outside the Weary Head.

The driver opened the conveyance door. The retinue arranged themselves — not theatrically, but practically, the way people arrange themselves around someone who sometimes needs things — and the Mistress Valdaine descended.

She was tall. This was the first thing, unavoidable and immediate. Tall in the specific way that suggested a heritage not entirely human — the proportions slightly different, the movement carrying a quality of precision that Vamir associated with elven blood, though diluted and expressed differently than in pure-blooded elves. Her hair was dark, streaked with something that might have been early silver or might have been a deliberate choice. Her clothing was severe and architectural in a way that was clearly intentional, every line considered.

She looked at the square with the assessing quality of someone who had looked at a great many places and had well-developed criteria.

Then she went inside without speaking to anyone, and the door of the Weary Head closed behind her, and that was all anyone saw of the Mistress Valdaine for the remainder of the day.

———

The retinue, however, talked.

This was, Vamir reflected, perhaps the defining characteristic of the situation: the central figure was entirely absent while her people were thoroughly, enthusiastically present. By midday he had heard three separate fragments of conversation from three separate locations in the square, all concerning the Mistress Valdaine, and none of them containing a single piece of information that could not have been — in the right light, with the right foreknowledge — interpreted in at least two completely different ways.

The first fragment came from the bakery, where two of the retinue — a young woman with close-cropped hair and a young man with ink-stained fingers — were purchasing enough bread to suggest they were provisioning for the full party.

"She sees things others can't," the young woman was saying to Makota, with the earnest intensity of someone who had thought about this and wanted to explain it correctly. "The shape of what's coming, before it arrives. I've watched her walk into a room and know — just know — what it needs."

"What sort of room?" Makota asked, with the focused attention she brought to information that might be significant.

"Any room," the young man said. "But especially the difficult ones. The ones that resist."

Makota looked at Vamir, who had arrived for his morning roll at exactly the wrong or right moment.

The second fragment came from Galhani's, where another retinue member — older than the others, perhaps thirty-five, with the quality of someone who had been with the group long enough to have developed perspective on it — was having tea and seemed inclined to talk.

"Working with her isn't easy," she said, to Galhani, who was inclined to listen to anything. "She takes everything you have and gives it back transformed. You don't leave her employ unchanged. Nobody does."

"Is that — good?" Galhani asked.

The retinue member considered this with genuine thoughtfulness. "It's necessary," she said. "She has standards that most people find excessive. Until they see the result." She paused. "I've given her three years of my life. I'd give her three more."

"Three years," Galhani said, and Vamir, who had stopped in the doorway ostensibly to check whether Galhani had the citrus blend ready, heard the weight she was putting on the number.

The third fragment came from the square itself, where the youngest of the retinue — barely twenty, with the wide-eyed quality of someone recently arrived in the orbit of something that had changed their understanding of what was possible — was talking to one of the travelers near the fountain.

"She doesn't seek out clients," the young one said. "They find their way to her eventually, if they're ready. She told me once that she's been doing this longer than anyone knows." He paused. "Longer than she'll admit."

The traveler, who had been on his way to somewhere else, had stopped with the specific quality of someone whose attention had been caught against their will.

Vamir walked past, filed all three fragments, and went to find Leota.

———

Leota was on her bench, which he had expected, and she had her embroidery, which he had also expected, and she said "sit down" before he had finished crossing the green, which suggested she had been waiting for him.

"You've heard," he said.

"I've heard," she said. "Jen came by twenty minutes ago with three specific things people had said and a question about whether we should be concerned."

"What did you tell her?"

"That I didn't know yet." Leota set a stitch. "What do you think?"

Vamir sat with the question for a moment, genuinely. He thought about the archive's field records and the compiler's note and the origin stories that were too neat. He thought about the pattern he had been constructing for months — the adversarial function, the threshold-guardian, the specific quality of the genuine article that Dardrad had identified without knowing he was identifying it.

He thought about Sam's gift.

"I don't know," he said. "Which is interesting in itself."

Leota looked at him. "You're not certain she isn't."

"I'm not certain she is," he said. "Which is different from certainty in the other direction." He paused. "The retinue's descriptions are — they fit a pattern. But they fit more than one pattern."

"She doesn't give you what you want," Leota said. "She gives you what you need."

Vamir turned to look at her. "Where did you hear that?"

"The older one — Caress, she says her name is — was talking to Sam this morning." Leota returned to the embroidery. "Sam looked thoughtful afterward."

"I'll talk to Sam," Vamir said.

"Yes," Leota agreed. "Do that."

He found Sam at the Broken Claw, doing the opening work with a quality of distraction that was, for Sam, significant.

"The retinue," Vamir said.

"Yes," Sam said. She set down the glass she was polishing. "I talked to the one who's been with her three years. Caress." She paused. "My gift was—" She stopped, and the stopping was its own kind of information. "Not what it usually is," she said carefully. "Not the clear signal I get with questers. Not the absence of signal I get with ordinary travelers." She looked at him. "Something in between. Which I don't have a good category for."

"What does in between feel like?" Vamir asked.

Sam considered this with the seriousness it deserved. "Like — a real thing, seen through obscured glass," she said finally. "Something is there. I can't tell exactly what." She picked up the glass again. "Could be her. Could be something about the people around her that's real, that I'm picking up on rather than her." She paused. "Could be that she's real in a different way than the questers are real."

Vamir held this. "She's barely been seen," he said.

"I know." Sam polished the glass with rather more attention than it needed. "The biggest room at the inn. Meals sent up. The retinue handles everything." She paused. "Which could mean she's protecting herself from being recognized. Or it could mean she's accustomed to being managed around. Or it could mean she simply prefers not to be social."

"All of which are consistent with someone significant," Vamir said. "And all of which are consistent with someone ordinary who has built significant habits."

"Yes," Sam said. "Exactly."

They sat with the uncertainty for a moment, in the way they had both become accustomed to sitting with things that didn't immediately resolve.

"We watch," Vamir said.

"We watch," Sam agreed.

———

The evening at the Broken Claw had the quality of a room with something unresolved in it, which the regulars felt without being able to name. The retinue came for dinner — all six of them, filling a corner table with the easy familiarity of people who spent a great deal of time together — and their conversation, by design or accident, continued to accumulate.

Vamir sat at his usual spot and listened with the full peripheral attention of the archivist.

The ink-stained young man — Pell, he was called — was explaining to a traveler who had asked about their group that the Mistress Valdaine's work was not for everyone. "You have to be ready to see things differently," he said. "Her vision of the future is unmatched. But the future she shows you isn't always the one you thought you wanted."

"The future she shows you," Dardrad repeated, from two stools over, in the tone he used when he was cataloguing something.

"What she produces," Caress said, from the corner table, apparently having heard, "changes what's possible. For the people who receive it." She picked up her drink. "The show she's planning in the eastern king-doms — it's going to be unlike anything they've seen."

"A show," Galhani said, and there was a quality in it that Vamir recognized — the tea-maker's instinct for the thing that was almost-right-but-not-quite, the sense of a blend that was one element away from what it wanted to be.

"What kind of show?" Vamir asked, from across the room.

Caress looked at him with the assessing quality she brought to things. "The kind that changes how people see themselves," she said. "How they present themselves to the world." She paused. "She has a gift for seeing what something could be, rather than what it is."

"And the eastern courts aren't ready for her?" Sam said, from behind the bar.

Caress smiled, with the warm certainty of a true believer. "The eastern courts are never ready for her," she said. "They never are, until they are."

The room absorbed this.

Vamir looked at Sam. Sam looked at Vamir. The look between them contained the full complexity of the situation — the genuine uncertainty, the not-knowing, the specific quality of something that might be significant seen through the obscured glass Sam had described.

He filed it. He held it. He did not resolve it, because it did not yet resolve.

———

They left the next morning, early, before the square had fully woken. Vamir watched from the window with his first tea of the day as the retinue loaded the sleek dark conveyance with the efficiency of people who had packed and departed many times. The Mistress Valdaine descended from the Weary Head with the quality she had descended with the day before — the height, the precision, the severe architectural clothing — and entered the conveyance without speaking to anyone or looking at anything except, briefly, the square itself.

She looked at the square the way Vamir looked at it. With full, specific attention. The kind of attention that records rather than merely sees.

Then she was inside, the door was closed, and the conveyance was moving, and the retinue followed, and in less than five minutes the party had left the square by the eastern road and North Pointe had returned to its ordinary morning.

Vamir stood at the window for a while.

He did not know. He had not known yesterday and he did not know this morning and the not-knowing had a specific texture that was different from his usual relationship with uncertainty. It was not the not-knowing of insufficient information. It was the not-knowing of information that could not yet be resolved — a question that was genuine, held in good faith, waiting for an answer that would come or would not come in its own time.

He was, he thought, comfortable with that. He had been becoming comfortable with it for a long time.

He went to open the shop.

fifteen

. . .

THEY ARRIVED ON A TUESDAY, which was the day the trade
road tended to deliver its more complicated packages.

Vamir saw them from the bookshop window before anyone else
had cause to notice them — four figures coming in from the eastern
approach in the mid-morning, moving with the compressed efficiency
of people who had been traveling hard and had not softened their
pace just because a town had appeared. Their gear was functional and
well-maintained in the way that spoke of professional use rather than
preparation for a specific journey. The tallest of them — the one who
walked slightly ahead, who carried himself with the unconscious
authority of someone accustomed to being the point of any formation
— had the particular quality of stillness that Vamir associated with
people who had spent a long time learning to be dangerous and had
not spent an equivalent time learning to set that aside.

He watched them cross the square without moving from the
window.

Poly, on his shoulder, was very still.

He noted this. He noted that his own response to the four figures
was not the alarm he would have felt a year ago, not the sharp instinct
that something was wrong that Yoren had provoked in Poly and in

him. What he felt instead was something more like recognition — the quiet click of a piece fitting into a space that had been waiting for it. He had read the field observations in the archive. He had read the compiler's dry accounting of what adversarial figures were for. He had been thinking about the Enchantress as threshold, as forge, as the thing that separated those who were ready from those who were not.

These four were walking toward that threshold.

He did not know yet whether they were the kind who would be made by the encounter or unmade by it. He suspected the tall one, Brasham — he did not know the name yet, but there was something in the set of the man's jaw that suggested a name with weight to it — would be the determining factor. Groups like this tended to be what their leader made them, for better or worse.

He turned from the window and went back to the ledger.

———

He heard about the Holdkin women from Makota, who had heard about them from Sora, who had heard about them from Kene, who had apparently been witness to an exchange outside Prudence's shop that had left him unsettled enough to report it to his mother in detail. This was, Vamir thought, the town's information network operating with its usual efficiency.

He went to look.

The two women were seated on the bench opposite Prudence's shop with the deliberateness of people who had chosen that particular bench for reasons that had nothing to do with comfort. They were dressed conservatively — plain wool, dark colors, the kind of clothes that made a statement about the wearer's values by studiously refusing to make a statement about anything. They had the look of Holdkin women of a certain stripe: the particular combination of composed certainty and watchful disapproval that he associated with the more enclosed communities in the eastern valleys, the ones that maintained their internal coherence through the careful management of what was acceptable and what was not.

Through Prudence's window, he could see her moving in the shop

— her black dress, her measured steps, the way she positioned herself always with her back to the wall and her face toward the door. She had noticed the women. She was managing herself carefully, the way she always managed herself, with the specific economy of someone for whom self-management had become a form of survival.

He had never known Prudence's full story. He knew the outline of it — the arrival with a toddler and no one else, the immediate and unusual certainty about the shop, the way she had integrated into the town with the thoroughness of someone who intended to stay and had made that intention structural. He knew, in the way you know things about people you see every day without ever discussing them directly, that she had come from somewhere that had not been kind to her, and that North Pointe had been chosen with the deliberateness of someone who needed to be somewhere safe and had found it.

He knew Holdkin communities. He had books about them — their social structures, their particular doctrines, their management of women who stepped outside the defined roles. He had several records of what happened to women who left such communities without permission, who took children with them, who set up in trade without a husband's sanction. He knew what the two women on the bench were doing there. He knew exactly what their presence meant to Prudence, and what the particular quality of their composed attention was intended to communicate.

He stood on the walkway for a moment and felt the instinct rise — the impulse to cross the square, to sit with Prudence, to make his presence a statement. He knew, without asking, that she would not want this. She was managing. She had been managing for a long time, and management was her method, and an intervention — however well-intentioned — would shift something she needed to remain undisturbed.

He also knew that this was not his story.

Not because he didn't care. He did. But the Holdkin women had come for Prudence, and Prudence would deal with them in her own way, and the outcome of that dealing was hers to determine. He could no more resolve it for her than he could resolve Barnaba's Change, or Leota's history, or any of the other stories he witnessed from the careful peripheral distance of the person whose function was to hold them.

He filed what he'd seen. He noted the women's presence, the quality of their attention, the way Prudence moved in the shop behind them. He noted that he had felt the impulse to act and had set it aside.

Then he walked past the bench without stopping, not looking at the women directly, and went back to the bookshop.

The feeling he carried with him was not comfortable. He did not expect it to be. He had said to Sam, in the beginning: *I do, a little. But not in the way you mean.* He had been talking about Yoren then. He thought about it now, in relation to Prudence, and found the feeling was in the same register but with a different weight to it. With Yoren, the risk had been Yoren's. With Prudence, the discomfort was a slower thing, more specific, a knowledge of what was happening and a deliberate choice not to intervene in it.

Both were true to his function. Neither was comfortable. He thought perhaps they shouldn't be.

————

The afternoon brought Leota to the bench outside her house, which was where Leota went when she had decided to watch something. Vamir had learned, over years of living in the same square, that Leota's choice of bench was itself information — she positioned herself based on what she wanted to observe, and the angle she chose told you almost as much as what she said about it afterward.

Today the bench faced the Broken Claw.

"They're inside," she said, when Vamir settled beside her. "The four. They've been in there since mid-afternoon."

"How did they seem to you?"

Leota considered this with the care she gave to assessments that mattered. "Purposeful. Not reckless — they're not thrill-seekers. The tall one has been here before, I think. Not to the Claw, but to the valley. There's a quality to how he looks at the mountains." She paused. "He's not afraid of them."

"Should he be?"

"Everyone should be, a little. The mountains don't care." She set a stitch, examined it. "The others take their cue from him. If he's steady, they're steady. If something shifts him—" She left the rest unfinished in the way she did when the rest was obvious.

Vamir looked at the Claw's closed door. "Sam's gift?"

"Real," Leota said. "I asked her this afternoon. She said it clearly." She turned a page in the embroidery without looking at him. "Clearer than usual, apparently. She said it had the quality of something that had been building for a long time."

He thought about the archive's field records — the parties that had been traveling toward a threshold without knowing that's what they were doing. "They've been on this road for a while."

"Yes." Leota's needle moved. "The question that interests me is whether they'll listen."

"To what?"

"To whatever the town has to tell them." She looked at him sideways. "You're already thinking about whether you have anything to give them."

He was. He had been since he'd seen them from the window. "The shop might."

"The shop," Leota said, with the precision she used when she was acknowledging what she was hearing and noting what it didn't say. She returned to her embroidery.

They sat in the particular comfortable silence that Vamir associated with Leota — not empty, but settled, the silence of someone who had been present in the same town for long enough that silence had become one of her primary modes of communication. After a while she said, without preamble: "The Holdkin women are staying at the inn."

"I saw them this morning."

"And?"

"And I noted it," he said.

Leota's needle paused. It was a brief pause, but specific — the pause of someone who had heard something that required acknowledgment but not comment. The needle resumed.

He appreciated this about Leota. She understood the distinction between things that required intervention and things that required witness, because she had spent a long time learning to make the same distinction about her own history. She did not agree with every choice he made on that axis. But she understood the axis.

"Prudence will manage," she said.

"She always does."

"Managing is not the same as thriving," Leota said, with a flatness that was not unkindness. "But sometimes it's the available option, and she knows the difference." She paused again. "Her gift will show itself eventually. When the time is right."

Vamir looked at the tailor's shop, where the closed sign had been in the window since mid-afternoon. "I know."

"It's a considerable gift," Leota said. "Worth waiting for."

He filed this, as he filed everything Leota said — not because he could use it immediately, but because Leota did not offer observations without reason and the reason usually became clear eventually.

———

The Broken Claw in the evening had the quality of a place that was holding two conversations simultaneously — the ordinary one, warm and familiar, and a second one underneath it that nobody was quite acknowledging. The four hunters occupied a table near the back wall, which was where people sat when they wanted to see the room without being seen, and they had the particular focused quietness of people who were assessing rather than socializing.

Vamir arrived early enough to claim his usual spot and to watch the room settle around the newcomers. The regulars did what the regulars always did with strangers who carried that quality of professional purpose — they made space, maintained their own conversations, and directed enough peripheral attention to the hunters' table to know exactly what was happening there without ever appearing to watch.

Dardrad watched with less peripheral attention than most.

The dwarf had positioned himself at the bar with the specific quality of planted-ness that meant he was not planning to move, and was monitoring the hunters' table with the frank assessment of someone who had spent enough time in the kind of company that carried that kind of gear to have opinions about what it meant. He said nothing for a long time. Then he said, to Vamir, in the low voice he used when he wanted to be heard by one person and not others:

"Those four are trouble."

"They're hunters," Vamir said.

"I know what they are." Dardrad's eyes didn't move from the table. "I know what kind of hunters. The kind that's been told what the quarry is and hasn't asked enough questions about why." His voice had dropped further. "The tall one's done this before. He's got the look of a man who's delivered something he shouldn't have delivered and is still telling himself the person who asked him to do it was telling the truth."

Vamir looked at Dardrad. "That's specific."

"I've known a lot of men with that look." Dardrad finally turned from the hunters' table and picked up his mug. "None of them were bad men, exactly. That's the problem with that look. Bad men don't usually have it."

Vamir held this. Dardrad was not an imprecise observer, and his history — abbreviated, never discussed in full, present in the scars on his knuckles and the particular way he sat with his back to nothing — had given him a calibrated eye for the quality of other people's moral compromises.

He looked at the tall man's table again, with this in mind.

Brasham — he had the name now, from an exchange he'd overheard when they came in — was not watching the room with the alertness of someone who expected trouble. He was watching it with something more complicated: the careful attention of a man who had been to enough places and seen enough things that every new room was a calculation, not of safety exactly but of what kind of place this was and what kind of place it required him to be. He was doing the same thing Vamir did, he realized — reading the room, cataloguing it. But where Vamir's cataloguing was for the archive, Brasham's was for survival, and the difference in purpose produced a different quality of attention.

The woman beside him — Vamir mentally tagged her as the second-in-command, from the way the other two deferred to her when Brasham was speaking but deferred to Brasham when she was — was watching Sam. Not suspiciously. More with the recognition of one professional acknowledging another.

Sam, for her part, was pouring drinks with her usual exactness and displaying no more interest in the hunters' table than in any other table, which meant she was paying close attention to all of it.

Galhani arrived, as she did most evenings, with Lara and the particular energy of someone who had been working through several things at once and was ready to set them all down. She slid in beside Vamir, read the room in the quick instinctive scan she always made, and registered the hunters' table.

"Who are they?" she said, low.

"Hunters," Vamir said. "They're headed to the Mistrals."

Galhani looked at them with the specific evaluative attention she reserved for people who were going to need something from the town. "They look like they know what they're doing."

"Yes," Vamir said. "That's part of what concerns me."

She looked at him. He didn't elaborate, and she let it go, which was one of the things he valued most about her — the ability to receive a partial answer and trust that the rest was coming when it could.

The evening progressed. The regulars settled into their patterns. The hunters ate and drank with the thoroughness of people replenishing after a long road, and the quality of their conversation — mostly low, occasionally pausing to consult something one of them produced from a coat pocket — was not the conversation of people planning violence. It was the conversation of people planning a very difficult journey, which was not the same thing, though the line between them was sometimes thinner than it looked.

Makota arrived late, coming from the bakery with the slightly harried quality of a woman who had been dealing with the tail end of a complicated day. She took a stool at the bar near Dardrad, accepted a drink from Sam, and looked around the room with the practical efficiency of someone assessing the current state of things.

Her eyes landed on the hunters' table. Stayed there for a moment. Then she looked at Vamir.

He gave her the small gesture he used when he wanted to communicate *I know, I'm watching, not yet.* She held his gaze for a moment, then looked away, satisfied or at least contained.

What Vamir was feeling, watching all of this — the town reading the situation, the careful management of concern, the specific quality of Dardrad's flat disapproval and Makota's contained alertness and Leota's earlier precision — was something he had not fully felt before in relation to the hunters and questers who passed through. He had watched them all from his usual peripheral distance and catalogued them and let them go. He had felt the appropriate concern and the appropriate equanimity.

What he felt tonight was the gap between what the town felt and what he felt, and it was specific enough to examine.

The town felt threatened. Not gravely, not existentially, but the particular unease of people who recognized a quality of purpose in these four that exceeded the usual quester's mix of hope and desperation. These four were not people who had come to ask the Enchantress for help. They had come to find her and remove her, or to find her and stop her, or to find her and deliver her to someone whose plans for her were not good. The town did not know this with certainty, but it felt it, the way the town felt things, through the accumulated instincts of people who had been watching questers come and go for long enough to know the difference between a pilgrim and a hunter.

Vamir knew it with something closer to certainty, because he had read the archive's field records. The Enchantress — whatever she was, whoever she was — was serving a function. She was the threshold, the forge, the filter. She existed, in the way the archive described, as a necessary component of a system that had been operating for longer than anyone currently alive could remember. And these four, with their professional gear and their too-quiet competence and the specific quality Dardrad had identified in Brasham's face, were walking toward that function with intentions that had nothing to do with being made or tested or refined.

He did not feel threatened. He felt concerned, in the way he felt concerned when he saw someone about to make an error of categorization — about to treat one kind of thing as though it were another kind of thing and suffer the consequences of the confusion. The Enchantress was not a threat to be neutralized. She was a threshold to be crossed or not crossed, depending on what the crosser brought to it.

He could not make Brasham understand this. He was not going to stand up in the Broken Claw and explain the archive's observations on the function of adversarial figures. And it was not, strictly, his role to intervene in the stories of the people who passed through.

But the shop always had the book a customer needed.

He turned this thought over carefully, with the attention it deserved.

The shop's gift was not passive. It was not merely reactive. Poly led customers to books before the customers had fully articulated their needs, because the shop understood needs at a level beneath what the customer could express. The gift was anticipatory. It met people where they were going, not just where they were.

Brasham needed something. Not a book, not exactly, but something the shop could provide — information, specifically the kind of information that might redirect a hunter who was not a bad man toward an understanding of what he was walking toward. The map Vamir had been compiling — the old Mistral routes, the high passes, the keeps — would serve as the gift's instrument. But the gift's actual content was the warning.

And the warning was the shop acting through him, not him acting through the shop.

He sat with this distinction for a while. He was aware that it was doing a particular kind of work — the work of making an act feel sanctioned rather than chosen, the archivist's ancient method of keeping himself outside the story by framing every action as the story acting through him rather than him acting on the story.

He was also aware that this time, it was simply true.

———

He waited until Brasham went to the bar alone.

This was partly calculation — he wanted the exchange to be private, without the second-in-command's assessment or the other two's witness — and partly instinct, the particular instinct he'd developed over years of knowing when a customer needed to be approached and when they needed to approach. Brasham went to the bar to refill a cup, and there was a quality to the way he moved that suggested he'd needed a moment out of his companions' orbit, a brief pause in which he was simply himself rather than the point of the formation.

Vamir was at the bar already, which required no maneuvering. He had simply placed himself there, with his drink, in the way that required no explanation.

He waited for Brasham to settle, then said, quietly: "You're going to the Mistrals."

Brasham looked at him with the assessment he applied to everything. "Most questers are, this season."

"Most questers aren't carrying what you're carrying," Vamir said. Not an accusation. An observation.

Brasham was quiet for a moment. Sam was at the far end of the bar, occupying herself with something that required her full attention, which was Sam's way of creating privacy. "And what do you think we're carrying?"

"A commission," Vamir said. "And a set of assumptions about what you're going to find that may not match what's actually there."

Brasham turned to face him fully. He was doing the calculation Vamir recognized — assessing whether this was a threat, a warning, a play of some kind, or the thing it appeared to be on the surface. He came to a conclusion. "Who are you?"

"The bookseller," Vamir said. "The shop has the books everyone in this valley has used to prepare for the Mistrals, for a long time. I know the routes and the history and the stories." He paused. "I also know that the stories about the Enchantress are not accurate accounts of what she is."

"And you know what she is."

"I have a better understanding than most," Vamir said. "Enough to tell you that she is not what your commission describes her as. Whatever you've been told — that she is a danger, that she is malevolent, that she is doing harm to the people who seek her — the records don't support it. The people who come back from her are changed. That's not the same as harmed."

Brasham was listening. Vamir had the attention of a man who had come to the valley with his conclusions formed and was, despite himself, hearing something that gave him a different shape to try.

"You're going to tell me not to go," Brasham said.

"No," Vamir said. "I don't tell people not to go. That's not what I do." He reached into his coat and produced the map — a single folded sheet, the high pass routes marked in his careful hand, the keeps indicated, the approaches noted with the seasonal accuracy Barnaba had taught him to think about. "I'm going to give you this. The most accurate map of the approaches that exists. And I'm going to tell you one thing, which you can do with as you choose."

Brasham took the map. He unfolded it, looked at it with the professional attention of someone who read maps the way Vamir read texts. "What's the one thing?"

"She is not the thing your commission says she is," Vamir said. "Whatever you've been told to do, consider whether the person who told you has been to the Mistrals themselves and seen what she actually does. Consider whether the stories that commission is based on are the stories of people who sought her and were tested and found wanting — and called that harm, because it felt like harm, even though it was something else." He folded his hands around his cup. "I don't know what you'll do with that. It's yours to do what you choose. But the shop always has what the traveler needs, and what you need is not just a map."

Brasham was quiet for a long moment, looking at the map. Then he folded it and placed it in his coat with the care he gave to things he intended to keep.

"You're not going to try to stop us," he said.

"No."

"Why not?"

Vamir considered the honest answer. "Because it's not my role. And because the Enchantress is better defended than you know." He picked up his drink. "But mostly because you're not a bad man, and I think if you go up there knowing what I've told you, the outcome will be different than if you go up there without it."

Brasham looked at him for another long moment — the assessment, the calculation, the conclusion. Then he nodded, once, and returned to his table.

Vamir stayed at the bar. His drink was in his hand and he was looking at it rather than at the room. He was aware of having just done something, and of the particular quality of discomfort that came with it — not regret, not guilt, but the mild vertigo of someone who has moved from one position to another and has not quite found their footing in the new one.

He had acted. Through the shop's gift, acting as its instrument, but he had acted.

The shop would have found Brasham the map eventually. Would have placed it at his hand, the way it placed things at the hands of travelers who needed them, through Poly's guidance or the quiet rearranging of the shelves. Vamir had simply — accelerated it. Had recognized the need before the customer had crossed the shop's threshold. Had brought the gift to where the customer was rather than waiting for the customer to come to him.

That was still the shop's function. He believed that.

He also believed that the choice to do it now, privately, in the bar, without witnesses, had been his. Not the shop's. His.

He did not know yet what to do with the difference.

Sam appeared beside him, refilled his cup without comment, and said, very low: "That was a good thing."

"The shop would have done it anyway," Vamir said.

Sam looked at him with the expression she used when she had heard an answer and was noting what it didn't say. "Yes," she said. "But you did it now."

She moved back down the bar. Vamir sat with his drink and the mild vertigo and the particular quality of the evening, which had the feeling of a fulcrum — a moment on which other moments would balance, in ways that were not yet visible.

———

Leota left early, which he had expected. She came to the bar to say goodnight to Sam, and on her way past Vamir she paused and said, without looking at him: "I noticed."

"I know," he said.

She went. He stayed.

The hunters left a candlemark later — Brasham last, pausing at the door with the quality of a man committing the room to memory. He didn't look at Vamir. He didn't need to.

After they were gone, the room had the slightly lighter quality of a space that has been holding its breath and has now released it. Dardrad made a sound that was not quite approval and went back to his drink. Makota caught Vamir's eye and gave him the smallest nod. Galhani, who had missed the bar exchange entirely, was in the middle of a lively discussion with Lara about the sourcing of a particular dried flower and paid the hunters' departure no mind.

Sam cleared the hunters' table with her usual efficiency and returned to the bar.

"They'll go tomorrow," she said.

"Yes," Vamir said.

"The map was right." It wasn't a question.

"The map was accurate," Vamir said. "As accurate as I could make it."

Sam was quiet for a moment. "And the warning?"

He looked at his drink. "Also accurate."

"Will he listen?"

"I don't know," Vamir said. "I told him what I could. What he does with it is his."

Sam nodded, and the nod had a quality he associated with her when she had assessed something and found it correct — not effusive, not even warm exactly, but present. The nod of someone who has witnessed something and has decided it should be witnessed.

He stayed until the last of the regulars had gone, partly because the evening had earned a slow close and partly because he was still processing the mild vertigo of the bar exchange and the Claw was the right space for that kind of processing. When Sam finally began to close up, he gathered his coat and his notebook and the specific interior quiet that had settled in him over the last mark.

Outside, the square was cold and still. The hunters' wagon was still at the stable — they would leave at first light, or just before it. The Holdkin women's window at the inn was dark. Prudence's shop was dark. The mapmaker's sign was lit by the lamp across the walkway, Barnaba's name still in its precise letters.

He walked home thinking about the difference between the shop acting and him acting, and about whether the difference mattered as much as he had always believed it did, and about whether the question itself was the thing he was supposed to be sitting with right now rather than resolving.

He thought it probably was.

He went inside, fed Poly, and stood for a while in the quiet of the shop before bed.

The blue volume was on its shelf. The wall behind it held what it held. He did not descend tonight — the archive's time was its own, and tonight belonged to the surface, to the processing of what had happened in the ordinary world and what he had chosen to do in it.

He went to bed with the question still open, which was, he thought, the right way to carry it.

sixteen

. . .

HE DID NOT PLAN to go down that night.

The bar exchange with Brasham had left him in a specific interior state — not unsettled exactly, but unfinished, the way a text feels when you've read it carefully and understood it and still know there's something in it you haven't reached yet. He had sat with it for two days, doing the ordinary work of the shop, teaching the children, eating with Galhani and Makota at the bakery and saying nothing about the hunters or the map or the particular quality of discomfort the exchange had left him with.

On the third morning he woke before the light and lay in the dark and understood that the unfinished quality was not going to resolve itself at the surface. It was an archive question. It had always been an archive question. He had been waiting, in his careful way, to be certain he was ready.

He was ready.

He rose, dressed, went down to the shop, and lifted the blue volume from its shelf.

———

The altar was different tonight.

Not physically — the basalt was the same, the sigils the same, the folded paper offering still precise at the base. But the quality of the stone's warmth when he pressed his palm to it was different. Not warmer. More present. As though the altar had been attending to something and had now, at his touch, redirected that attention to him.

He stood before it for a long moment.

He had been pressing his palm to this stone for moons now, in the way he had seen done at shrines of this age — acknowledgment, not prayer, the gesture of someone noting a presence rather than petitioning it. It had felt right. It had felt like the appropriate register for where he was in his understanding.

Tonight the gesture felt insufficient.

He did not think about it. He did not consult his notebook or look for a reference in the archive's texts or reason his way toward the decision. He simply understood, in the way Forest Elves understood things that had no words yet, that this moment required something more than acknowledgment.

He reached into his coat pocket for the small knife he carried for opening packages and cutting cord. He made a clean, shallow cut across the heel of his left palm — the tool hand, the recording hand, the hand that held the pen — and pressed it flat against the sigils. Against both of them: Nimarith's compressed peaks, and the open eye above the quill that he now knew to be the Lady of Script's mark.

The blood was warm against the cold stone. He held the pressure steady, the way his people held a hand to the cut bark of a tree that had been wounded — not to heal it, but to acknowledge the wound, to offer something of yourself in recognition of what the tree had given. His grandfather had done this. His grandfather's grandfather. The gesture was older than anything he had read, older than the archive's oldest texts, older than the trade road and the waypoint and the town that had grown up around the crossing.

I see you, he thought, which was what his people said. *I am seen by you. I offer what I have.*

The stone's warmth changed. It did not intensify — it deepened, which was different, the difference between a fire burning higher and a fire burning more completely. Something in the altar recognized what had been offered and received it, and the quality of the recognition was not distant or impersonal but specific, individual, the way a person looks at you when they know who you are.

He held the pressure until the bleeding slowed, then wrapped the hand in the cloth he'd brought for the purpose. He was not, he thought, surprised. He had known this was coming in the way he knew things that lived below the level of reasoning. He had simply needed to be in the right place at the right time with the right quality of understanding.

He continued down.

———

The archive received him differently.

He noticed it immediately — a quality in the ambient light that was neither the cool clarity of working visits nor the warm gold of evenings when the archive was at its most comfortable. It was something older than either, the light of very deep places that have their own sources and do not depend on the weather above. It fell on the shelves and the stacks and the long curving rows of texts with the patient evenness of something that had been burning unchanged for a very long time.

He did not go to the usual table. He stood at the threshold and let the archive orient him, the way he had learned to wait for Poly's guidance rather than impose his own direction.

The tea was there, as it always was. He did not drink it immediately. He set his notebook on the table and stood, thinking about what he had come for.

The mechanism, he thought. *Who shapes the antagonist. How it works.*

Nothing moved. The archive was attentive but still.

He sat, opened the notebook, and began to write — not questions but observations, the way he would approach any text he was trying to understand. The field records from previous visits. The treatise on adversarial function. The compiler's note about origin stories being community narratives rather than accurate accounts. The marginal question, underlined and carried for sennights.

He wrote his way through what he knew and found the edge of it, which was where he always found it: the function was clear, the origin stories were insufficient, and somewhere in the archive was the answer to the question of mechanism, the answer to who shaped the antagonist and how and why.

He looked at the shelves.

Nothing came.

He waited.

Still nothing.

He refilled his tea and returned to the notebook and tried a different approach — working backward from the Enchantress specifically, from what the travelers had described, from what Sam's gift confirmed, from what the archive had shown him about the town's history as waypoint and stage. He wrote a careful analysis of the Enchantress as a figure, her function in the cycle, the specific qualities that distinguished her from the origin-story versions of adversarial figures —

He looked up. The shelves were exactly as they had been. Nothing had been presented, nothing had moved, nothing had appeared at his elbow.

The archive was not responding.

He sat with this for a while. In all the previous visits, the archive had led — Poly guiding, texts appearing, the shelves rearranging in the direction of what he needed. He had never had to force it. He had never had to demand. The process had been collaborative, mutual, the archive offering and him receiving and the gap between those actions closing as his relationship with the space deepened.

Now the archive was waiting.

Not withholding — there was no hostility in the stillness, no sense of a door closed against him. It was simply waiting, the way a very good teacher waits when a student has been given everything they need to take the next step and has not yet taken it.

He thought about what he'd been writing and understood what was wrong.

He had been writing about the Enchantress. He had been approaching the question as a scholar approaches a subject — from the outside, with the tools of analysis, maintaining the distance between the examiner and the examined. He had been treating the archive like a text to be decoded rather than a conversation to be had.

He set down the pen.

All right, he thought. *What's the actual question?*

Not the Enchantress. Not the mechanism. He had been asking the wrong question all along, or rather he had been asking the right question in the wrong register. *Who shapes the antagonist* was a question about the world. But the archive was not responding to questions about the world. It was responding to questions about him.

He had known this, in some sense, since the first visit. The archive was not a library. It collected observations made by people like him — people whose function was to stand outside the story and hold the record. Every text he had found, every observation from every anonymous field recorder, had been written by someone like him. The archive had been built for people like him. It was speaking his language, and he had been answering in a different one.

He looked at the blood-wrapped hand in his lap.

What am I, he thought, *in relation to this?*

He picked up the pen and began to write again, but differently this time. Not about the Enchantress. About himself.

I am an archivist. I was born to it and I have chosen it and those two things have become indistinguishable in me. I stand outside the story. I watch and record and hold the memory of what happened so that it will not be lost. I do not steer. To steer is to enter the story and to enter the story is to compromise the record.

He looked at what he'd written.

The archive did not respond.

He knew why. He had just written something that was partly true and partly comfortable — the version of his position that he had been examining for moons, the one that Sam had questioned and Barnaba had challenged and the bar exchange with Brasham had complicated. He had written it as though it were settled, as though the past moons of questioning had resolved rather than clarified.

He crossed out the last two sentences.

I stand outside the story. I watch and record and hold the memory.

He paused. Then he wrote:

Or I have told myself this. And the telling has been useful and mostly accurate and sometimes a way of avoiding the accountability that comes with choosing rather than simply being.

He stopped. The archive was still.

He was getting closer to something and moving away from it simultaneously, which was the particular frustration of a thought that required honesty to complete and kept encountering the edges of his willingness to be honest.

He stood, walked to the nearest shelf, looked at the spines without seeing them. He walked back. He stood at the table and looked at the notebook and the crossed-out sentences and the bandaged hand.

What is the price, he thought, *of choosing this?*

Because that was the question. Not whether he was an archivist, not whether the role was valid, not whether Barnaba's freedom to rewrite herself was something he envied or Sam's directness was something he admired or the Holdkin women's presence outside Prudence's shop was something he should have acted on. Those were all approaches to the question. The question itself was about accountability.

He had given Brasham the map. He had given him the warning. He had done it as the shop's instrument and he had done it as himself and the distinction between those two things was real but it was not the point. The point was that he had made a choice and the choice had consequences and the consequences were Brasham's to navigate and he, Vamir, would never know how they resolved. He had acted and then he had returned to the position of witness and the record he was keeping of the hunters' visit had a gap in it — his own action — that he could describe but could not fully account for from outside.

That was the price.

The witness who chose to witness was accountable for what their witnessing failed to prevent. Not responsible for it — that was a different thing — but accountable. He held the record. The record included the things he had seen and noted and filed and not acted on.

Prudence managing in her dark dresses while the Holdkin women sat on the bench outside. Yoren walking into the mountains with his dangerous errand and his raw hands. Barnaba's Change progressing in the night while he watched from careful peripheral distance.

He had chosen to hold those. Not been compelled to. Chosen.

And the cost of that choosing was that he carried them. Not with guilt — guilt was not the right register, not the thing he was reaching for. With weight. The specific weight of a person who had been present at something and had understood it and had made a decision about their relationship to it. The weight was not punishment. It was just the honest mass of the choice.

He sat down, picked up the pen, and wrote:

I am a witness because I choose to be. The choice is real and it has a cost and I accept the cost. The cost is that I carry what I witness without the relief of having acted. The record I keep is not neutral. It is the record a person makes who has chosen a particular relationship to the world and lives inside that choice every day.

I am not outside the story. I am the part of the story that holds the story.

That is what I am.

He set down the pen.

The archive moved.

Not dramatically — not the shelves rearranging or the light blazing up or any of the gestures a library might make in a story about magical libraries. What happened was subtler and more specific: a section of the archive's back wall, which he had understood for moons to be shelving extending into the deeper dark, resolved itself differently. Not a new thing appearing, but a thing he had been looking at for moons showing itself to be what it was — a door, set so perfectly into the surrounding shelves that its edges were invisible unless you knew they were there.

The ambient light, which had been holding its old quality, shifted toward the deeper warmth he associated with the archive when it was at its most present and attended. The tea on the table — he had not touched it since the early part of the evening — was, when he picked it up, warm.

He looked at Poly, who had been still on the table's edge for the past mark and was now standing, alert, third eye fully open and blazing a clear, steady blue.

Vamir stood, picked up the lantern, and walked toward the door.

The room beyond was small.

This surprised him, somehow. The archive's main space had spent moons impressing him with its impossible scale, and he had absorbed that scale until it was simply how he experienced the place — vast, layered, extending beyond any reliable geometry. The room behind the door was the size of a study, low-ceilinged, with the quality of a space that had been finished with care rather than expanded by magic. The walls were dressed stone. The floor was swept. There was a table, a chair, a lamp that was already lit.

On the table: a single book.

Not the largest in the archive. Not the most imposing. A medium volume, bound in what appeared to be undyed leather, its cover bearing only the two sigils he had been looking at for moons — Nimarith's peaks and the Lady of Script's eye above the quill, paired on the same surface, the same size, equal in the arrangement.

He sat down. He placed his hands flat on the table, on either side of the book, the bandaged hand and the whole hand both. He did not open it immediately. He sat with it, with the fact of it, with the specific quality of having worked his way to this room through several wrong turnings and the one right one.

Then he opened it.

———

The book was written in a language that was not quite any language he knew, but that he could read nonetheless — or rather, that read itself to him, in the way things sometimes worked in the archive, meaning arriving without the intermediate step of decoding. He had learned not to question this.

It was a dialogue. Two voices, clearly distinguished by the texture of their thought if not by any marking in the text — one vast and specific, the way stone is specific, concerned with permanence and the long view of things that did not change on human timescales. The other fluid and recursive, interested in everything including itself, the voice of something that had spent a very long time thinking about thinking and had arrived at considerable precision about what it knew and what it didn't.

He understood, reading the first exchange, that he was hearing Nimarith and the Lady of Script.

Not a record of their words. Something closer to a transcript — the actual shape of a conversation, preserved with the fidelity that only an archive could provide. He felt the weight of this and accepted it without dramatizing it, the way he accepted the warm tea and the books that appeared at his elbow. The archive had been built for this. He had been brought to this room for this. The conversation had been waiting here for the person who arrived at it the right way.

He read.

The dialogue was not about the Enchantress specifically. It was older than any specific Enchantress — older, he understood, than several cycles of the figure, old enough that the current iteration would not have been known to either speaker at the time of the conversation. It was about the principle of the thing.

Nimarith's position was this: that the valley's gifts — the icosagon, the waypoint, the shops' particular capacities — were not intended to make things easy for the travelers who came through. They were intended to make things possible. The difference was specific and important. Easy would corrupt the gift. Possible preserved its meaning. The traveler who received what they needed and no more, who was sustained rather than transported, who left the waypoint with the resources to continue but not with the journey already done — that traveler arrived at their destination as themselves, changed by the road rather than bypassed by it.

But the road, Nimarith said, required testing.

Not the arbitrary testing of an indifferent universe — the storm, the cold, the random obstacle. The specific testing of a gatekeeper who understood what was being sought and what the seeker would need to have become in order to receive it well. The testing of something that had been placed there, that was in some sense a function rather than a person, though persons were how the function expressed itself in the world.

The Lady of Script's response was careful. She asked about the persons. She asked about the cost to them — the woman or man who became the function, who lived as the adversarial figure at the threshold of significant things, who was in some ways inside the story and in some ways outside it, who served a purpose that the world needed and that the world would never fully understand.

Nimarith's answer was long and Vamir read it slowly.

The function chose the person, not the other way around. But the choosing was not coercive — it was recognitive. The function found the person in whom it could best express itself, the person whose particular nature and history and quality of presence made them the right vessel at the right time. And the person — always — had the choice to accept or refuse.

Those who accepted knew, in some part of themselves, what they were accepting. They felt the rightness of it, the way Vamir had felt the rightness of the archive on his first descent, the way Bartram had felt the rightness of the bench and the shop and the blue sign. Not a compulsion. A recognition.

And they were, Nimarith said — and here Vamir stopped and read the sentence twice — *not alone in it.* The function was expressed through a person but it was held by something larger, managed, attended to, the way a waypoint was attended to. The Enchantress — any iteration of the figure, in any generation — served the function with the support of the divine management that had placed her there. She was not abandoned to the role. She was accompanied in it.

Vamir set the book down for a moment.

He thought about the questers' stories — the too-neat origin narratives, the Evil Wizardess denied her inheritance, the Old Hag whose grief had curdled. The compiler's note: *these are what people say when they do not know what to say.* The actual person inside the function was not the story the world told about them. She was someone who had recognized a rightness and accepted it and was accompanied in it by something that understood what she was carrying.

He thought about the warning he had given Brasham. *She is not what your commission describes her as.* He had not known, when he said it, the full weight of what he was saying. He had known the archive's observations about adversarial function. He had not known this — that the function was not imposed but accepted, not punitive but managed, not isolated but held.

He thought about Leota, and Leonard the Weaver, and the marginal note: *but who shapes the antagonist?* The answer was the gods. The answer was Nimarith, who had placed the valley and its gifts and its creed, and who had also placed the figure at the threshold — the necessary testing, the filter and the forge and the balance — because the gifts of the waypoint could not function without something to ensure they were received by those capable of using them.

The town's passive gifts and the Enchantress's active testing were not separate systems. They were the same system. North Pointe and the keep in the Mistrals were two expressions of the same divine management.

He was sitting in the archive of the first. She lived in the keep of the second.

He opened the notebook and wrote, carefully:

The gods shape the antagonist. Nimarith places the function and the function finds its person. The person chooses. The person is not alone. The origin stories are wrong — not because there is no person but because they reduce the person to the story the world needs to tell about them. The actual truth is that the Enchantress, whoever she is, accepted a recognition and is held by something larger than the role. She is not a villain. She is not a victim. She is a keeper. Like me.

He stopped. Read the last sentence.

Like me.

He had not expected to write that. He looked at it for a while, in the quiet of the small room with the lamp burning its steady light.

He was not the same kind of keeper. His function was to hold the record. Hers was to test the seekers. Both served the waypoint's larger purpose — the sustainable passage of significant journeys through a specific place in the world. Both were chosen rather than compelled. Both carried a weight that the people around them did not fully understand.

Both, he thought, were accompanied. Whatever the Lady of Script's mark on the altar meant — whatever it meant that he had pressed his bleeding hand to it tonight, that the archive had existed for people like him for longer than the town had stood — he was not the first keeper and would not be the last, and the function he served had been placed and managed with the same care as the function across the mountain.

He was not outside the story. He had written it himself, upstairs, and here it was again: *I am the part of the story that holds the story.*

He was not separate from the divine management. He was an expression of it. The Lady of Script and Nimarith had built this place together — had carved their marks side by side into the altar at the threshold — because the archive required both, because the record required both the permanence of the mountain and the fluidity of the word, because a keeper needed to be both held and free.

He sat in the small room for a long time, with the lamp and the book and the bandaged hand and the quality of understanding that was not resolution but was something better: clarity. The clear-eyed apprehension of what the thing actually was, without the distortion of comfort or fear.

He was a witness who chose to witness, and the choice had a cost, and the cost was the weight of what he held, and the weight was also the meaning, and the meaning was also the gift.

He had known this. He had written his way to it, upstairs, under pressure from Sam's questions and Barnaba's philosophy and the discomfort of the Holdkin women and the vertigo of the bar exchange. But he had known it the way you know a thing before you can say it — imprecisely, incompletely, with the frustrating sense that the true version of the understanding was just out of reach.

He knew it now with the archive's specificity. The kind of knowing that had a texture and a weight and would not soften with time or convenience.

He closed the book. He left it on the table, which felt right — this was not a book to be carried upstairs. This was a book to be returned to.

He stood, picked up the lantern, and looked at the room for a long moment: the table, the chair, the lamp still burning, the two sigils on the cover of the book.

"Thank you," he said, to both of them. To the mountain god and the librarian. To the valley and the record. To the long line of unnamed keepers who had left offerings at the altar and folded paper and herbs bound in blue thread, who had done this work in the dark for as long as the dark had held the archive.

He went back through the door.

———

The main archive received him with its oldest light, the light he now recognized as what the space looked like when it was fully itself — neither the working clarity of research visits nor the warm gold of comfortable evenings, but the deep, sourceless illumination of a place that had been doing its work since before the town above it had existed.

He walked slowly back toward the stairs, through the long curved rows, the stacks rising on either side. The rustling in the deep reaches — brief, deliberate, the archive's housekeeping — had stilled. The space had the quality of something that has completed a necessary thing and is now at rest.

He paused at the table near the stairs where the tea always was. The cup was there. He drank it, standing, looking at the shelves. He thought about everything the archive had given him, across all the visits: the waypoint records, the founding documents, the Everkin texts, the Leonard/Leota chronicle, the field observations, the adversarial function treatise, the compiler's honest admission of not knowing, the sealed room.

The archive had not lectured. It had provided. And it had made him work for the most important thing — had waited until he arrived at the right question in the right register before it showed him the door.

He appreciated this about it. He had said so before, and it was still true, and it was more specifically true now: the archive had been built for people who did not need to be handed understanding but needed to be given the materials to arrive at it. His predecessors had been the same. The anonymous field observers. The Keeper of the High Pass Record. The earlier hand that had written in the margin of the chronicle. All of them had been brought to what they needed to find by working for it, and the archive had held their work and held the work of everyone who came after, and would hold his.

He was in that record now. He had been since the first descent, probably. The archive added to itself.

At the altar he stopped. The blood he had left was dry on the stone — a thin dark mark between the two sigils, the most personal thing he had ever left anywhere. He looked at it for a moment, then placed his whole hand — the bandaged one — against the stone. Not pressing this time. Just resting.

The warmth was there. Deeper than before. Not different in nature but in degree, the difference between an acquaintance's acknowledgment and a friend's. Something had changed in the exchange, something in the relationship between him and the altar and whatever the altar represented. Not a transaction completed — an ongoing thing deepened.

He climbed the stairs.

The shop received him in its ordinary dark. The stained glass held the absolute black of deep night — it was later than he had realized, the archive's time being what it was, and the square outside was silent and lamp-lit and still.

He replaced the blue volume on its shelf. He stood for a moment, his bandaged hand held loosely at his side, the notebook under his arm. He felt the particular quality of exhaustion that came after the archive's deepest work — not fatigue exactly, but the tiredness of a person who has been larger than usual for several marks and is now returning to their ordinary size.

He was not outside the story.

He was the part of the story that held the story.

He went upstairs, lay down, and slept without difficulty, and the dream he had — if he had one — was of the small room, the lamp, the two sigils on the book, and the steady warmth of the stone under his hand.

seventeen

. . .

HE DID NOT SLEEP after returning from the archive.

Not from agitation — the quality of the wakefulness was not anxious but inhabited, the way a room feels when something has just happened in it and the air hasn't settled yet. He lay in the dark with the bandaged hand resting on his chest and the understanding from the sealed room moving through him in the slow way that genuine understanding moved, finding the places it needed to reach and reaching them.

At some point the sky shifted from black to the particular dark blue that preceded dawn, and he rose, dressed, and went down to the shop.

He made tea. He stood at the window.

The square was empty and lamp-lit and very still. The hunters' wagon was at the stable, its outline just visible at the edge of the light. They would leave soon — he had the sense of it the way he had the sense of many things now, not premonition exactly but the accumulated reading of patterns, the archivist's ability to see a shape before it had fully declared itself.

He stood at the window and drank his tea and did not go to the archive.

He had been given what he needed. The work now was integration

— the slow settling of the sealed room's understanding into the ordinary texture of his days, the way significant things always had to be absorbed rather than simply known. He had written *she is a keeper, like me* and the sentence had surprised him and still surprised him when he returned to it, and he was not yet finished being surprised by it.

He was still at the window when the stable doors opened and the hunters came out.

They were efficient about it, which he had expected. No ceremony, no delay. The pre-dawn ritual of people who had been leaving places for a long time and had reduced the process to its necessary elements. Gear loaded, horses ready, the formation assembling itself with the unconscious precision he had noticed the day they arrived.

Brasham came last.

He stood for a moment at the edge of the stable yard, looking at the square. Not at anything specific — just looking, the way people looked at places they were leaving, the quick inventory of a space that was about to become a memory. His gaze moved across the shop fronts, the old stone, the lamplight on the fountain.

It moved across the bookshop window.

Vamir stood still, his cup in both hands, watching.

For a moment Brasham's gaze rested on the window. Whether he could see Vamir in the pre-dawn dark, behind the stained glass, was uncertain. Whether he was looking for him or simply looking was uncertain.

Then he turned, mounted, and the four of them moved out of the square and onto the eastern road.

Vamir watched until they were gone. Then he watched the empty road for a while, the way you watch a door after someone has gone through it. Then he put down his cup, put on his coat, and went to find Jen.

She was at her desk, which was where Jen was anytime circumstances that did not specifically require her to be elsewhere. She looked up when he came in, read something in his face, and said: "The hunters left."

"Just now." He sat in the chair across from her desk, which he rarely did — their conversations usually happened standing, at doorways, in passing. Sitting meant something different. She registered this.

"Tell me," she said.

He had been thinking, on the walk across the square, about how to do this. He had arrived at an approach that was honest without being complete — the sage's method, the archivist's method, the method of someone who understands more than they can say and is responsible about the gap between the two.

"The Enchantress," he said, "is not what the hunters think she is."

Jen waited.

"She is not a threat. Not in the sense they mean. She is — a function. Something that was placed where she is because the valley requires it. Because the quests that come through here, the significant ones, need something that the town can't provide. The town sustains. It resupplies. It gives people what they need to continue." He looked at his hands. "But it doesn't test. It doesn't determine whether what's being sought is going to a person capable of receiving it well. The Enchantress does that."

Jen was still. Her pen was in her hand but not moving.

"I gave Brasham a map," Vamir said. "And a warning. That's the most I could do."

"You told him she wasn't what he thought."

"Yes."

"And you think he heard you."

"I think he's a man who has been told one story long enough that he's built his sense of himself around it, and I gave him the materials to question the story, and what he does with those materials is his." He looked at her. "That's the limit of my role."

Jen set the pen down with the deliberateness of someone who has decided to give a conversation her full attention. "What do you know, Vamir, and how do you know it?"

He had expected this question. He had expected it in some form from the moment he decided to come here. Jen was a constable. Her professional instinct was to establish the source of information before acting on it, because the source determined the reliability and the reliability determined the appropriate response.

"I know it from research," he said. "From records. From a long time of reading histories that most people don't have access to and connecting things that don't present themselves as connected." He paused. "I'm a Forest Elf, Jen. I've been alive for a considerable time. Some of what I know comes from having been awake for enough cycles of the world to recognize a pattern when I see one."

This was true. It was not the whole truth. He felt the gap between them as a specific weight — not guilt, because he was not deceiving her, but the particular accountability he had written about in the sealed room. He was choosing to hold this, and the choice had a cost.

Jen looked at him for a long moment with the assessment she brought to everything. "You're not going to tell me everything."

"Not yet," he said. "Not because I don't trust you. Because some of what I know isn't mine to share in a way that would be useful right now, and because — the story needs to play out. The hunters need to be allowed to do what they're going to do. The Enchantress needs to be allowed to do what she does. My knowing the shape of it doesn't mean I should alter the shape of it." He met her eyes. "I'm asking you to trust that, and I know that's an unusual thing to ask of a constable."

Jen was quiet. Outside, the square was beginning to come to life in its morning stages — the first deliveries, the distant clatter of the bakery.

"You've met Nimarith," he said. "Or his avatar. You know what it means when a god is managing something in this valley."

Something shifted in her expression. Not softening — Jen didn't soften — but a recognition, the specific quality of someone who has been given a piece of information that connects to other pieces they were already holding.

"You're saying this is that," she said.

"I'm saying the Enchantress is to the valley's larger purpose what the shops are to the town's smaller purpose. She's part of the same system. Placed, managed, tended to." He paused. "Which means the hunters are walking toward something that Nimarith has arranged. And North Pointe's role in that — our role — is to have given them what they needed to make the best choice they can when they get there. Nothing more."

Jen picked up the pen, set it down again. "You gave Brasham the map."

"The shop gave him the map," Vamir said, and heard himself saying it, and heard also the conversation in the sealed room — *I am not outside the story* — and held the tension of both things being true.

Jen heard something in it too. "The shop," she repeated, with a precision that indicated she was noting what the distinction was doing rather than accepting it uncritically.

"He needed it," Vamir said. "It was the shop's function to provide it. I was the instrument."

"And the warning?"

He was quiet for a moment. "Also the shop's function. The shop has what the traveler needs. Sometimes what the traveler needs is not a book."

Jen looked at him steadily. "You're going to tell me eventually," she said. Not a question. Not a demand. An observation with a timeline attached.

"Yes," he said. "When I understand it well enough to tell it accurately, I'll tell it." He looked at her. "That's the most honest thing I can offer you."

Jen was quiet for a long moment. Then she nodded — not the nod of someone who is satisfied, but the nod of someone who has assessed a situation and determined that the course of action available to them is to wait. It was, he thought, the most Jen thing she could have done, and he felt a specific gratitude for it.

"North Pointe," she said, after a moment, "has always been adjacent to the story. Not in it."

"Yes."

"We supply. We sustain. We send people on their way with what they need." She looked at the window, at the square outside. "We've given people everything they needed to fail, when failure was what the road required. We don't stop them. We give them the tools and we let the road do what the road does."

"Yes," Vamir said.

"So this isn't different," she said. "Except that you're telling me there's a god managing the other end of it."

"There's always been a god managing the other end of it," Vamir said. "We just don't usually have cause to think about it."

Jen made the sound she made when she had arrived at a conclusion she didn't like but accepted. "I don't like it," she said. "I want you to know that. I don't like sending four people into the mountains with nothing but a map and a bookseller's warning between them and whatever's up there."

"I know," Vamir said.

"But I understand it," she said. "And I'll hold it." She looked at him directly. "I want you to tell Sam."

———

He found Sam opening the Claw, which she did every morning with the particular ritual efficiency of someone who considered the opening of her pub a civic act as much as a commercial one. The chairs down from the tables. The fire set and lit. The taps checked. The bar wiped.

She looked up when he came in and said, without preamble: "They left at dawn."

"Yes."

"Sit down," she said. "I'll make tea."

This was how Sam offered care — practically, without announcement, the gesture folded into the action so seamlessly that declining it would have required more effort than accepting. He sat at the bar and she put the kettle on and continued the opening routine with the unhurried competence of someone who could do this in their sleep and sometimes had.

He told her what he had told Jen, in approximately the same form, watching her face as he did. Sam listened differently than Jen — less analytical, more visceral, her responses registering in her expression and her hands rather than in questions. When he reached the part about Nimarith's management, about the Enchantress as function rather than threat, he saw something in her face that was neither surprise nor easy acceptance but something between them — the recognition of a person who has been told something that coheres with what they already knew at a level below articulation.

"Your gift," he said. "When you feel a quest. It tells you it's real."

"Yes."

"This one was clearer than usual. You said it had the quality of something that had been building for a long time."

"It did." She poured the tea, set the cup in front of him. "It felt like — something that had been moving toward a conclusion for longer than any of us had been watching it. Something that had been arranged." She looked at him. "I didn't know what to do with that at the time."

"You do now?"

Sam considered. "I know what it means when I feel that quality in a quest. It means the story is real and the stakes are real and whatever happens at the end of it has been meant to happen." She set down her own cup. "I've tried to stop a quest like that before. Not recently. When I was younger and more confident that I understood what was good for people." A pause. "It didn't go well. Not because I failed, but because succeeding was the wrong thing. The story needed to complete and I delayed it and the delay had costs."

Vamir looked at her.

"So I know," she said. "What you're asking me to hold. I've held it before." She picked up the cloth and turned it in her hands. "That doesn't mean I like it."

"I know."

"Those are four real people walking into the mountains with a commission from someone who either doesn't know or doesn't care what the Enchantress actually is." Her voice was flat with the specific flatness she used for things that cost her something to say evenly. "And we gave them a meal and a map and let them go."

"We gave them more than that," Vamir said. "I gave Brasham —"

"I know what you gave him." She looked at him. "I watched. I made space for it." She set the cloth down. "It was the right thing. I'm not saying it wasn't." She looked at the window, at the morning square. "I'm saying it doesn't make the rest of it comfortable."

"No," he agreed. "It doesn't."

They sat in silence for a moment — not the settled silence of people who have finished talking but the specific silence of people who have arrived together at the edge of what can be done about a thing and are standing there, looking at it.

"He took the map," Sam said.

"Yes."

"And the warning."

"Yes."

"Then we did what we could do." She picked up her cup. "That's what the town does. We do what we can do and we let the road do the rest." She paused. "It doesn't always feel like enough."

"No," Vamir said. "It rarely does."

Sam drank her tea and looked at the square where the hunters had been and were no longer. Her face had the quality it had when she was holding something — not suppressing it, but holding it, the way a strong person holds a heavy thing: fully, without complaint, with the understanding that putting it down was not an option but that the holding could be done with dignity.

"You need to tell me," she said, "when you can. Whatever you know that you're not saying."

"I will," he said.

"And Vamir." She looked at him directly. "The warning you gave him — the map — don't tell me that was the shop and not you. I was here. I made space for you to do it. I know what it looked like."

He held her gaze. "It was both," he said. "I think those two things may be less separate than I've been treating them."

Sam nodded once, slowly, with the expression of someone who has heard an honest answer and is giving it the weight it deserves. "Good," she said. "That's good."

She refilled his cup. He stayed until the morning was properly established and the first customers appeared at the door, and then he crossed the square to the bookshop, turned the sign to OPEN, and let the day's work find him.

———

Leota was waiting on the bench outside her house when he came out at midday. He had not arranged this. He had not needed to. Leota positioned herself where she needed to be.

He sat beside her. The square was in its noon configuration — full light, full activity, the town going about its ordinary business with the thoroughness of a place that had decided to be ordinary on purpose.

"They're gone," she said.

"Since before dawn."

"I know. I heard them leave." She was working on the embroidery, which had progressed since the last time he'd seen it — the small angry owl was nearly complete, its expression now of a piece with Leota's general assessment of the world. "Jen told me you'd spoken to her."

"And Sam."

"And now me." She set a stitch. "You gave the tall one a warning."

"I gave him a map and a context for what he was walking toward."

"Yes." Another stitch. "And you're going to tell me that it was the shop's function."

"I'm going to tell you it was both the shop's function and mine, and that I'm less certain than I used to be about the distance between those two things."

Leota's needle paused. It was brief — a half-second — and then it resumed. "That's more honest than I expected."

"I've been doing a great deal of thinking," he said. "About the nature of the role. What it requires. What it costs."

"And?"

"And I think I've been treating the witness position as more external than it actually is. You can choose to observe. You can hold the record. But you're still in the world that you're observing, and the observing is itself an act with consequences." He looked at the square, at the ordinary business of the town. "I think I knew this. I think I've been working my way toward saying it clearly."

Leota set the embroidery in her lap and looked at him with the full attention she reserved for things that warranted it. He met it.

"You know something about the Enchantress," she said. "More than you're saying."

"Yes."

"And you're not going to tell me what it is."

"Not yet. Not in the form I currently hold it."

"Because?"

"Because the story needs to play out, and I don't know yet what telling it would do to the shape of the playing." He paused. "And because some of what I know involves understanding that I'm still — absorbing. Telling it before I've finished absorbing it would be telling it wrong, and telling it wrong would be worse than not telling it."

Leota was quiet for a moment. When she spoke, her voice had the specific flatness of someone delivering a precise observation rather than an opinion: "You've met Nimarith. Or something that speaks for him. In the recent past."

It was not a question.

He looked at her. "Not directly," he said. "But — yes. Something in that register."

She nodded, and returned to the embroidery. He understood, from the quality of the nod, that this was the piece she had needed — not the details, not the full account, but the confirmation that what he was holding had a divine weight to it, that his caution was not the archivist's habitual discretion but something more specific. She had her own experience of Nimarith. She knew what it meant to be given knowledge that couldn't be freely shared.

"You could warn her," Leota said. The needle moved. "The Enchantress."

There it was.

He had known it was coming — had known since the sealed room that this question existed and that Leota was the person most likely to ask it. He had sat with it for two days and had not resolved it and was not going to resolve it now.

"I don't know how to reach her," he said.

"That's not an answer."

"No," he agreed. "It isn't." He was quiet for a moment. "She is — held. What she is, she chose, and what she chose is supported by something larger than either of us. She is not alone in it." He felt the weight of the words as he said them — not performance, but the genuine texture of what he had read in the sealed room. "The hunters are coming, and she knows her function, and she has resources I don't have access to and don't fully understand. I don't know that warning her would change anything except my own comfort."

"Your own comfort," Leota repeated.

"Yes. The warning would be for me. So that I had acted. So that the record showed I had done something." He looked at his hands. "And that's not the right reason to act."

Leota was quiet for a long time. The embroidery moved. The square continued its noon business. From somewhere across the green came the sound of Makota's kits in some dispute that would resolve itself without intervention.

"That is," Leota said finally, "either the most honest thing you've ever said to me or a very elegant way of not doing something uncomfortable."

"It might be both," he said.

"Yes," she said. "It might." She examined the owl's expression with the critical eye of a craftsperson checking their work. "I don't like it either, for what it's worth."

"I know."

"But I've lived long enough to know when something is in the hands of the gods and when it isn't, and when it is, the correct response is to be useful in the ways you can be and still about the ways you can't." She set the final stitch and held the hoop at arm's length. "Even when the stillness is indistinguishable from cowardice from the outside."

"Even then," Vamir said.

"You're sure," she said. Not a question. Not quite.

"I'm sure that what I know points in this direction," he said. "I'm not sure the direction is comfortable. I'm not sure it will resolve the way I'd choose if I were writing it." He looked at the mountains, visible above the roofline, the Mistral range pale and specific in the noon light. "But I don't think I'm writing it."

Leota lowered the embroidery hoop and looked at the mountains too.

"No," she said. "None of us are."

They sat for a while in the specific quality of silence that follows a conclusion that isn't a resolution — the silence of people who have looked at a hard thing together and have not looked away from it and have not fixed it and have decided to continue anyway. The noon light moved across the square. The ordinary business of the town continued around them, indifferent and sustaining.

After a while, Leota said: "The owl is finished."

"It's excellent," Vamir said. "It looks exactly like you."

Leota made a sound that was not quite a laugh but was in the same family. She tucked the hoop under her arm and stood, in the way of someone whose bench time was complete.

"Come to supper," she said. "Tonight. Nothing elaborate. I want to feed you something."

"Yes," he said.

"And Vamir." She paused, not looking at him. "Whatever you're carrying from that archive of yours — and yes, I know there's an archive, I've known for some time, the building has a particular quality when you've been in it — whatever it is, it's making you more yourself rather than less. I want you to know that I've noticed."

He was quiet for a moment.

"Thank you," he said.

She went inside. He sat for a while longer on the bench, looking at the mountains, carrying what he carried, in the specific weight that was also the meaning that was also the gift.

eighteen

. . .

THE MORNING WAS unremarkable in every way that mornings could be unremarkable, which Vamir would later think of as appropriate. The light through the stained glass was doing its usual thing with the blues and golds. Poly was on its perch with the alert satisfaction of a creature that had already accomplished something and was prepared to be modest about it. The kettle had just come to the boil.

He was in the middle of the entirely ordinary act of pouring water over the mesh pouch when the shop door opened — the firm twist, the gentle shove, the three-note chime — and Elspeth Riverpine came in from the morning.

He had not seen her in… it felt like a moon or more. He had thought about her occasionally, in the way you think about people who leave a specific impression — the quality of her attention, the bawdy song, the way she had said *that's all any of us can hope to do* with the particular warmth of someone who meant it entirely. The nagging-pleasantly feeling he had carried home across the dark square, the half-remembered song waiting to resolve.

She looked exactly as she had: silver hair pinned with wooden sticks, the broad kind face, the dimple that appeared when she smiled. The heavy wool shawl. The hands that had lived a long life in them.

She smiled when she saw him, and the dimple appeared, and she said: "There you are. I was hoping you'd be in."

"I'm always in," Vamir said. "Tea?"

"Please," she said, and settled onto the stool at the end of the counter with the ease of someone returning to a familiar place rather than entering a new one, and Vamir poured a second cup and slid it across and thought: *she moves like someone who knows this building.*

He noted this and said nothing.

"I wasn't sure you'd remember me," Elspeth said, wrapping both hands around the cup.

"You sang the miller's daughter song in the Broken Claw and brought the whole pub along on the chorus," Vamir said. "I remember everyone who does that."

She laughed — the round pleasant sound he remembered. "Fair enough."

They drank tea for a moment in the companionable way of people who had been comfortable with each other before and found that the comfort had survived the interval. Poly descended from its perch and walked along the counter with the deliberate steps it used when it was paying close attention to something, and came to rest at the end nearest Elspeth, and regarded her with all three eyes open.

Elspeth regarded it back, with an expression that was not surprise but was something adjacent to recognition. "Hello," she said, to Poly. "I wondered if you'd remember me too."

Poly made a sound Vamir could not immediately categorize.

"He doesn't forget many people either," Vamir said.

"No," said Elspeth. "I imagine he doesn't." She looked at Poly for another moment, and something in the quality of the look — specific, settled, the look of someone who understood what they were looking at — registered in Vamir's peripheral attention without fully declaring itself.

He waited.

Elspeth set down her cup, folded her hands on the counter, and looked at him with the expression of someone who has decided to say a thing and is simply choosing the moment.

"I have a confession to make," she said.

"All right," Vamir said.

"I wasn't entirely honest with you, the first time I was here."

"You told us you were a widow seeing the world," Vamir said. "Was that not true?"

"Oh, it was perfectly true," Elspeth said. "I am a widow and I do enjoy seeing the world. Those parts were accurate." She paused. "I may have omitted some relevant context."

"Such as?"

She picked up her cup again, looked into it, set it down. It was the gesture of someone who has been holding a thing for a while and is now putting it on the table, and Vamir recognized the gesture because he had made it himself, across this counter, more times than he could count.

"I live in the Mistrals," she said. "In the old keep. I've lived there for—" She made a small movement with one hand that indicated a duration she wasn't going to specify precisely. "Some time."

Vamir looked at her.

"I'm the Enchantress," Elspeth said, in the tone of someone clarifying a minor administrative point. "In case that wasn't clear."

The shop was very quiet.

Poly made the sound it made when it had known something for a while and was pleased that everyone was now catching up.

Vamir looked at Elspeth — at her broad kind face, the dimple that had appeared again at his expression, the hands wrapped around the teacup. He looked at the particular quality of settled-ness she carried, the way she had always seemed utterly at home no matter where she was, and understood now what he had been looking at. She was at home because she knew this valley in the way he was beginning to know the archive — not from visiting it but from being in constant relationship with it, from having held it for longer than most of its current inhabitants had been alive.

He thought about the sealed room. About the book with the two sigils on the cover. About the understanding he had written by lamplight in the small space behind the locked door: *she is a keeper, like me.*

The archive had told him what she was.

Elspeth had just told him who.

The two pieces of understanding met in him with the specific quiet click of things that had been moving toward each other for a long time and had finally arrived. Not a collision. A completion.

He became aware that he had been silent for slightly longer than the conversation required.

"You're not surprised," Elspeth said, watching him with the accurate attention she had always applied to people.

"I'm—" He considered the honest answer. "I'm not surprised in the way you might expect," he said. "I've been doing some research. About the Enchantress. About what she is and what she does." He met her eyes. "I had arrived at the understanding that she was—a person, specifically, doing a specific job, for reasons that made sense in the context of the valley's larger purpose. I had not connected that understanding to you."

Elspeth tilted her head. "Research," she said.

"I've been alive a long time," he said. "I've had access to records most people don't. And I had reasons to look."

She studied him with the expression of someone revising an assessment. "I knew about North Pointe, of course. I've known about the town for—well, for as long as I've been where I am. It's the waypoint. Anyone in the valley knows about the waypoint." She paused. "I didn't know about a bookseller who did research into the valley's structural arrangements."

"I didn't know there was an Enchantress who occasionally came to the Broken Claw and led the pub in song," Vamir said.

Elspeth's mouth curved. "In my defense, it had been a long time since I'd had a proper evening out."

"How long?"

"Longer than I'd like to admit," she said. "The work is—" She paused, looking for the right word. "Absorbing. In the way that important things are absorbing. But it can become all-consuming if you're not careful, and I find I need to come down from the mountain occasionally and be among people." She looked around the shop with a warmth he recognized now as something more specific than affection — it was the warmth of one professional recognizing the quality of another's work. "This is a good town," she said. "It always has been. The shops do what they're meant to do. The people are genuine." She looked at him. "You especially. You were kind to me when I was just a wandering old woman, and I noticed that."

"You weren't just a wandering old woman," Vamir said.

"No," she agreed. "But I was being one, for the evening. And you treated me accordingly. That matters more than you might think, when most of your interactions involve people who know—or think they know—what you are before they've met you."

Vamir thought about the questers, with their origin stories and their terrified reverence and their too-neat narratives of who she was and why. He thought about Brasham and the commission and the map he had pressed into the man's hands in the dark of the Broken Claw.

"Four hunters left here three days ago," he said. "Headed for the Mistrals."

Elspeth's expression shifted — not dramatically, but specifically, the way a professional's face shifts when a conversation moves from the social register to the working one. "I know," she said. "I felt them cross the valley boundary this morning."

"They have a commission. Someone sent them to—" He paused, choosing the word. "Remove you."

"Yes," she said, with the equanimity of someone who has been receiving this kind of information for a considerable time. "That happens periodically. Someone decides the Enchantress is a problem to be solved rather than a function to be respected." She picked up her cup. "It generally resolves itself."

"You're not concerned."

"I'm—" She considered. "I'm appropriately cautious. I'm not panicked." She looked at him. "You gave one of them a warning."

It was not a question.

Vamir was quiet for a moment. "You know about that."

"I know the town gave them what it gives everyone — what they needed, rather than what they asked for. And I know there's a book-seller here who understands more about my situation than most people do." She set the cup down. "What did you tell him?"

"That you aren't what his commission described. That the people who have sought you and found the experience difficult have described harm that was actually testing. That he should consider the source of his commission before acting on it." He paused. "And that you are better defended than he knows."

Elspeth was quiet for a moment, looking at him with an expression he couldn't fully read — not quite gratitude, not quite assessment, something that contained both and something else as well.

"Thank you," she said. "For what it's worth."

"It may not be worth much," he said honestly. "I don't know what he'll do with it."

"No," she agreed. "Neither do I." She was quiet for another moment. "But someone telling the truth about me, to someone who was walking toward me with wrong information — that is worth something. Even if the telling doesn't change the outcome." She looked at him steadily. "You understand that, I think. The value of the record being accurate, regardless of what the record produces."

He did understand it. He understood it in the specific way of someone who had spent moons arguing for exactly that value, against his own doubts and other people's practical objections. Hearing it named back to him by the person who had, without knowing it, been the subject of his research for the better part of a year had a quality he would not have been able to fully describe.

"I do," he said.

The door opened.

Sam came in with the unhurried directness of a woman who had seen the light on and decided to investigate, carrying a cloth she was using to dry a glass, which was Sam's equivalent of casual. She looked at Vamir. She looked at Elspeth. She looked at Vamir again.

"Elspeth," she said, in the tone of someone confirming an identification.

"Sam," Elspeth said warmly. "I was hoping I'd see you."

Sam set the glass on the counter, hung the cloth over her shoulder, and pulled up a stool. "Tell me," she said, to both of them, and the precision of the request indicated she already knew that there was something to be told and was simply indicating that she was ready to receive it.

Elspeth told her. She told it with the same matter-of-fact clarity she had used with Vamir, slightly compressed now that the initial telling had already happened, with the air of someone who has been keeping a secret for a long time and finds that telling it a second time, to a second person, carries a different but not lesser relief. Sam listened with the still attention she brought to things that mattered, and her expression moved through several things that were not quite surprise and not quite recognition but were somewhere between them — the expression of a woman whose gift had been telling her something for two years and was now being shown what it had been pointing at.

When Elspeth finished, Sam was quiet for a moment. Then she said: "Your quest-sense. When those hunters came through, it was — different. Clearer."

"Yes," Sam said.

"That's because the thing they were hunting has a specific quality. It's — placed. Intentional." Elspeth looked at the counter. "I've always found it interesting that the pub has that gift. A gift for knowing what travelers need to hear. And the person who carries it is a former mercenary who has been places and done things and knows what it means when someone is walking toward something that could unmake them." She looked at Sam. "Nimarith chooses his instruments carefully."

Sam absorbed this. "You've met him."

"I've met his representative," Elspeth said. "Some years ago. It was —" The pause was brief but specific. "Clarifying."

"Yes," Sam said. "That's the word."

They were quiet for a moment, the three of them, in the particular quality of silence that follows the acknowledgment of shared experience — not identical experience, but experience in the same register, the same divine context.

Vamir thought about what he had written in the sealed room: *she is a keeper, like me.* He thought about the altar, the two sigils, the understanding that Nimarith and the Lady of Script had built this place together. He thought about the waypoint and the keep and the two ends of the same system, sitting at opposite ends of a bookshop counter and drinking tea on an ordinary morning.

He did not say any of this. The understanding was his to hold for now, and Elspeth's disclosure had been hers to make, and the moment had its own completeness without requiring him to add to it.

"The hunters," Sam said.

"Will be dealt with," Elspeth said, and the confidence in it was not arrogance but the specific confidence of someone who has been doing a job for a long time and knows the range of outcomes. "They may turn back. They may arrive and find the experience—educational. They may succeed in whatever their commission requires, in which case—" A pause. "The function will find its next expression, in time. It always does."

"You're not worried," Sam said.

"I'm cautious," Elspeth said. "I'm not panicked." She picked up her tea. "I've been doing this for long enough to know that the ones who arrive with commissions are usually the ones the testing is most important for. They've been told what to think before they've had the encounter. What they find, if they're honest with themselves, rarely matches what they were told."

"And if they're not honest with themselves?" Sam said.

Elspeth's expression was steady and not unkind. "Then the testing tells them something true about themselves that they would not otherwise have known," she said. "And they carry it home, and what they do with it is their own business."

Sam nodded, slowly, with the nod she used when she had heard something that cohered with things she already understood but had not previously been able to articulate.

"I want to ask you something," Vamir said.

Elspeth looked at him.

"The evening you were here. The singing. You stayed the whole night and you were — genuinely here. Not performing it. Not gathering information." He paused. "Why did you come?"

She looked at him for a moment, and the expression on her face had the quality of someone being asked a question they had not expected and finding it — not unwelcome, but unexpected in its accuracy.

"I needed a good evening," she said. "I hadn't had one in a while."

She looked at her cup. "The work is important and I believe in it and I chose it and I would choose it again. But it is — isolating, in ways that are sometimes harder than others. The keep is very large and very quiet, and the people who come to it are generally not coming for conversation." She paused. "I came to North Pointe because I knew the town. I knew it would be — " She searched for the word. "Genuine. The people here are what they are. They don't perform the town. They live it."

"And the confession?" Vamir said. "Why now?"

"Because I've been carrying it since the evening I was here, and it's been sitting in my chest the way things sit when they want to be said, and — " She looked at him. "You're the right person to tell. You were the right person when I was just a wandering widow at the bar, and you're still the right person now, for reasons that are becoming somewhat clearer to me as we talk." She held his gaze. "Your shop always has what the traveler needs."

"Yes," he said.

"I think," she said carefully, "that I may have needed this. The telling. More than I knew before I started telling it."

He thought of the questers' faces — the exhaustion and the relief of people who had been carrying something toward a threshold and were now, finally, at it. He thought of Bartram, in the square, with the blue sign and the dream of the bench. He thought of Barnaba, the night she had told him about the Change, with the specific relief of a thing that had been sitting in the chest being set down somewhere else for a while.

The shop, he thought, always had what the traveler needed.

Elspeth finished her tea, set the cup down, and stood with the easy movement of someone who had done what she'd come to do and was at peace with it. "I'll let you get back to your morning," she said. "Both of you." She looked at Poly, who had not moved from the end of the counter. "And you," she said.

Poly made the ceremonial sound.

"Goodbye, Vamir," she said. "Thank you for the tea. And for the warning you gave the tall one, whether or not it does what you hoped."

"Travel safely," he said. "And come back when you need another good evening."

She smiled — the broad smile, the dimple, the warmth of someone who has been genuine in a room and is leaving it having been genuinely received. She went to the door, did the firm twist and the gentle shove, and the chimes sang.

Sam and Vamir sat in the quiet of the shop for a moment, listening to her footsteps on the walkway outside. Then Poly turned from the door, walked back along the counter, and settled between them with the expression it had when all relevant matters had been properly attended to.

"Well," Sam said.

"Yes," Vamir said.

They sat with that for a moment.

"She needed the evening," Sam said.

"Yes."

"And we gave it to her." Sam looked at the door. "The town gave it to her. Without knowing that's what we were doing."

"The town always—" he started.

"I know," Sam said. "I know what the town always does." She picked up her cloth. "I'm just — noting it. That we served the function. Unknowingly. Doing what we do." She stood. "Which is what the town does."

"Yes," Vamir said.

"I'm going to go open the pub," she said. "And I'm going to think about this for a long time." She paused at the door. "The toast," she said. "At the end of the evening. When she said *to villains, to stories.*"

"Yes," Vamir said.

"She was toasting herself," Sam said.

"Yes," Vamir said. "I think she was."

Sam made a sound that was somewhere between a laugh and a acknowledgment, and went out into the morning.

———

He was cataloging the afternoon's new arrivals — three crates, the usual mixed lot — when he heard the door again. Firm twist. Gentle shove. The chimes.

He looked up.

Elspeth stood in the doorway, one hand on the frame, the other at her throat where the wool shawl was wrapped.

"I almost forgot," she said.

"Your scarf?" Vamir said.

"My scarf," she agreed, though she was wearing it, which they both noticed simultaneously, which produced a small pause.

"Ah," said Elspeth.

"Ah," said Vamir.

She came in properly and closed the door, and the shop was quiet, and Poly was on the counter between them, and the morning light was doing its particular thing with the colored glass.

"I wanted to say something," she said. "Without Sam here, though I like Sam very much."

"All right," he said.

She looked at him with the full attention she had always brought to this particular space, this particular person. "You know more than you said this morning."

He did not deny it.

"You've been in places," she said, "that tell a person things about how the valley works. And you've been there recently." She paused. "Not the mountains. Something closer." She looked at the shop, at the shelves, at the ordinary ordinary surface of it. "Something in this building."

He held her gaze. "Yes," he said.

"And you're not going to tell me what."

"Not today," he said. "Not yet. When I understand it well enough to tell it accurately." He paused. "You told me something today that I wasn't sure you would tell me. When I have something equivalent to offer in return, I will."

She looked at him for a long moment. He had the sense, under her attention, of being assessed by someone who had been assessing people at significant moments for a considerable time and was very good at it. Not the testing-function assessment of the threshold-guardian — something more personal than that, the assessment of one person deciding how much to trust another.

"You're a keeper," she said. Not the word he had used, but the right word.

"Yes," he said.

"Of the waypoint's record."

"Yes."

She was quiet for a moment, absorbing this — not with surprise, he thought, but with the specific quality of someone fitting a piece into a picture that had been missing it. Her expression had the completion he had felt in his own chest when she had said *I'm the Enchantress* and the two years of archive research had acquired a face.

"I wondered," she said, "for a long time, whether there was someone like that. The town has all its other keepers — the constable, the tavern-keeper, the baker who feeds everyone. It seemed like the kind of place that would also have someone who — held the larger shape of it. Remembered." She looked at him. "I'm glad it's you."

He did not know what to say to this. He found, examining the feeling, that he did not need to say anything — that the statement had its own completeness and adding to it would only reduce it.

"The tall hunter," she said. "The warning you gave him."

"Brasham."

"Brasham." She turned the name over. "He's a good man in a complicated position." She paused. "I know the type. They come up the mountain carrying instructions that don't match what they find. What they do with that mismatch — " She paused. "That's the test, isn't it. Not the obstacle I put in front of them. The gap between what they were told and what they see."

"Yes," Vamir said. "I think that's right."

"The map was the right thing to give him."

"The shop thought so."

She looked at him, and he heard himself, and they both held the small familiar tension of a person who had just made the distinction between themselves and their function and was not entirely sure the distinction held.

"The shop thought so," she repeated, gently.

"I thought so," he said. "And the shop agreed."

Elspeth smiled — the full smile, the dimple, the warmth. "That's better," she said.

She adjusted the scarf she had allegedly forgotten, which they both understood now to be a pretext so thoroughly established that it had acquired a kind of fondness, and moved toward the door.

"Come back," he said. "When you need another good evening. Or when you don't need one but would like one anyway."

"I will," she said. And the quality of the promise was the quality of something she intended to keep.

The door opened. The chimes sang. She stepped out into the morning and crossed the square in the direction of the eastern road and the mountain pass, an old woman with wooden sticks in her silver hair, utterly at home in the world.

Vamir stood at the counter and watched until she was out of sight.

Then he went back to the cataloging, and the morning continued, and the shop was warm and quiet and full of the specific quality it had when something important had happened in it and the importance was still settling.

Poly sat between the crates and the counter and watched him work, all three eyes half-closed in the expression it had when it was content.

"I know," Vamir said. "You knew the whole time."

Poly made a sound that did not dispute this, and turned its attention back to the shelves, and the morning went on.

nineteen

. . .

THE MORNING after Elspeth's visit had the quality of a morning after a significant thing — not subdued, but attentive, as though the day itself was paying closer attention than usual. The light was good. The square was doing its ordinary business. The bookshop smelled of tea and old paper and the particular mineral ghost that had begun to accompany Vamir after archive visits, faint enough that only he noticed it.

He had slept well. He had not expected to, given the weight of the previous day, but the sleep had been deep and dreamless and he had woken with the specific clarity of someone whose mind had been doing its quiet integration work while his body rested. The pieces were in their places. Elspeth was the Enchantress. The Enchantress was a keeper. The hunters were in the mountains. The archive held the record of all of it, and he held the archive, and the holding was his function and his choice and the cost of the choice was the weight of what he held and the weight was also the meaning.

He made tea. He opened the shop. He waited for the morning to bring him what it had.

What it brought him, a candlemark after opening, was Leota, which was not a surprise. She appeared in the doorway with the specific quality of arrival she had when she had decided to have a conversation rather than been moved to have one — deliberate, unhurried, the black dress and the pale hands and the expression of someone who had been thinking about something and had concluded that thinking about it alone had gone far enough.

"Walk with me," she said.

————

They ended up on the bench outside Makota's, which was where the morning light was best at this time and where the square's activity provided the kind of comfortable ambient noise that made private conversation easier rather than harder. Makota appeared at the window briefly, registered them, and produced two cups of tea and a plate of the small seeded biscuits that appeared only on mornings she judged to require them.

"Thank you," Leota called, without turning.

Makota waved and disappeared.

They sat for a moment with the tea and the morning light. A delivery cart came through the square, its wheels on the old stone producing the particular rhythm Vamir had memorized without intending to. One of Makota's kits emerged from the bakery's side door, conducted a brief transaction with a small customer, and disappeared again. The fountain ran clear.

"Elspeth came to see you yesterday," Leota said.

"Yes."

"And told you."

"Yes."

Leota picked up her cup. "How did it land?"

Vamir thought about the specific quality of the click — the archive's understanding acquiring a face, the two halves of the system meeting over a counter in an ordinary bookshop on an ordinary morning. "Like completion," he said. "Like something that had been moving toward a conclusion for a long time arriving at it."

"Not surprise."

"Surprise at who," he said. "Not at what."

Leota looked at him with the measuring quality she brought to assessments that mattered. "You'd worked out the what."

"Most of it." He drank his tea. "Not all. She told me things I didn't know. I told her things she didn't know." He paused. "It was — a meeting of two people who had been in the same system without knowing the other was there."

Leota was quiet for a moment, turning this over. "She's been in the valley a long time," she said. "I've known about the Enchantress since before I came to North Pointe. Not who she was. What she was." She paused. "Nimarith's management tends to be consistent. The forms change. The function doesn't."

"No," Vamir agreed. "The function doesn't."

The cart had passed and the square had settled back into its mid-morning rhythm. A group of travelers was gathering near the inn — not questers, from the look of them, but merchants, the kind who moved through with the regularity of tides, familiar with the town and comfortable in it.

"The hunters," Leota said.

"In the mountains by now," Vamir said. "Two days out, perhaps three."

"And you feel—"

"What I feel," he said, "is that I gave Brasham the most accurate account I could of what he was walking toward, and that the rest of it is between him and her and the function she serves." He paused. "I feel the weight of that. But I don't feel that I've failed in what was mine to do."

Leota turned her cup in both hands. "No," she said. "I don't think you have." She was quiet for a moment. "I've been thinking about what you said yesterday. On the bench. That the warning would have been for you — so the record showed you had acted."

"Yes."

"It's a truthful thing to say." She set the cup down. "I've noticed that you've been saying more truthful things lately. More precise things. About what the role actually costs." She looked at him. "You've been doing that for a few moons now. Something changed in you."

He thought about the sealed room. About *I am the part of the story that holds the story.* About the blood drying on the altar stone in the dark.

"Yes," he said. "Something changed."

"Good," she said. Not pressing for the what of it. Simply receiving the confirmation and finding it sufficient.

They sat for a while in the good light. The biscuits were eaten. A second cup was produced from somewhere, because Makota ran the bakery the way Sam ran the pub — she saw what was needed before it was requested.

"I want to ask you something," Vamir said.

"All right."

"The equanimity," he said. "The way I hold the witness role. The — steadiness about things that other people find alarming or unbearable." He looked at the square, not at her. "You said yesterday that it's easier for me. That I've never had a mob with torches at my door."

"Yes," she said.

"I want to understand what you mean by that."

Leota was quiet. Not a resistant quiet — a considering one, the quiet of someone deciding not whether to speak but how.

"I mean," she said finally, "that your equanimity about staying outside the story comes from a position that has never been seriously threatened. You chose the witness role. You've held it under philosophical pressure — Sam's questions, Barnaba's arguments. You held it under the practical pressure of the hunters, and Prudence and the Holdkin women, and I think you paid a real cost for some of those." She paused. "But you've never been inside a story that tried to consume you. You've never been the thing the story was about, against your will, with consequences you couldn't step back from." She looked at her hands. "The equanimity looks different when you've been there."

He held this. He held it without interjecting, without offering the thing he knew — the chronicle, the Siege, the phrase *citing exhaustion* doing its enormous work in a single line of text. He held the asymmetry with the care it deserved.

"I know," he said. "That what I have is easier."

"Not worse," she said, quickly and precisely. "Not lesser. Easier."

She looked at him. "The witness role is real and it has value and I am not saying you haven't paid for it. I'm saying that the paying has been of a particular kind, and there are other kinds." She paused. "And that the people who have paid those other kinds of cost sometimes find the equanimity of the witness — difficult to be near. Not because it's wrong. Because it's a reminder of what they couldn't have."

He sat with this for a long moment.

"I don't want you to be different," she said. "I want you to understand what the steadiness looks like from the outside. From certain outsides." She picked up her cup again. "Elspeth, for instance. She's been inside the story in ways that don't allow the witness position. What she does requires being the thing that happens to people, not the person who records it. The cost of that is—" She paused. "Not mine to describe. But it's real."

He thought about Elspeth at the bar, leading the pub in song with the reckless joy of someone who had been alone for a long time and was briefly, completely, not alone. *I needed a good evening.* The keep, large and quiet, the people who came to it not coming for conversation.

"Yes," he said. "I understand that better now than I did a year ago."

Leota looked at him with the expression she had when she was revising an assessment upward. "Good," she said. "That's the right direction."

They were quiet for a while. The morning moved through its stages. The merchants at the inn finished their preparations and moved out, eastward, with the efficiency of people for whom this particular road was entirely familiar. One of them waved at Sam, who was standing in the Claw's doorway with a cloth, and Sam waved back with the ease of long acquaintance.

"The town," Vamir said. "The way it holds people. The way it held Elspeth, that evening, without knowing what it was holding." He paused. "I've been thinking about what the archive —" He stopped, corrected himself. "What I've found in my research, about the town's designed purpose. That it serves the passage. That it sustains rather than transforms. That it gives people what they need to continue without doing the continuing for them."

"Yes," Leota said. "I know what the town is for."

"But it also — held her. Let her be just a person for an evening. Let her sing a bawdy song and accept a room at the inn and not be the Enchantress." He looked at the square. "I don't think that's incidental. I think that's part of the function. The spiritual restoration the waypoint provides — it applies to the people who serve the valley's larger purposes as much as it applies to the travelers passing through."

Leota was still.

"Elspeth needed the evening," he said. "And the town gave it to her. Without knowing that's what it was doing. The town always—"

"Has what the traveler needs," Leota said quietly.

"Yes."

She was quiet for a long moment. When she spoke, her voice had a quality he didn't hear in it often — not softened, because Leota didn't soften, but something in it that was less armored than usual. "The town has given me things I didn't know I needed," she said. "Over the years. Without announcement. Without requiring me to ask." She looked at the square. "I came here for reasons that had nothing to do with kindness and everything to do with — needing a place that would not require me to be what I had been." She paused. "The town gave me that. Still gives me that. Every ordinary morning."

Vamir said nothing. He received this with the full attention it deserved and held it without adding to it, because it was complete.

After a moment Leota picked up a biscuit, examined it, ate it with the deliberateness of someone returning to the ordinary world from a less ordinary one.

"Rost is back," she said. Her voice was back to its usual register, the brief opening closed as cleanly as it had appeared. "His party returned yesterday evening. You'll want to talk to him."

"Yes," Vamir said. "How do they seem?"

"Changed," she said. "The way people are changed when they've been somewhere that required more of them than they expected." She paused. "Rost specifically has the look of a man who has been wrong about something important and is still working out what to do about it."

Vamir thought about Brasham's face in the stable yard, the quick inventory of the square before he turned and mounted. He thought about what the archive's field records had described: the parties that succeeded were the ones that had been broken and rebuilt. *Not destroyed — rebuilt.*

"That's not a bad look to have," he said.

"No," Leota agreed. "It isn't."

————

Rost was at the Broken Claw when Vamir found him. seated at a corner table with a mug and the particular quality of stillness that people had when they had been moving for a long time and had only recently stopped. He was a broad-shouldered man of middle age with a farmer's hands and a traveler's eyes — the combination that appeared when someone had spent most of their life in one place and then, for reasons the place couldn't provide, had left it.

He had come to North Pointe eight moons ago with a quest. He had not said what the quest was for, in the way questers often didn't, and Vamir had given him maps and supplies and the books he needed and had watched him go without asking. He had returned with two of his original four companions and the look Leota had described.

He looked up when Vamir sat down across from him.

"Bookseller," he said.

"How was the road?" Vamir said.

Rost looked at his mug. "Long," he said. "And — not what I expected."

"It rarely is."

"No." He was quiet for a moment. "She's not what the stories say."

Vamir held this carefully. "What did the stories say?"

"That she was dangerous. Malevolent. That she took things from people without — " He stopped. "That she was something to be survived." He looked at Vamir. "She's not that."

"What is she?"

Rost turned the mug in his hands. He had the look of a man searching for words for an experience that had not provided him with its own language. "She asked me questions," he said. "Not — hostile questions. Precise ones. About what I wanted and why I wanted it and what I intended to do with it if I got it." He paused. "I'd been traveling for four moons. I'd thought about those questions on the road. I thought I had answers." Another pause. "I didn't have the right answers."

"What happened?"

"She sent me away," he said. "Not harshly. She said — what I was looking for wasn't wrong to want, but I wasn't ready to have it. That there were things I needed to understand first." He looked at his hands. "She told me what they were."

"And?"

"And she was right," he said, with the flatness of someone who has checked this conclusion multiple times and keeps arriving at the same answer. "I didn't want her to be right. But she was." He looked at Vamir. "I'm going home. To do the things she said. And then—" He paused. "Maybe try again. When I'm ready."

Vamir looked at this man — his farmer's hands, his traveler's eyes, the specific quality of a person who had been broken in a particular direction and was beginning to understand the shape of what he was being rebuilt into.

"That seems right," Vamir said.

"Does it?" Rost looked at him with a directness that had something raw in it. "You ever met her?"

"Once," Vamir said. "Briefly. In a different context."

Rost looked at him for a moment. "She's — kind," he said, as though the word surprised him. "Under the rest of it. Under the testing and the questions and the—" He paused. "She's doing something she believes in. You can feel it." He shook his head. "Not what I expected."

"No," Vamir said. "She rarely is."

He stayed for a while, talking with Rost about the road and the mountains and the practical matters of the return journey — what provisions he needed, whether his companions required anything from the shop, the best route west at this season. The ordinary work of the waypoint. The sustaining rather than transforming. The giving of what was needed to continue.

When Rost left, a mark later, he had maps and supplies and a small bundle of books he hadn't known he needed until Poly had deposited them at his feet with the quiet certainty of something that understood the difference between what was asked for and what was required.

Vamir stood in the doorway of the shop and watched him cross the square.

Changed, Leota had said. The way people are changed when somewhere has required more of them than they expected.

He filed it. He held it. He let the square's ordinary afternoon close around the moment and carry it forward.

———

He was closing the shop for the evening when Sam appeared, leaning in the doorway with the cloth over her shoulder and the look of someone who had something to say and had chosen the moment.

"Rost came to the Claw after he left you," she said.

"How did he seem?"

"Like someone who'd been told a hard truth by someone who meant well," she said. "And is starting to think the truth might be worth the difficulty." She paused. "He asked me about her. The Enchantress."

"What did you tell him?"

"That she had a gift for knowing what travelers needed to hear," Sam said, with the faint quality of someone enjoying the precision of a true thing that was also funny. "He thought about that for a while." She straightened from the doorway. "He left a good tip."

"He's a good man," Vamir said.

"Most of them are," Sam said. "That's what makes it hard, sometimes. When the testing is hardest for the good ones." She paused. "She's kind, he said to me. Under the rest of it."

"Yes," Vamir said. "She is."

Sam looked at him for a moment with the expression she used

when she had assessed something and found it correct. Then she nodded, the nod that meant the observation was complete, and went back across the square to the Broken Claw, where the evening was beginning and the first customers were arriving and the ordinary life of the town was doing what it always did.

Vamir closed the shop, turned the sign, and stood for a moment in the quiet of the building.

The archive was below him, patient, its deep quiet a constant now rather than a surprise. The shop was around him, warm, the stained glass holding the last of the evening light in its hundred uneven panes. Elspeth was somewhere on the eastern road, heading back to the keep in the mountains, carrying the conversation in her chest the way you carried things that needed time to settle. Rost was at the inn, reading whatever Poly had found for him, working through the questions the testing had given him.

He thought about Leota on the bench: *you never had a mob with torches at your door.*

He thought about the sealed room: *she is a keeper, like me.*

He thought about Elspeth at the counter, the scarf she hadn't forgotten, the two of them holding what they held across the ordinary surface of a bookshop morning.

He was the part of the story that held the story.

The holding had weight, and the weight had meaning, and the meaning was also the gift.

He went upstairs to make tea, and the evening settled around the town, and the story moved on.

twenty

. . .

THE DAY BARNABA came back was mid-sennight, which Vamir
was beginning to think was simply the day the trade road delivered its
most significant packages.

He saw them from the window — two figures coming in from the
eastern approach in the mid-morning, moving at the unhurried pace
of people who had nowhere they urgently needed to be. One of them
he recognized immediately, because Elspeth Riverpine walked the way
she always walked, with the absolute ease of someone who had been
at home in the world for a very long time and had stopped needing to
announce it. The other he recognized more slowly, in the way you
recognize someone whose fundamental quality has remained constant
while everything else has undergone a thorough revision.

He stood at the window for a moment, the morning's cup of tea
cooling in his hands, and felt the pieces assemble themselves.

Barnaba. Changed. Walking into the square with Elspeth at her
side, and Elspeth's presence here was information — the Enchantress
and the mapmaker, together, which meant that whatever had
happened in the sennights since the shuttered shop and the brass plate
and the silence, it had happened in the mountains, in or near the keep,
and had resolved itself into this: two people walking into North Pointe

on a Tuesday morning with the quality of people who had somewhere specific to be and knew it.

He set down the tea. He went out to meet them.

————

Barnaba was taller.

Not dramatically — two inches, perhaps three, the kind of height that announces itself in the changed proportion of a person rather than in any single measurement. She moved differently too, which was the first thing Vamir noticed when she was close enough to notice properly: the quick, contained precision of her old movement had opened into something longer and more deliberate, the way a stream opens into a river when the channel widens. She was not slower. She was more settled in the space she occupied, the way a tree is more settled in the ground than a sapling.

Her face had arrived.

He had been watching it arrive for moons — the sharpness softening, the jaw broadening, the cheekbones moving toward a different geometry. Now the process was complete, or near enough that what remained was refinement rather than transformation. The face that looked back at him was not the absence of the old Barnaba. It was something that the old Barnaba had been becoming, the destination toward which all those moons of Change had been traveling. Broader, yes, and smoother in some places and more marked in others, with a quality of openness that the old face — precise, angular, always about to make a point — had not had room for.

The eyes were the same. The measuring quality in them, the precision that had always made Vamir feel seen rather than simply observed. The eyes were exactly the same.

The ink stains on the hands were in different places than he remembered. The hands themselves were the same.

"Hello, Vamir," Barnaba said, and the voice was lower than it had been, settled in a register that suited the new proportion of things, and hearing it was the confirmation his mind had been waiting for — the same voice, differently housed, the Barnaba-ness of it unmistakable underneath the changed pitch.

"Welcome home," he said, and meant it in the specific way, the way the town meant it — not *welcome back to where you were* but *welcome to where you belong*, which was not necessarily the same place twice.

Barnaba looked at him with an expression that was the old expression wearing the new face — the quick intelligent calculation, the slight upward movement at one corner of the mouth. "You're not surprised," she said.

"Not by you," he said. He looked at Elspeth. "Her, a little. Though I probably shouldn't be."

Elspeth beamed. "I told you he'd know," she said, to Barnaba, in the tone of someone winning a minor domestic argument.

"You told me he'd probably guess," Barnaba said. "That's not the same as knowing." She looked at Vamir. "She said you were perceptive."

"She's generous," Vamir said.

"She's accurate," Elspeth said, firmly, and took his arm with the ease of someone who had decided they were on friendly terms and saw no reason to revisit the decision. "Walk with us. I want tea, and I want to see what Galhani's done with that citrus blend she was working on, and Barnaba wants to see the square."

"The square hasn't changed," Vamir said.

"I know," Barnaba said. "That's why I want to see it."

———

They crossed the square at the pace Elspeth set, which was the pace of someone who intended to see everything and was in no hurry about it. Vamir walked between them and felt, with the specific quality of things that were both ordinary and not, the particular configuration of the morning: himself, the Enchantress, and the changed mapmaker, moving through the town on a Tuesday in late spring.

He did not announce them. He did not need to.

The first person who saw Barnaba was Kene, emerging from the bakery's side door with an empty basket, who stopped and looked and then went back inside at a pace suggesting the information needed to travel faster than he could carry it calmly. The second was Tyran, who appeared in the smithy doorway with the unhurried certainty of a very large person who moves when he's ready and not before, and who looked at Barnaba for a long moment with the assessing quality he brought to structural problems, and then nodded once — the nod of someone confirming that what they're looking at is sound.

"Lastmaker's in," Tyran said, by way of greeting. "He'll want to see you."

"I'll want to see him," Barnaba said.

The bakery door opened.

Makota came out with the directness of someone who has received information and has decided what to do about it, wiping her hands on her apron. She stopped a few feet away, and for a moment she simply looked — the measuring look, the inventory, the Makota assessment of people she knew against people who had arrived — and then something in her face that had been tight since the morning of the shuttered shop and the brass plate and the absence released, quietly and completely.

She crossed the remaining distance and put her arms around Barnaba, who was taller now and broader and stood differently in the world, and Makota was not a tall person and had to reach, and she reached without hesitation.

Barnaba stood for a moment with the expression of someone receiving something they had not been certain they would receive. Then her arms came up and she held on, and Vamir observed this with the full attention it deserved and noted it and held it, the archivist doing his work, the witness being present at the thing he was witnessing.

"You could have written," Makota said, into Barnaba's shoulder.

"I know," Barnaba said. "I should have. I'm sorry."

"You're here now." Makota stepped back and looked at her with the frankness of someone who has had moons to formulate an opinion and has arrived at it decisively. "You look well. Different." She tilted her head. "Good different."

"Thank you," Barnaba said, and the gratitude in it was specific —

not for the compliment but for the willingness to see, for the refusal to treat the Change as something that required management or accommodation. She had said to Vamir, in the long-ago evening in the map shop: *I'd still have to be a story, and I'm tired of being a story.* Makota was not making her a story. Makota was simply glad she was standing there.

"Come in," Makota said. "Both of you." She included Elspeth in the gesture with the warmth she gave all newcomers who arrived in the company of people she loved. "Everyone needs feeding."

———

The bakery had the quality it always had when something significant was happening in it — not louder or more formal, but more itself, as though the occasion had clarified rather than changed its essential character. Makota fed them with the thoroughness she brought to people she was glad to see, which meant the bread was the good bread and the preserves were from the back of the shelf and the tea was Galhani's, summoned from next door by some mechanism that involved Kene and two minutes and no apparent inconvenience.

Galhani arrived with the tea and stayed, because Galhani always stayed, and she received Barnaba with the specific energy of someone who had been worried and was now converting the worry directly into joy without stopping at relief. She asked seventeen questions in the space of the time it took to pour the tea, and listened to the answers with the concentrated attention of someone who intended to remember all of them.

Bartram appeared from across the square — he had, in the sennights since his arrival, developed the shopkeeper's awareness of significant events in the square, which was one of the gifts the town gave its keepers — and greeted Barnaba with the warm directness of someone who had heard about the mapmaker and was meeting them now without the complication of prior expectations. They talked maps within three minutes, which Vamir had expected and which seemed to please Barnaba in the specific way that conversations about maps always had.

Jen came in, as Jen always came in — appearing without announcement, absorbing the room, positioning herself at the edge of things. She looked at Barnaba for a moment, and Barnaba looked at her, and then Jen said: "Good. You're well."

"I am," Barnaba said.

"Good," Jen said again, and that was Jen's entire response to moons of absence and return and the visible evidence of the Change, which was exactly right and which Barnaba received with a recognition that suggested she had understood Jen well in the time she'd been in North Pointe and had not expected anything different.

Sam arrived last, with the timing she had for significant gatherings, and looked at Elspeth across the room with the specific expression of someone who has information that most people in the room don't have and is choosing to simply be present with it rather than deploy it.

Elspeth met her eyes and gave her the small nod of one person acknowledging another who is in on a thing, and Sam returned it, and that was the entirety of their exchange on the subject, which was exactly the right amount.

———

It was Galhani who made the tea. This was not unusual — Galhani was constitutionally incapable of being in a room where tea was being made without being involved — but this particular pot was significant in ways she didn't yet know. She had brought the blend from next door, the green-with-citrus she had been developing since before Barnaba left, the one that had been almost-right for moons.

She poured it with her usual flair and set it in front of Vamir first, because she always used him as her test case.

He drank it.

He set down the cup.

"You found the citrus," he said.

Galhani looked at him. She picked up her own cup, drank, and went very still in the way of someone experiencing a thing they have been working toward for a long time.

"It's right," she said.

"Yes," Vamir said.

She drank again. The expression on her face moved through several things — the craftsperson's satisfaction, the surprise of something arriving when you had stopped expecting it, and then something quieter, a recognition of what the rightness meant in the context of this particular morning. She looked at Barnaba, who was deep in a conversation with Bartram about altitude and paper quality and the particular challenges of mapping spaces that didn't stay still. She looked at Vamir.

"It came back," she said.

"It was always there," he said. "You just found the right element."

Galhani was quiet for a moment, turning the cup in her hands. "It's been tasting like nothing," she said. "For moons. I thought it was my blends. My sourcing." She looked at the cup. "But it wasn't. '

"No," he said. "It wasn't."

She looked at Barnaba again, and the look had in it everything that the hug had had and several things the hug hadn't been able to hold, and then she returned to the tea with the absorbed satisfaction of a craftsperson whose craft has been restored to her, and did not say anything else about it, because she didn't need to.

Later, when the bakery had settled into the comfortable configuration of a gathering that had done its necessary work and was now simply being, Vamir found himself beside Elspeth at the end of the counter, both of them with fresh cups, watching Barnaba hold court at the center table.

The new Barnaba was not the old Barnaba performing in a new body. The new Barnaba was someone for whom the body and the person had arrived at the same address at the same time, and the result was a quality of ease that the old Barnaba — precise, angular, always slightly at odds with the space she occupied — had never quite had. The gestures were larger. The laugh was different — lower, less contained, more willing to be heard. The way Barnaba listened to Bartram's questions had the same quality the maps had always had:

total engagement, the sense of a mind fully applied to the problem in front of it, but the engagement was warmer now, less defended.

"She's good," Elspeth said, quietly, beside him.

"Yes," Vamir said.

"She was good before. Now she's—" Elspeth paused, looking for the word. "Correctly sized." She sipped her tea. "The keep was very good for her. Dreadful for me, having someone so relentlessly interested in all the passages."

Vamir looked at her. "She maps the keep."

"She maps the keep," Elspeth confirmed, with the expression of someone who has arrived at a complicated relationship with a domestic fact. "Every morning. Which would be perfectly fine, except that the keep rearranges itself. It's done it for as long as I've been there. So there is no definitive map of the keep, and never will be, and I have explained this." She paused. "She finds this a feature rather than a problem."

"She would," Vamir said.

"She keeps the maps anyway," Elspeth said. "She's building an archive of what the keep has been, rather than what it is. Every configuration it's ever taken, as completely as she can document it." She looked at her cup with an expression that was fondness wearing the costume of mild complaint. "There are rather a lot of maps already. The keep, at least, is large enough to store them."

Vamir thought about the archive below the bookshop — the deep record, the accumulation of observations across centuries, the keeper's task of holding what had been rather than what was. He thought about Barnaba in the map shop, the drawings carpeting the floor, the same keep rendered from a hundred angles. He thought about the Change preparing her not for a new place but for a new kind of work — not the finished map of a fixed territory, but the ongoing record of a place that refused to stay still.

"She was always going to do that work," he said.

"Yes," Elspeth said. "I think she was." A pause. "I didn't know that when she arrived. She turned up in the middle of a particularly frustrating sennight — I'd had three questers in as many days, all of them convinced they knew what they wanted, all of them wrong — and there she was at the keep's lower gate with a pack full of surveying equipment and that expression." She smiled. "You know the expression."

"The one that means she's already decided and is merely waiting for the world to catch up," Vamir said.

"That one precisely." Elspeth's smile deepened. "She said she'd come to map the passes and had taken a wrong turning. I said the keep was not a pass. She looked at the keep the way she looks at everything — the total inventory — and said that it looked like it might be more interesting than a pass anyway." A pause. "She was right."

They watched Barnaba sketch something on a scrap of paper for Bartram — a quick technical diagram, the hands moving with the old precision, the new ease — and Bartram lean over it with the focused attention of a craftsperson recognizing quality work.

"She told me about the town," Elspeth said, more quietly. "About what it was like here. The people. The evening she remembered — this evening, in the pub, the singing." She paused. "I had not thought about that evening from her point of view. I knew it was a good evening. I didn't know how she'd carried it."

"How had she carried it?"

"As home," Elspeth said simply. "Even knowing she was leaving. Even knowing the Change was taking her somewhere new. She carried this town as home." She looked at the room — Makota behind the counter, Galhani with her tea, Jen at the edge, Sam having arrived quietly at some point and taken up her usual observational position. "She still does, I think. Just from further away."

Vamir was quiet for a moment. "You could come back," he said. "When you need a good evening. You know that."

"I know," Elspeth said. "I will." She paused. "It's a peculiar thing, living where I live. You become the place, in people's imaginations. They have a very clear idea of who you are and what you are and where you belong, and it's usually somewhere remote and frightening and fundamentally separate from ordinary life." She gestured at the room. "And then you come here and drink tea in a bakery and nobody requires you to be the Enchantress at all, and it's—" She paused. "Restoring," she said. "In the technical sense."

"The waypoint's function," Vamir said.

"Yes." She looked at him with the expression she had worn in the bookshop — the keeper recognizing another keeper. "Your town is very good at what it does."

"It's been practicing for a long time," Vamir said.

Elspeth laughed — the full laugh, the round pleasant sound he had first heard across a crowded pub, and the dimple appeared, and she was just an old woman drinking tea in a bakery on a Tuesday morning, entirely at home.

———

The gathering dispersed in the natural way of gatherings that have done their work — gradually, without announcement, each person peeling away when the moment was right for them. Jen first, because Jen had circuits to complete and had received what the morning offered. Bartram back across the square to the shop, with a new conversation started and an appointment made to continue it. Galhani to her next steeping, already working through the implications of the citrus discovery in a way that would probably produce three new blends before evening.

Barnaba and Elspeth stayed the longest, and when they finally rose to go it was with the ease of people who have nowhere they urgently need to be except back, eventually, to where they live — which was, Vamir now understood, the keep in the mountains, large and cold and drafty and full of accumulated maps of every configuration it had ever taken.

He walked them to the edge of the square.

"The passes are good this time of year," Barnaba said, settling her pack with the old efficiency. "The north route is faster but the east route is better for stopping and looking at things."

"Which will you take?" Vamir asked.

Barnaba looked at Elspeth. Elspeth looked at the mountains. "The east," Elspeth said. "We're not in a hurry, and there's a formation I want her to see. She hasn't mapped it yet."

"A rock formation?" Vamir said.

"An interesting one," Elspeth said, with the mildness of someone who has spent a long time developing opinions about geology. "It changes depending on the angle you view it from. Barnaba has a theory."

"The theory is that it's actually three separate formations that overlap spatially in a way that makes them appear to be one thing," Barnaba said. "I need more angles to confirm it."

"It's one formation," Elspeth said, serenely.

"It's three," Barnaba said. "I have preliminary sketches."

"You have preliminary sketches of everything," Elspeth said. "It proves nothing."

Vamir looked at the two of them — the Enchantress and the mapmaker, arguing about a rock formation on the road back to the keep in the mountains, with the ease of people who had been arguing about things that mattered to them for long enough that the argument had become a form of affection.

"Send word," he said. "When you can."

"Barnaba will draw you a map," Elspeth said. "She draws maps of everything."

"I will," Barnaba said, not denying this. She looked at Vamir with the old measuring quality in the new face. "Thank you," she said. "For —" She paused. "For being here. For the shop being here. For the town being what it is." She paused again. "I needed to come back and see it before I could fully go."

"I understand," Vamir said. Because he did — the Everkin record in the archive, the departure not as leaving but as arriving elsewhere, the old place needing to be seen and held and carried as home from the new distance.

She embraced him, which was not something the old Barnaba had done — the old Barnaba had expressed warmth through proximity and shared silence and the occasional precise word. The new Barnaba was apparently a person who embraced people, and the embrace was warm and specific and brief and exactly right.

Then they went. East road, unhurried pace, the two of them side by side with the quality of people who had found, in the large cold keep in the mountains and in each other's company, a form of ordinary life that suited them.

Vamir watched until they were out of sight.

Then he stood in the square for a moment, in the good late-morning light, with the particular quality of the day which had the feeling of a thing completed — not ended, but completed, the way a piece of music is completed, the themes resolved into a form that could hold them.

The fountain ran clear. The bakery was warm and lit. Across the square, Bartram's shop had the quality it had been developing since his arrival — settled, occupied, the window showing the careful display of a craftsperson who understood that the way a thing was presented was part of what the thing was. The boot-shaped sign caught the light.

He went back to the bookshop.

————

The afternoon was ordinary in the way that afternoons after significant mornings were ordinary — the ordinary feeling earned rather than default, the specific pleasure of the everyday following hard on the specific weight of the significant. Travelers in and out. The ledger. The lesson with the children, which produced, among other things, a lengthy debate about whether a map of a place that kept changing was still a map or was something else, which Vamir let run considerably longer than the curriculum required.

Tannos had opinions. He always had opinions.

At the end of the lesson, when the children had gone and the shop was quiet, Vamir stood at the window and looked at the square in the late-afternoon light. The day had given him what it had given him — Barnaba returned and thriving, Elspeth present and ordinary and warm, Galhani's tea restored, Makota's hug, Jen's two words, the geological argument on the eastern road.

He thought about the archive below his feet, its patient deep quiet, the altar with the blood-dark mark between the two sigils. He thought about the sealed room, the small table, the lamp that was always lit. He thought about the book with the two sigils on the cover, waiting for his return.

He was not going down tonight. Tonight was for the surface, for the ordinary pleasures of the restored town, for the specific quality of an evening that had earned its ease.

He went to the Broken Claw, because Sam had already predicted he would and would have something poured before he sat down.

She did.

"Elspeth and Barnaba left?" Sam asked.

"East road," Vamir said. "They're arguing about a rock formation."

Sam looked at him. "About a—"

"Barnaba thinks it's three separate formations that overlap. Elspeth thinks it's one."

Sam absorbed this. "Barnaba is probably right," she said.

"Almost certainly," Vamir said. "Elspeth knows this. She's enjoying the argument."

Sam made the sound she made when something was exactly what she expected and also somehow better. She refilled his glass before he'd asked, which was the Broken Claw's particular form of affection, and moved back down the bar.

The evening gathered. The regulars arrived in their usual sequence. The fire was lit. Galhani appeared with Lara and the energy of someone who had made three new blends since morning and needed willing subjects, and Vamir submitted to the tasting with the thoroughness it deserved.

The third blend was extraordinary.

"There it is," Galhani said, watching his face.

"Yes," Vamir said. "There it is."

She beamed with the satisfaction of a craftsperson whose craft had come home, and poured everyone a second cup, and the evening was warm and the fire was good and the town was whole.

twenty-one

. . .

THREE SENNIGHTS after Barnaba and Elspeth walked back into the square on a Tuesday morning, the town had settled into the particular quality of itself that Vamir thought of as full — not complete in the sense of lacking nothing, because the town was always in motion, always losing and finding and adjusting, but full in the sense of a chord that has all its notes. Bartram's shop had its sign and its gift and its particular smell of worked leather and beeswax that had become part of the square's composite scent. Galhani's tea was right. The scale at Pavati's weighed what it weighed. The beer poured clean.

The trade road was busy in the way of late spring, which was to say constantly and with purpose, travelers moving through with the urgency of people who had been waiting out the last of the cold and were now making up for lost time. Vamir opened the shop in the mornings and let the day find him, and the day reliably did, and Poly was in good form, and the archive below was patient and present and waiting for him when he had something new to bring to it.

He was, on the whole, well.

———

Elspeth came down on a Wednesday this time, which suggested she was varying her schedule deliberately or that Wednesdays had simply arrived at their turn. She appeared at the bookshop door in the mid-morning — firm twist, gentle shove, three-note chime — with the wool shawl and the wooden sticks and the expression of someone who has done something she is quietly pleased about and would like to share it with the right audience.

"Tea," she said. "And I have news."

Vamir put the kettle on. Sam arrived eleven minutes later, which was either coincidence or the gift at work, and Vamir suspected the latter. Leota materialized shortly after, which was simply Leota.

They settled at the back table — the four of them, tea distributed, Poly on the counter with the alert patience of a creature that had decided this was worth attending to — and Elspeth folded her hands and looked at the middle distance with the expression of someone ordering a narrative.

"The hunters," she said.

"Yes," Sam said.

"They arrived in the second sennight," Elspeth began, with the tone of someone who has been looking forward to telling a story and intends to tell it properly. "Which was faster than I expected, given the season. The tall one — Brasham — had apparently pushed the pace. He wanted to arrive before his resolve softened." She paused. "That was the first piece of information."

"That he was worried about his resolve softening," Leota said.

"Yes. A man who is certain of his righteousness doesn't worry about losing it on the way." She picked up her cup. "So I led them around."

Vamir looked at her.

"Not cruelly," she said, with the mild defensiveness of someone anticipating a misunderstanding. "Not dangerously. I simply — arranged that the paths they took were longer than they appeared, and that the landmarks were not quite where they expected them to be, and that every time they thought they had their bearings the mountain helpfully provided them with new and more interesting bearings to be confused by." She sipped her tea. "It's a very obliging mountain, Nimarith's. It seems to enjoy that kind of thing."

"How long?" Sam asked.

"Four days," Elspeth said. "Which is not excessive, for the kind of certainty they arrived with. They were devout men in the way that is less about devotion and more about the comfort of not having to think about whether the thing you've been told to do is the right thing to do." She paused. "That kind of certainty is very efficient and very brittle. The mountain is patient. It simply waits."

"And?" Leota said.

"And on the fourth day, the youngest one sat down on a rock and said he was done." Elspeth's expression softened slightly. "Not done with the quest. Done with pretending. He told the others that he'd been thinking about what the bookseller had said—" She looked at Vamir with something warm in it. "—and that he didn't actually know whether what they'd been told about the Enchantress was true, and that he'd been following the commission because following commissions was what he did, and that sitting on a wet rock on a mountain in the fourth day of being thoroughly lost had given him occasion to wonder whether the commission deserved the following."

"What did Brasham say?" Vamir asked.

"Nothing, at first," Elspeth said. "He sat with it for a while. Which was, in my assessment, the most promising thing he'd done since arriving." She set down her cup. "Then he said that he'd had the same thought, more or less, since the bookseller had said what he'd said in the pub. That he'd been carrying it the whole way up the mountain and hadn't been able to put it down." She paused. "He asked, out loud, whether anyone was listening."

The back table was quiet.

"I led them down more gently after that," Elspeth said. "A different path — shorter, easier, with the kind of views that make a person feel that the world is larger and more interesting than they'd been treating it. By the time they reached the valley floor they were cold and tired and considerably less certain than they'd started, which is exactly the right condition for going home and reconsidering one's assumptions."

"Did they see you?" Leota asked.

"Brasham did," Elspeth said. "Briefly. At a distance, at the point where I shifted the path back to the easier route. He looked at me for a moment." She paused. "He didn't look like a man who had found what he came to find. He looked like a man who had found something else instead and wasn't yet sure what it was." She picked up her cup again. "That's usually the better outcome, in my experience."

"What became of the commission?" Sam asked. "The person who sent them."

"That," Elspeth said, with a serenity that contained something flintier underneath it, "is between them and whoever sent them, and I expect Brasham will have some questions for that person that the person will find uncomfortable." She paused. "He struck me as a man who, once he has decided something was wrong, becomes quite thorough about addressing it." She looked at her tea. "He left his company's mark on a stone at the valley boundary, which is an old custom — it means they passed through and were changed by the passing and acknowledge it. I haven't seen that in some years."

The table absorbed this. Vamir thought of the mark in the stone, and Brasham's face in the pre-dawn square, the quick inventory before he mounted and rode. He thought of the four days on the mountain, the cold rock, the youngest one deciding he was done pretending. He thought of the field records in the archive — the parties that had been broken and rebuilt.

"Rebuilt," he said, quietly.

"Yes," Elspeth said. "I think so." She looked at him directly. "Your warning helped. I want you to know that. The seed was planted before they arrived, and it made the mountain's work easier." She paused. "The youngest one specifically mentioned the bookseller's words. Several times, apparently. By the fourth day Brasham had heard them enough that he could have recited them."

Vamir was quiet for a moment. He thought about the distinction he had been working with for moons — the shop acting, him acting, the line between them thinner than he had believed. He thought about the warning that had been both the shop's function and his choice, and Sam's observation: *you did it now.*

"The shop had what he needed," Vamir said.

Elspeth looked at him with the keeper's look — the specific recognition between two people who are in the same system and know it. "The shop did," she said. "And so did you."

He held her gaze for a moment and then nodded, once, and let it settle.

Sam picked up her cup. "To villains," she said, quietly. Not a toast exactly. A private acknowledgment of the thing she knew that most of the room knew, the echo of an evening in the Broken Claw, a song about a miller's daughter.

Elspeth smiled — the full smile, the dimple. "To stories," she said.

They drank.

———

The first of the two travelers came on a Friday, late afternoon, when the shop had the particular quality it had at that time — the light shifting from the active gold of mid-day to something longer and more amber, the day's business mostly done, the shelves in the specific state of mild disorder that meant they had been used.

She came alone, which was not unusual, but she had the quality of someone whose aloneness was circumstantial rather than essential — a person who had left someone behind who mattered and was moving with the particular efficiency of someone who intended to return as quickly as possible.

She was perhaps thirty, with the practical clothing of a person who had been traveling for some days without much thought for appearance, and she had the expression Poly responded to with its most direct attention — not the hunger of the seeker or the anxiety of the desperate, but the clear-eyed purposefulness of someone who knows what they need and why they need it.

"The bookseller?" she said.

"Yes," Vamir said.

"I need a medicinal text," she said. "Specifically northern mountain ailments, specifically the kind that affects children in high valleys in late winter, specifically the kind that our village healer hasn't encountered before and doesn't know how to treat. Three children sick already. Two more showing early signs." She met his eyes. "I've been traveling for six days. I'll travel six more if I need to. I need the right book."

Vamir looked at her for a moment — the clear eyes, the six days of road, the two more if needed — and felt the shop attend to the moment with the specific quality it had when what was being asked for was something it had been holding for exactly this.

"Poly," he said.

Poly was already moving.

It went directly — none of the browsing quality it sometimes had, the consideration of options. It went to the far end of the medical texts, to a shelf that Vamir had not opened in some time, and placed its wing on a spine with the certainty of something that had known exactly where this was and had been waiting for the right person to come for it.

The book was old — older than most of what he had in the medical section, the binding repaired at least twice, the pages dense with both printed text and handwritten annotations in several different hands, each generation of healers adding what they had learned to what they had inherited.

He carried it to the counter and opened it to the index. Mountain ailments, late winter presentation, children, high valley. The relevant section was substantial, specific, annotated.

"How much?" she said, before he had finished checking the entry.

"It's yours," he said.

She looked at him.

"The shop has what travelers need," he said. "Sometimes the need outweighs the commerce." He closed the book and slid it across the counter. "The annotations in the third section are particularly relevant to what you're describing. There's a treatment on page two hundred and fourteen that was added by a healer from a valley two ranges east of here, about forty years ago. She notes it worked consistently."

The woman picked up the book with both hands, the way Poly retrieved things — complete attention, the understanding of what was being held. She looked at him with an expression that had several things in it, none of which she seemed to find words for immediately.

"Thank you," she said, finally. Simply. The way people said it when they meant the whole of it.

"Travel safely," Vamir said. "The north road is faster around now."

She went. The door chimed. Poly watched her cross the square with three-eyed satisfaction and then returned to its perch with the air of a job correctly done.

Vamir stood at the counter for a moment in the amber late-afternoon light, his hand resting on the empty space where the book had been.

The shop always had what the traveler needed. And sometimes the traveler needed it so purely, so cleanly, with such uncomplicated selflessness, that the shop produced it with something that felt less like a transaction and more like a recognition — one right thing meeting another right thing in the ordinary space of a bookshop on a trade road in a small northern valley.

He filed it. He held it. He went back to the ledger.

———

The second traveler came the following Tuesday — Vamir was beginning to accept that Tuesdays were simply the designated day for things that mattered — and she came as half of a pair, which the shop sometimes preferred.

The pair were the two women Leota had mentioned, returning from the Mistrals with the specific quality of people who had been thoroughly tested and had not passed, and knew it, and were making their peace with the knowing. They were not broken by the experience. They were the kind of people the testing found honest — people who, confronted with the gap between what they thought they wanted and what they actually needed, chose honesty over persistence.

They came for maps. They needed to understand where they had been, in the way that people sometimes needed to see a journey on paper before they could understand what the journey had meant. Poly found them the relevant surveys and Vamir spread them on the back table and they spent a mark tracing the routes they had taken, and the conversation was practical and specific and occasionally punctuated by one of them saying something that was clearly about more than the map and then returning to the map with the deliberateness of someone who had said what needed saying and did not need to say it again.

When they left they had the maps and a history of the Mistral passes that one of them had noticed on the shelf near the door and asked about quietly, and a small volume of local poetry that Poly had deposited at the other one's feet without being asked, which she had looked at and then tucked under her arm without comment.

Vamir watched them go. They walked with the ease of two people who had been through something together and had come out on the same side of it, which was its own form of completion even when the thing they'd been through had not resolved the way they'd hoped.

The shop had given them what they needed. Not what they'd come for. What they needed.

He noted the distinction, as he always did, with the satisfaction of someone whose function was still, after all these years, capable of surprising him with its precision.

———

The evening was Galhani's, which was how the best evenings tended to be — she arrived at the Broken Claw with Lara and the energy of someone who had been waiting all day to tell everyone about the fourth new blend, which was somehow better than the third, and the conversation moved through its usual channels of warmth and mild argument and the particular pleasure of people who had known each other long enough to be genuinely interested in what the other one thought.

Makota brought pastries, because Makota always brought pastries to evenings that deserved them. Jen arrived and took her usual position at the edge of things and contributed two observations that were precise enough to reframe the whole conversation each time, which was Jen's particular gift in social settings. Bartram had been invited for the first time and arrived with the slightly formal quality of someone who knew they were being included and intended to be worthy of it, and within half a mark was in a deep discussion with Dardrad about leather treatment that Vamir suspected would continue for some sennights.

Sam poured and listened and occasionally said the thing that needed saying, which was her function and her gift and the thing she did better than almost anyone Vamir knew.

Vamir sat in his usual spot, the one that gave him the room and the bar equally, and let the evening settle around him. He was present in it — not cataloguing from the outside, not taking his careful peripheral notes, but in it, the way Galhani had pulled him into the center of Bartram's welcome and the way the singing always caught him if he stayed long enough.

He thought about the sealed room and the small lamp burning, and the understanding that had arrived there: *I am not outside the story. I am the part of the story that holds the story.*

He thought about Elspeth's voice: *to stories.*

He raised his glass slightly, to no one visible and everyone present, and drank.

Galhani caught the gesture and raised her own, not knowing what she was raising it to, and that was exactly right — you did not need to know the full meaning of a toast to participate in it genuinely. The town had been doing this for longer than anyone could remember: sustaining, witnessing, holding the record of itself through every departure and arrival and disruption and restoration, returning to function as its fundamental nature required.

He was part of that. He had always been part of that.

He let the evening be what it was.

———

The morning that ended the book was an ordinary morning, which was the only kind worth ending on.

The light came through the stained glass in its usual way — the blues and golds, the hundred uneven panes, the checkered warmth that moved across the floor as the sun climbed. The shop smelled of old paper and leather and the particular topnote of linden and apple blossom that rose from the kettle Vamir had set on the stove behind the counter.

Poly was on the endcap of the "Forgotten Epics" shelf, eyes half-closed, one stubby wing-arm draped over a battered spine in the way it had when it was keeping a text company rather than retrieving it. Its blue feathers caught the morning light.

Vamir moved through the opening ritual with the ease of something done ten thousand times and still, somehow, not diminished by the repetition. The returns bin. The ledger. The shelves, which had arranged themselves in the quiet way they sometimes arranged themselves overnight, texts that belonged together finding their way to proximity.

He paused at the "Histories — Local & Regional" section. The slim blue volume was there, at the end of the bottom row, flush with its neighbors. His grandfather's book. The key to the archive below, the thing that had been in this building for years before he understood what it was.

He touched the spine, the way you touched a familiar thing without meaning to.

Then he crossed to the window.

The square was coming to life in its morning stages — the deliveries first, then the early errand-runners, then the slow accumulation of the day's business. Makota's kits raced something around the fountain. Warren's forge was already lit, the first pale smoke rising in the still air. Bartram's shop window showed the careful display of the morning's work, the boot-shaped sign bright in the early light.

He watched the square the way he always watched it — with the full peripheral attention of the archivist, the witness, the keeper of the record. Not from outside the story. From the place in the story that held the story.

The town was whole. The trade road ran. The mountain stood where it had always stood, patient and specific, Nimarith's long presence in the stone. Somewhere up the eastern pass, in a keep that rearranged its rooms and accumulated maps of itself, Elspeth was beginning her morning and Barnaba was noting the overnight configuration of the corridor outside the east gallery and adding it to the archive of what the keep had been.

The questers would come today, as they came every day, with their hope and their fear and their not-quite-right understanding of what they were walking toward. The shop would have what they needed. Poly would find the books before the customers had finished asking. The town would sustain and the road would test and the mountain would wait, and the record would be held by the person whose function it was to hold it.

He had chosen this. He chose it again, now, in the ordinary light of an ordinary morning, with the full understanding of what the choice cost and what the cost meant and why the meaning was worth the cost.

He went to the door.

He turned the sign to OPEN.

Outside, the square went about its business, indifferent and sustaining, the town being what it was, as it had always been, as it would continue to be when the current keeper had been replaced by the next one and the record passed on and the blue volume sat in its place on the shelf waiting for the hand that would recognize it.

The chimes above the door rang as it swung open — three notes, the usual greeting.

Poly lifted its head, all three eyes open.

The first customer of the day was already coming up the walkway.

Vamir smiled and waited for what the morning would bring.

epilogue

. . .

THEY CAME BACK ON A FRIDAY, three weeks later, from the eastern road, without the conveyance and without the Mistress Valdaine.

Vamir noticed them from the window in the late afternoon — six figures, recognizable by their collective quality rather than any individual feature, moving with the specific energy of people who had a great deal to say and had been saving it for an audience. He watched them cross the square toward the Broken Claw with the purposeful stride of people who needed a drink and a sympathetic ear, not necessarily in that order.

He put on his coat and followed at a reasonable interval.

———

Sam had already poured by the time he arrived. This was either the gift or simple experience, and at this point in his relationship with the Broken Claw, Vamir had stopped trying to distinguish between them.

The six retinue members occupied the corner table with the quality of people who had been through something together and were not yet finished processing it. Caress, the eldest, had the expression of someone who had foreseen an outcome and was experiencing the specific exhaustion of having been right. Pell, the ink-stained young man, was in the middle of a sentence that had apparently been going for some time.

"— and the thing is, she was right about all of it," Pell was saying, with the fervent sincerity of someone defending a position under pressure. "The silhouettes, the fabric weights, the whole direction — she was right. The eastern courts are simply not ready—"

"The eastern courts," said the young woman with the close-cropped hair — Maret, Vamir recalled — "threw a roll at her."

"At her work," Pell said. "There's a distinction."

"The roll landed on the gown," Maret said. "I'm not sure the gown would agree that the distinction matters."

Sam set a fresh pitcher on the table with the efficiency of someone who had assessed the situation and determined that the primary need was logistical. "Start from the beginning," she said, in the tone she used when she wanted information organized properly.

Caress picked up the pitcher. "The Mistress Valdaine," she said, with the dignity of someone delivering a formal report while also slightly needing to laugh, "presented her spring collection to the court of the Eastern Reach three days ago."

Vamir settled onto a nearby stool and did not announce himself, which was unnecessary because Sam had already seen him and the retinue was too absorbed in the narrative to pay attention to anyone outside it.

"The collection," Caress continued, "was extraordinary. Genuinely. The draping alone — the way she'd worked with the mountain silks—"

"Tell them about the hems," said the youngest one, whose name Vamir had not caught.

"The hems were revolutionary," Caress said. "She's been seeing it for two seasons — the direction everything is moving, before anyone else can see it. The dropped hem, the structural shoulder, the whole vocabulary—"

"Her vision of the future is unmatched," Pell said, with feeling.

"Her vision of the future," Maret said, "was approximately four years ahead of what the eastern courts are currently prepared to wear to a formal occasion."

A pause.

"The Countess of Aldermere," Caress said carefully, "described the collection as 'an affront to the traditions of civilized dress.'"

"And threw a roll," Maret said.

"Someone in her party threw a roll," Caress said.

"She didn't discourage it," Maret said.

Sam refilled glasses with the equanimity of someone receiving information she was going to be thinking about for some time.

Vamir looked at the table — the six of them, their various expressions of loyalty and exhaustion and the specific resilience of people who had hitched their wagon to a visionary and were accustomed to the particular turbulence that came with it. He thought about the things they had said in the square three weeks ago: *she sees things others can't. The shape of what's coming, before it arrives.*

The shape of what was coming, in the world of fashion, before the eastern courts were ready for it.

Her vision of the future is unmatched. But the future she shows you isn't always the one you thought you wanted.

The dropped hem. The structural shoulder. The whole vocabulary.

She doesn't give you what you want. She gives you what you need. Which is sometimes the same thing.

He pressed his lips together against a smile.

"And the Mistress Valdaine?" Sam asked.

"Dismissed us," Caress said. "All of us. On the road back." She said it without apparent rancor — the resignation of someone who had seen this before and knew it wasn't personal. "She said she works better alone when she's reconceptualizing. That we were useful for the execution phase but the visioning required solitude." She paused. "She'll have six new people by autumn. She always does."

"You don't seem—" Sam began.

"Devastated?" Caress smiled, with the warmth of a person who had genuinely learned something from the experience and knew it. "She takes everything you have and gives it back transformed. She was right about that. I know things about proportion and line that I didn't know three years ago, and I'll know them wherever I go next." She looked at the table. "She's brilliant. She's also — not easy to work for."

"She has standards that most people find excessive," Pell said, with slightly less conviction than he'd had three weeks ago.

"She does," Caress agreed. "Which is a real thing, not a problem. Just — a real thing."

Maret, who had been quiet for a moment, looked up with the expression of someone who had been doing calculations. "Renvale is looking for an atelier head," she said. "In the western cities. I heard it from the Countess's second before the roll-throwing incident. He was perfectly civil, actually." She paused. "The Countess throws rolls. He does not."

"Renvale's work is extraordinary," the youngest one said.

"Renvale's eye for architecture is unparalleled," Pell said, with the speed of someone whose interests were already pivoting.

"Renvale," Caress said thoughtfully, "does occasionally present in the eastern courts."

"With, presumably," Sam said, "no roll incidents."

"No roll incidents on record," Caress confirmed.

The conversation moved into the specifics of Renvale's recent collections and the western cities' fashion landscape, and Vamir sat for a while longer, listening with the satisfaction of someone who has been holding an unanswered question for three weeks and has just watched it answer itself.

Sam appeared beside him, cloth over her shoulder, and did not say anything for a moment.

"She was real," Sam said, finally. "Just not that kind of real."

"No," Vamir agreed.

"My gift was picking up something genuine," Sam said. "The work. The — actual quality of what she does, and what the people around her are experiencing." She paused. "A real gift, just a different one."

"A gift for seeing the shape of what's coming," Vamir said. "Before it arrives."

Sam looked at him. "Before anyone else can see it," she said.

"Yes," Vamir said.

They sat with that for a moment — the specific pleasure of a question resolved not through drama but through the accumulated comedy of the eastern courts and a roll thrown at a revolutionary hem, and six loyal people at a corner table already planning their next orbit.

"To stories," Vamir said, very quietly.

Sam made the sound she made when something was exactly right, and went back to the bar, and the evening gathered around the Broken Claw with the warmth it always had, and the town was what it was, and the record held it all.

award-winning fiction

Daniel Scratch: a story of witchkind

- Kirkus Starred Review
- Winner, American Fiction Awards—Best Fantasy (2023)
- Finalist, American Legacy Book Awards—Best Fantasy (2024)

———

Clara Thorn, the witch that was found

- Winner, American Fiction Awards—Best Young Adult (2023)
- Runner-Up, American Fiction Awards—Best Fantasy (2023)
- Finalist, American Legacy Book Awards—Best Fantasy (2024)
- Finalist, American Legacy Book Awards—Best Young Adult (2024)

———

Find these books and more at DonJones.com

about the author

Don Jones spent two decades writing tech books before he finally penned his first sci-fi novella, *A History of the Galactic War*. His well-reviewed and award-winning novels span fantasy and science fiction, with a focus on world building and relatable characters.

Connect, get free novels and short stories, and learn about upcoming releases by visiting Don's author website at DonJones.com.